REIGNING KINGDOMS,
BOOK ONE

I0588005

SWORD
OF
RAGE

JENNIFER ANNE DAVIS

Cover Design by KimG-Design
Editing by Jennifer Murgia
Proofreading by Appalachian Proofing

ISBN (Paperback): 978-1-7344947-7-8
eISBN: 978-1-7344947-4-7

Library of Congress Control Number: 1-10174997371

ALSO BY JENNIFER ANNE DAVIS

The
Mainland

MARSDEN

MELENIA
Royal Castle
Kreng
Penlar

Royal Castle

RUSSEK
Clovek

FREN
Feldiva

WENDAN OCEAN

(LANDANIA)

(KRICOK)

(FIA)

Bizantek Forest

TELMENA

Lumar

(ROMEK)

(ELEK)   EMPERION

LAKESIDE

APETHAGA

(SAREK)   (KROSEK)

EMPEROR'S CITY

(LANEK)

DROMIEN

GREAT OCEAN

GREENWOOD ISLAND

NELL

N

W   E

S

CHAPTER ONE

HARLEY

The door to the bedchamber swung open. Harley pretended to remain focused on the vanity mirror while surreptitiously watching Lyle's reflection as he rushed into the room. He would be irritated she wasn't ready for the party. Harley quickly looped another curl of her long blonde hair on top of her head, pinning it in place, trying to act as serene as possible with him in the room. Lyle stopped a few feet behind her, his eyes narrowing. The hairs on the back of her neck rose, and she had to force herself not to shiver. "By the time you change out of your captain's uniform, I'll be ready," she assured him. Her hands started to shake so she shoved them in her lap, thankful her voice remained sweet and steady, not revealing her true emotions.

"I won't be changing." His fingers slowly curled around the hilt of the sword strapped to his waist.

The king and queen would never approve of her husband arriving in his captain's uniform. "I thought my uncle asked no

1

one don military attire this evening?" She prayed Lyle didn't take offense to her reminding him of that, otherwise she'd suffer for it tonight. However, she didn't want him to be humiliated by her uncle. If that happened, Lyle would find a way to make her pay for his embarrassment tenfold.

"The king asked me to oversee the castle's main gate. Far more people than expected are arriving."

She adjusted one of her curls, carefully watching her husband in the mirror, praying he didn't notice the relief she felt at him not hovering over her all night. Maybe that was why her uncle had asked Lyle to man the gate. Neither he nor the queen were particularly fond of him. The corners of her lips rose as she fought a smile. Not even she cared for him. "I'm surprised you're working tonight since you were on duty all day."

Lyle finally looked away from her. Harley sucked in a breath of fresh air, thankful she'd have a respite and could celebrate her cousin's birthday without having to constantly worry about what she said and did.

"So am I," he mumbled as he surveyed the room, probably to ensure they were alone. When they arrived yesterday, he'd immediately dismissed the lady's maid that had been assigned to Harley, claiming he didn't want anyone snooping around their room. Even back home, he refused to allow servants in their house.

As he walked across the room, Harley noticed his stiff shoulders and twitchy movements. Something had to be bothering him. "I'll miss you this evening." The words felt like cow dung to say; however, she needed to placate him.

At the window, Lyle let go of his sword and shifted the curtain, peering outside. "Since my father is still gone, the king is short men." His words were clipped, indicating he was

2

irritated. "King Coden insisted I stay an extra fortnight with my unit until Commander Beck returns."

Harley tried not to shiver at the mere mention of Commander Beck. She'd never liked Lyle's father. The few times she'd been around him, he'd been too friendly, placing his beefy hand on her shoulder, waist, or even her cheek. She made sure to never be alone with him. Thankfully, he'd left Melenia right after she and Lyle wed. The commander had accompanied Prince Owen to the kingdom of Marsden, taking a significant number of the king's soldiers with him. She wished he'd fall off the ship during the voyage home and drown.

Lyle released the curtain, then turned to face her. "His Majesty insisted you stay as well."

Glancing at her reflection, she made sure her face didn't reveal anything other than that of a doting wife. Once she was certain she appeared meek and mild, she asked, "If you remain here, who will protect our province?" Not that she cared. She'd simply asked the question so Lyle would know she was paying attention to him. If she didn't ask questions or engage often enough, he would assume something was wrong and keep a closer eye on her. The last thing she wanted was to draw attention to herself.

"You don't need to be concerned with such things."

Of course not. She was only a woman after all. Reining in her irritation, Harley gracefully stood from the chair, fixing the folds of her sky-blue dress. The one and only benefit of marrying Lyle had been him being granted the position of captain, in charge of the soldiers stationed in Penlar, the province her parents oversaw. She hadn't wanted to leave the safety of her family home, let alone the countryside where she grew up. Still, she would have preferred to marry someone she enjoyed being around, someone kind and engaging—even if it meant leaving Penlar.

"The party has already started," Lyle said, extending his arm for her to take. "I'll escort you to the great hall before going on duty."

Even though they'd arrived at the royal family's castle yesterday, she had yet to see her uncle or aunt, the king and queen of Melenia. She hadn't even seen her cousins. It had been a few months since she'd spent any time here.

Sucking in her breath, Harley slid her hand on Lyle's arm, trying not to flinch. She loathed touching him. He led her from the bedchamber. Growing up, she'd always known her parents would choose who she married. On the surface, Lyle was handsome to be sure. He wore his blond hair in the typical military style, cut short on the sides with the top slightly longer and neatly combed back. His brown eyes matched the color of damp soil after a light rain. At the age of twenty-seven, he'd already earned the position as a captain in the Melenia army—one of only eight. Of course, his father was the commander of the king's army. But she'd seen Lyle wield a sword. He fought with a ruthless abandon that helped when training soldiers or dealing with uprisings throughout the province.

Since they'd only been married a couple of months, they didn't have any children. As much as Harley wanted to be a mother, she didn't intend to have children with Lyle any time soon—not that she had a say in the matter, but she wasn't ready. Harley shook her head, banishing all thoughts of that right now. It was her cousin's birthday, and she wished to celebrate with her. Since Harley was only two years younger than Oriana, Harley had spent every summer at the royal castle, serving as a playmate for the princess. Which meant she knew this place inside and out, like a second home.

At the end of the hallway, Lyle pulled her to a stop, squeezing her hand. "I need you to do something for me." He opened the door on the left, revealing a storage closet. "Wait in there until I return." He shoved her inside, then closed the door.

"I'm going to be late," she said, confusion rising within her. "My uncle will wonder where I am."

"I won't be long." There was a jingling noise and then a solid *thunk* as the lock slid into place.

With a shaking hand, Harley reached for the handle. It wouldn't budge. "Lyle?" Footsteps sounded as he left her there. "Lyle!" she repeated, this time louder. People were expecting her. The entire purpose of her trip to the royal castle was for the celebration this evening. She couldn't miss it because her husband decided to lock her in a closet. They weren't at home where he could do such things with no one knowing. Her uncle would notice her absence and send someone looking for her.

Tired of obeying Lyle's every command, she banged on the door, seething with anger. This was not how she pictured married life would be. Most days, she remained at home with nothing to do. Lyle didn't want her wandering the countryside while he was out working with his soldiers. Her parents had explained the importance of listening to her husband, whether she agreed with him or not. Since they were married, he owned her. Her dowry had been substantial, and she'd had several suitors. Her parents, Lord Silas and Lady Mayle, considered what each man had to offer before choosing the most advantageous match for their only daughter. Things like companionship, love, and compatibility had nothing to do with it.

"Who's in there?" a male voice demanded from the other side of the door.

"Hollis? Is that you?"

"Harley?" her brother asked, jostling the door handle. "Hang on."

Something clanked against the handle, then the door swung open. "I always wanted to do that," he said, holding his sword in one hand and the broken handle in the other. "What are you doing in there? The party already started."

Defiance and frustration filled her. "Lyle locked me in here," she blurted before thinking better of it. "He told me to wait here for him." Tears threatened. This would not end well.

Hollis's eyes darkened. "He locked you in this closet?" She nodded. He tossed the handle to the floor, then sheathed his sword. "Come on out."

Harley hesitated, not wanting to disobey her husband and pay the price later. Maybe if Hollis closed the door, they could pretend he hadn't seen her in there.

Hollis's eyes flashed with intense anger. "The king sent me to find you. The royal family is about to do a special toast to Princess Oriana. You need to be there." He took hold of her arm, dragging her from the closet. "Since I'm your older brother, I can escort you in place of your husband." His words were clipped and furious. They headed to the large wooden staircase. "Why did Lyle lock you in the closet?"

It probably wasn't a good time for her to mention that her husband did such things quite often back home. She shrugged, hoping to avoid the awkward conversation.

"Do you know where Lyle ran off to?"

"He's guarding the front gates tonight." She lifted her dress so she wouldn't trip as she descended the stairs.

"Is he?" Hollis eyed her sidelong. "I've barely seen you since you arrived. Is married life treating you so well that you don't have time for your favorite brother?" A loaded question. One he probably already knew the answer to given that he'd just found her locked in a closet.

"You're my only brother," she answered, purposely ignoring his implied question. Changing the subject, she said, "I barely recognize you since you're not wearing your uniform tonight." As a member of the royal guard, he spent most of his time in the castle with the king. But tonight, he was just Lord Hollis— an eligible bachelor with considerable wealth and high connections. At a time when poverty was rampant, someone like her brother was highly sought after.

"And I barely recognize you. You've lost weight." At the bottom of the staircase, Hollis headed to the right. The entrance to the great hall stood directly in front of them. "Ready?" he asked as they neared the doors.

"I wish Mother and Father were here." Even though she lived in the same province as them, Lyle rarely let her visit her family.

"You know Mother never comes to the royal castle, and Father's health has been declining. He can't afford to travel so far. It was one of the reasons he insisted on you marrying even though you're only eighteen. He needed to be sure you're taken care of."

The mere thought of her father's failing health made her stomach sour. Growing up, he'd read to her long into the night, insisted she have the same education as her brother, and he'd take her on rides throughout the countryside, ensuring she knew her way around the province. She couldn't imagine him not being there as she traversed her way through life.

Hollis patted her hand. "Because tonight is special, I won't press the matter about why you were locked in a closet. But tomorrow, you and I are going to have a conversation about Lyle." His jaw clenched.

"All right." Maybe it was time she confided in someone about what was going on. However, there was nothing Hollis could do to rectify the situation. She belonged to Lyle now, and he could do with her as he pleased.

When they neared the doors to the great hall, the two men standing guard bowed. The one on the right said, "Welcome Lord Hollis, Lady Harley."

The brother and sister entered the great hall, which had been transformed for the occasion. Garland hung from the beams of the tall ceiling, and flowers decorated the tables around the perimeter of the room. Dozens of people danced in the center of the hall while a group of musicians sat in the corner playing their instruments. The royal family stood on the dais—King Coden, Queen Martie, Prince Oliver, Prince Oakley, and Princess Oriana.

Hollis led Harley through the throng of people. "It doesn't seem right that Prince Owen isn't here," he mused.

"I agree." Owen had always enjoyed parties and dancing.

The king spotted Harley and smiled, waving his niece and nephew to the dais.

"There certainly are a lot of people here," Harley mumbled. So many that the air became hot from the bodies packed so closely together. Though there were many familiar faces, there were several she didn't recognize. However, every single person wore fine clothing, indicating the kingdom's richest and most influential families were in attendance for the birthday celebration.

When they reached the dais, the king wrapped Harley in a hug. "It's good to see you. How's your mother?"

"She's doing well. She sends her love."

"Cousin," Oriana said. "I've missed you. I'm so happy you came to my birthday party." The king released Harley, and Oriana squeezed her. Whispering, she said, "As soon as this toast is over, we need to catch up. I want to hear all about married life." She released Harley and wiggled her eyebrows, indicating which part of married life she wanted to know about.

Harley didn't want to discuss that aspect of her marriage. It was uncomfortable talking about such things. Especially when such things were unpleasant. Maybe if Lyle took his time and wasn't so rough, it would be different.

"Are you okay?" Hollis asked as the two of them moved to the side of the dais.

"I'm fine." She forced a smile on her face. Today was about Oriana. She shoved all thoughts of Lyle away and focused on what she did have—a loving brother, a doting uncle and aunt, and wonderful cousins. It was enough to keep her going.

A servant handed the royal family, along with Hollis and Harley, goblets filled to the brim.

King Coden took a step forward. "Thank you all for coming," he bellowed, capturing everyone's attention.

Holding a drink in hand, Harley watched Oriana beam as the king proceeded to announce how proud he was of his beautiful daughter. Harley wondered if any princes from the neighboring kingdoms were in attendance. Now that Oriana was twenty, it was time she married.

"Raise your drinks," the king said, holding his goblet high. "Happy birthday, Princess Oriana!"

As Harley took a sip, the door to her left banged open, garnering her attention. A hulk of a man with furs draped over his body stepped forward, filling the doorway. A collective hush descended over the great hall. At each entrance, a man of similar size and stature hovered with a sword in hand.

"What's the meaning of this?" King Coden demanded, his face turning red, furious at the untimely interruption.

The dozen or so men remained towering in the doorways, effectively blocking all exits. Like ocean water returning from the shore to the sea, the guests parted, an aisle forming in the middle of the hall. Three men strode toward the dais with lethal intensity. These foreigners were wolves in a room filled with bunnies.

Harley wondered where Melenia's guards were and why they hadn't they stopped these men from interrupting Oriana's party. Cold terror slid down her spine as she recalled Lyle saying that a significant number of the king's soldiers were gone.

Hollis leaned closer to her. "Hide," he whispered, his urgent voice leaving no room for arguing.

Shaking, Harley inched backward, easing off the dais, doing as Hollis commanded even though her mind screamed that this could not be happening. Surely her uncle would stop these men. He'd have them all arrested for their insolence. After setting her goblet on a tray held by a wide-eyed servant, she crept toward the nearest pillar. She forced herself to move slowly while still facing the crowd to avoid standing out.

Hollis remained on the dais with the royal family, angling his body to block her from sight. Scanning the faces of those in the great hall, Harley still didn't see a single Melenia soldier. At the pillar, she paused, watching the scene unfold before her. When the three foreigners reached the dais, the one in the middle stepped forward.

Her uncle shook his head. "I should have known King Drenton of Russek would be behind something like this. What does your father want, Prince Kerdan?" He practically spit the words out, each one laced with venom.

The man who'd stepped forward to address her uncle towered over everyone in the room. His wide shoulders gave way to heavily muscled arms pulling the fabric of his shirt taut. This man had to be a soldier, fighter, or killer. Not a prince. No crown adorned his head to indicate his position. His brown hair hung loose around his face. While Harley had heard rumors Russek's warriors sported black war tattoos, she'd never understood what people meant until now. Black swirls, as if someone had taken a paint brush, covered the man's cheeks and forehead, making him appear more animal than human. The thick furs draped over his shoulders only enhanced the image. Harley shivered.

"We are in need of soldiers," Kerdan stated, his voice thick as it rumbled through the hall. "I've been sent to acquire men."

"You won't get mine," the king spat. "I already told your father I won't align with Russek against Emperion." He took a step down off the dais and approached the warrior prince.

Harley used the opportunity to move closer to the curtain behind the pillar. As she slid back a step, Kerdan's eyes locked with hers, momentarily freezing her in place, before his attention returned to the king. "No one has to get hurt," Kerdan said. "I have the castle surrounded. You're vastly outnumbered." The king opened his mouth to respond, but Kerdan held up his hand, silencing him. "Cooperate and no harm will come to your loved ones."

Sweat beaded on Harley's forehead as the situation intensified. She glanced at her family. Queen Martie clung to Princess Oriana. Prince Oliver stood at the king's shoulder, his hand on the hilt of his sword. Prince Oakley and Hollis moved in front of the queen and princess, as if trying to shield them.

"This is my daughter's birthday celebration," the king seethed.

"Then I suggest you comply so she makes it to her next birthday." Kerdan withdrew his sword, the sound of steel slicing through the air.

Harley jerked as if the sword had cut her arm, a deep foreboding snaking through her. She needed to escape from the great hall and light the warning signal so soldiers from the neighboring towns could come to their aid.

Taking slow, measured steps, she finally reached the curtain off to the side of the dais. After a quick glance to make sure no one nearby watched her, she stepped behind it. A two-foot space separated the thick, heavy curtain from the wall. She'd done this so many times playing hide and seek as a child, that it came naturally to her. The fabric wouldn't sway unless she pushed against it. Regardless, she couldn't remain there. Her hands fumbled over the wooden wall until she felt the small latch, a little lower than she remembered. Pressing on it, a soft click sounded. Harley prayed the hinges wouldn't squeak as she pushed the door open and stepped into the secret passageway made for an event such as this. After shutting the door, she pressed her ear against the wood, trying to hear what was being said in the great hall.

"Take the six members of the royal family to the dungeon," Kerdan ordered. "Everyone else will remain in here. Seal the room."

Panic flooded Harley. Kerdan must have mistaken Hollis for

Owen. Would either the king or queen correct him? Or—Harley swallowed the lump forming in her throat—had Hollis willingly taken Owen's place in order to keep the prince safe?

Several people screamed, and shuffling noises came from the other side of the door. Harley took a step back, hitting the wall. This could not be happening. It felt as if the floor beneath her feet tilted and the walls spun.

Standing there like a frightened cat would not help those she loved. Pushing off the wall, she felt around until her hand came across an unlit torch hanging on the wall. Lifting it, she shoved her hand into the iron holder, grabbing the lighter. It took her several tries before it finally lit. Tears streamed down her cheeks. Hollis had forced her to learn how to do this when she was only eight years old. At the time, she thought it ridiculous torture. Now she understood the necessity.

The turret was at the west end of the castle. With the torch at her side, she traversed through the passageways, being sure to keep the flames as far from her hair and dress as possible. There were two ways to reach the top of the turret where the warning signal was located. Harley could either climb the ladder accessible from the secret passageways, which seemed difficult in a dress, or she could enter the main portion of the castle and use the servants' stairwell, which seemed the safer and quicker option.

When she came to the door closest to the stairwell, she pressed her ear against it, listening. Most exits were located behind large pictures or curtains, so when opened, no one would see. Playing hide and seek here as a child had been an all-day event. And even then, sometimes the cousins still couldn't find one another. She never thought a child's game would one day be vital to the survival of the royal family.

Not hearing any noise, she placed the lit torch in a holder

on the wall. She pulled the door open and slid out behind the curtain, being careful not to ruffle it too much in case someone lurked nearby. She was just about to take a step when footsteps came from the corridor to her right. Afraid to move and accidentally shift the curtain, she froze. Pinching her lips together, she breathed slowly and waited, trying not to shake from fright. This was just another game of hide and seek.

"I understand your concerns," a male voice said softly.

"I don't think you do," another male voice hissed. "Things have already deviated too far from the plan. Why is the royal family in the dungeon? They are supposed to be dead."

"That's because my stepbrother, Kerdan, is in charge."

"Why is he here?" the man whispered.

"His father asked him to plan this entire invasion. But don't worry, come morning, everything will be as it should and Kerdan will be dead. Once he's out of the way, no one will stop you from executing the royal family."

CHAPTER TWO

HARLEY

*H*arley started violently shaking. *Executed*. This man wanted her uncle, aunt, and cousins dead. Since Hollis was in the dungeon in Owen's place, he would be killed as well. She had to do something to prevent her family from being murdered.

"You're going to assassinate Prince Kerdan?" the man whispered.

"With immense pleasure," the other replied, his voice slithering like a snake.

"That wasn't part of the plan. I won't have you pin it on me." Panic laced the man's words.

A throaty chuckle rumbled a few feet away. "You forget who you're speaking to. If I were you, I'd watch my tone."

A shiver swept through Harley's body. She needed to get out of there, but she was too afraid to move with the men so close by.

Another shuffle sounded only a few inches away. "Of course, Prince Soma. My apologies."

"Don't use my name, you fool. Now take me to my supplies before someone sees me."

"I have everything you requested hidden in a room down this corridor." Footsteps headed to the left. "I'd like to set aside some time tomorrow for us to discuss a loose end."

"I won't be here tomorrow. After I do what needs to be done, I'm going to Emperion. There's someone there I need to deal with."

When the voices and footsteps faded away, Harley reached back, finding the clasp and opening the hidden door. She would have to reach the turret the other way since Prince Soma and the person he'd been talking to had gone down the corridor she needed to use.

Back in the passageway, she grabbed the torch, her arm shaking. It felt like she was going to vomit as the gravity of the situation overwhelmed her. Unable to waste a single minute, she forced her legs to move, heading toward the turret. Based upon the conversation she'd just overheard, Kerdan wanted the royal family alive, at least for now. He probably needed King Coden to sign a treaty or declaration. Since Kerdan had locked the nobles in the great hall, it seemed logical to assume he would try negotiating with the king, using the nobility as a bargaining chip. However, Prince Soma planned on assassinating Prince Kerdan. Once that happened, he'd said the royal family would be executed. A fierce determination filled Harley—she would save her family or die trying. She started jogging since there wasn't much time for help to arrive.

At the base of the turret, she examined the tall ladder positioned in the middle of the circular stone tower. After hanging up the torch, she wiped her sweaty hands on her dress, then grabbed hold of the first rung. She started climbing, trying not to step on the hem of her dress and slip.

Harley climbed five stories before reaching the top of the ladder. She flopped onto a small rectangular platform, panting as she looked out of the opening carved into the wall. She had to go through it in order to light the signal fire. Taking a calming breath, she climbed out to a narrow stairwell about five feet high that led to the top of the turret. Wind whipped around her face, causing her hair to unravel, making it hard to see. Afraid she'd plunge to her death, she gathered her hair together, tying it in a knot before kneeling next to the large pile of wood.

Not daring to look over the side for fear she'd become disoriented and fall, she grabbed the lighter, focusing on it. With shaking hands, she tried to get a spark. It didn't work. She attempted it again, doing it just as she'd been taught. Nothing happened. Tears filled her eyes. Her family was going to die if she didn't get help. All that stood between her and salvation was a single flame. Her brother's voice filled her head, calmly instructing her how to light the fire. Focusing on his words, she did as he said. An ember flared, catching on the kindling. Relief filled her as thick black smoke rose into the sky for the nearby towns to see. It was the signal that the castle was under attack and to send help.

The heat from the fire became intense, forcing Harley to crawl back to the stairwell. As she descended the steps, her breath caught. Surrounding the castle, hundreds of enemy soldiers dotted the landscape. She scanned the area looking for fellow Melenians. A group of about fifty stood huddled together in a hastily constructed pen surrounded by a half dozen spears sticking up out of the ground, a head skewered on top of each one. Bile rose in the back of her throat at the horror of Melenia soldiers being beheaded. What an awful way to die.

With shaky legs, she climbed back into the turret. As she descended the ladder, she heard men shouting the words *smoke* and *fire*. She needed to hide before someone found her in there. In too much of a hurry, her right foot slipped, her chin smacking one of the rungs, jarring her head. Tears streamed down her cheeks as she clutched onto the rung, hanging on for dear life. She frantically flailed about until her feet found purchase and she steadied herself. With a wildly beating heart, sweaty palms, and shaking arms, she hastily descended the rest of the ladder. When Harley neared the bottom, cold fingers curled around her ankle, startling her.

"Didn't expect to find a woman lighting the signal," a man with a thick accent mused. He yanked her.

She tumbled to the floor, her back stinging in pain and the air knocked out of her. The man reached down, grabbing her arms and lifting her upright. As she dangled in his grip, gasping for air, fear overrode the pain and she kicked at his stomach, trying to get him to drop her. If he'd just let go, she could run away and hide in one of the storage closets.

Tightening his grip, he slammed her against the wall of the turret, pinning her in place as he towered over her by at least two feet. "Who are you?" he demanded.

Her mind screamed in panic, trying to think of a way out of this mess. "I have information for Prince Kerdan," she blurted, a crazy plan forming. If Kerdan died, so would the royal family, which meant she needed to prevent the prince's assassination.

The Russek soldier raised his eyebrows. "You just lit the signal fire. You are no friend to Russek." He gripped her harder, as if trying to intimidate her.

Dangling above the floor, she shoved her fear away and summoned every ounce of arrogance she had. "One of your own plans on killing your prince. Apparently, no one is a friend to Russek."

The man loosened his grip, his brows furrowing. "Where did you hear that?" His deep voice rumbled with menace.

"I'll only speak to Prince Kerdan."

"How do you know that's not me?"

A good, loaded, dangerous question. Swallowing, she said, "Because I've met him before." She now understood why the prince chose not to wear a crown or clothing to indicate his position, thus allowing him to blend in with his soldiers. During a takeover or battle, it would be wise to switch places with another soldier to not stand out like a target.

The man set her on her feet and took a step back, observing her. Seconds went by. Harley raised her chin, refusing to cower before him.

He nodded. "Let's go." Clutching her upper arm, he dragged her out of the passageways and into the servants' corridor.

Fear flared inside Harley. She had no idea if this man was going to toss her outside the castle, take her to Kerdan, or do something far more nefarious with her. Not having any other options, she decided not to fight or argue with him, her mind scrambling to come up with a backup plan if this didn't go as she hoped.

Loud, boisterous voices of foreigners resounded up ahead. Harley stifled her panic. If she wanted to negotiate with Russek soldiers, she needed to be brave and bold.

"In here." The man led her into the kitchen where a dozen men sat around a rectangular table, talking with one another as they shoveled food in their mouths. All of them had large, squared shoulders with furs draped over them, confirming

Harley had just walked into a room full of enemy soldiers. The man escorting her shoved her forward, and she stumbled.

All twelve men turned to scrutinize her. "Who's this?" asked one of the soldiers toward the middle of the table.

Harley recognized him as Prince Kerdan. She tried to find her voice to respond; however, no words came out.

"I found her in the turret," the man behind her announced. "She lit the signal fire."

"Why did you bring her here?" Kerdan inquired, setting his spoon down.

"She has information for you."

Kerdan took a drink from his cup, then stood and approached Harley, his eyes scanning her from head to toe, assessing her.

She craned her head up, forcing herself to meet his eyes. "Prince Kerdan." Her voice came out shaky. She imagined her mother scolding her for being frightened before a group of brute soldiers. Clutching her hands together, she tried to keep her chin high, summoning her inner strength. In order to save her brother, she needed to convince Kerdan to let him go.

"You were on the dais with the royal family." He folded his arms, tilting his head to the side as he continued to observe her. "Are you related to them? Or perhaps you are engaged to one of the princes?"

She didn't want to reveal her relationship to the royal family quite yet, so she refused to answer.

"How'd you escape from the great hall?" he asked, his voice curious and not threatening as she'd anticipated.

Of course, that could be a ploy to lure her in to trusting him. She considered lying but decided against it because she didn't have much time. "The secret passageways." Since the man had found her at the bottom of the turret, the passageways must have been discovered. She felt better revealing information they'd already ascertained.

Kerdan considered her. "What's your name?"

"It's not important." Not that he would recognize her name anyway since her mother was related to the queen, not the king.

The corners of his lips pulled into a tight smile, and she realized her error. Only someone important would say that. Wanting to change the subject rather than reveal she was the king's niece, she said, "I overheard information you'll find vital to your survival."

"We just imprisoned Melenia's royal family and took over the castle. Why would you want to help me?" He raised his eyebrows, awaiting her response.

She found it interesting he didn't question the validity of her news, but rather, her reasoning behind wanting to aid him. She swallowed, considering her words carefully. It felt as if she stood on thin ice, small cracks splintering out from under her feet. "The royal family is alive because of you." She hoped the truth kept the ice from shattering completely. She needed him to keep her family alive.

"I gave strict orders that no harm will come to them. We are only here for soldiers."

As relieved as she was to hear that, she scoffed at the notion that needing soldiers justified the invasion. While the royal family hadn't been harmed, there were dead Melenians outside the castle. Families would be grieving from their losses.

"What information do you have for me?" He glanced over his shoulder at his fellow soldiers who remained at the table.

"After I tell you this information, what will you do with me?" He could have her thrown in the dungeon, taken to the great hall with the other nobles, or locked up outside in the pen holding the Melenia soldiers. None of these possibilities seemed particularly appealing.

"I don't plan to do anything with you. Once you tell me whatever it is you came here to tell me, you are free to go."

Her eyes narrowed, considering the reason he would simply release her when everyone else had been locked up.

"I have no use for you," he explained.

She studied this large man before her. His towering physique, tattoos, and furs all screamed of a bloodthirsty warrior. But his words seemed to contradict his appearance. "Why did you come here for our soldiers?" she inquired, curiosity getting the better of her.

He rubbed his face. "I'm tired and hungry. I'd like to finish my supper. Tell me your information and go. If other Russeks find you here, they may not be so accommodating."

The threat slithered down her back. Her legs shook, and she could feel the ice cracking beneath her. "While I was sneaking through the secret passageways, I overheard a conversation between Prince Soma and a soldier."

Kerdan's eyes narrowed. "Did you? I'm surprised, seeing as how Soma isn't supposed to be here."

Every single soldier at the table stopped eating, turning to watch the prince and Harley's exchange.

"Prince Soma doesn't want you to know he's here because he intends to assassinate you tonight."

"You heard him say this?" Kerdan demanded, his eyes blazing with fury.

"I did." Everyone in the kitchen remained so still she wondered if the soldiers were even breathing. At least she had their undivided attention, and Kerdan appeared to believe her.

"When?"

"Just before I lit the warning signal." No one here seemed particularly concerned that she'd lit the signal and neighboring towns would be sending their soldiers.

Kerdan spun toward the table. "Everyone back."

They all did as he instructed.

"Soma loves his poisons," one of the soldiers mumbled.

Kerdan went over to his plate, sniffing the food. If Soma had managed to poison Kerdan already, Harley would need to either find a way to save him or come up with another plan. Neither seemed doable at the moment.

"I don't smell anything," Kerdan said. "But Soma is sly and talented." When he stood upright, his face appeared whiter than before. "I need to get to my bags. The necessary provisions are in there."

The men started barking orders to one another.

Kerdan approached her again.

She assumed the provisions he mentioned were to counter the poison. "Are you going to be all right?" Once he took what was necessary, he could go after Soma, ensuring her family remained alive.

"Thank you for this information. If what you said is true, I can't guarantee the safety of the royal family."

"Why not?" she demanded. It was the only reason she'd told him about the assassination.

He reached under his fur wrap and withdrew a key. "This is for the dungeon. I suggest you free them immediately. We're leaving."

Her fingers curled around the key. "You can't leave." He was the only thing standing between her family and their deaths.

"My provisions aren't here with me. I stashed them a mile away." He grabbed her shoulders, forcing her to look into his eyes. "That is the only key. Use the secret passageways to get to the royal family. Then sneak them out of the castle under the cover of night. Get as far away from here as you can. Understand?"

She nodded, wondering why he couldn't get his provisions and then return here. "You're not coming back?"

The pupils of his eyes seemed as if they were getting wider. "I doubt I'll be able to do anything for days. By then, it'll probably be too late." He released her and exited the kitchen with his men.

Standing all alone, Harley clutched the key to the dungeon. She would have to come up with another plan—something to stall until help arrived. Since she'd lit the signal, it would only be a matter of time. She hurried from the kitchen, rushing back to the entrance of the secret passageways. When she reached for the hidden clasp, something smacked the back of her head, knocking her to the floor.

Cold hands pried her fingers open, plucking the key from her. "You almost ruined everything."

With her vision blurry, she couldn't make out the man who rolled her over and slid a piece of cloth over her mouth. When Harley breathed in, the cloth smelled funny. Complete blackness engulfed her.

Harley peeled her eyelids open, blinking against the bright light. She found herself lying on a bed in one of the guest suites in the royal castle. When she sat up, her vision blurred and her mouth felt sticky and dry. The back of her head throbbed, so she gently touched it, finding a lump. She remembered someone placing a cloth over her mouth and nose, drugging her. Before she'd passed out, the person took the key to the dungeon from her.

She shoved the covers off her body and slid out of bed. Rushing over to the window, she saw the sun already cresting the nearby hills. A sense of dread filled her as she imagined all that could have happened while she'd been passed out in bed. She ran to the door and grabbed the handle, trying to yank it open, but it wouldn't budge. Out in the hallway, she heard people running by. She pounded on the door, but no one stopped to help her. A few screams resounded from somewhere inside the castle. She needed to find her brother.

Something wet soaked through her shoes. Peering down, she saw blood flowing into the room from under the door, pooling around her feet. Horrified, she took a step back, vomit rising in the back of her throat. Last night, she'd lit the signal fire. Had no one come to help them? More screams echoed through the castle. The hair on the back of her neck stood on end. She needed to get out of there before someone crashed through the door and butchered her.

Running over to the window, she threw it open and climbed out, hanging by her hands. Since she was on the second floor, she didn't have far to fall. A bloodcurdling scream came from inside the castle. That was all the encouragement she needed to let go. Her stomach felt like it had worms crawling inside as she dropped to the ground, bending her legs to soften the landing.

Chaos ensued all around her. She sprinted as fast as she could away from the castle. Servants ran from Russek soldiers who wielded swords dripping with blood, boasting of the kills they'd already made. At the front of the castle, hundreds of Melenia soldiers stood in orderly lines, weapons at the ready. Relief filled Harley. These had to be men from the neighboring towns who'd seen the signal fire and came to help. She headed toward them, her eyes filling with tears. The person in charge needed to know that the royal family remained locked in the dungeon.

"Put down your weapons!" a loud voice boomed from the open gorge tower on the side of the castle facing the Melenia soldiers. That was where the royal family usually addressed their subjects.

Harley screeched to a halt, as did most of the people around her. Dozens of archers stood on top of the castle, all with armed bows pointed at the people below. She glanced at the Melenia soldiers, trying to decide if she could make it to them before someone struck her down with an arrow.

One of the Melenia soldiers took a step forward. "We only take orders from our king."

Pride swelled within Harley. She wanted to jump up and down in agreement before telling the Russek soldier to stuff it. If only she had a weapon and knew how to fight.

The man on the open tower smiled. "I'm so glad you mentioned your king."

A half-dozen Russek soldiers dragged King Coden, Queen Martie, Prince Oliver, Prince Oakley, Princess Oriana, and Hollis from inside the castle to the stone platform, visible for all below to see. The royal family had their hands tied behind their backs and their mouths gagged.

As Harley feared, her brother had been mistaken for Prince Owen. She wanted to scream that they'd made an error and to let her brother go. However, no words came out of her mouth. Instead, seeing her brother at the mercy of Russek soldiers paralyzed her with undiluted terror.

"We offered your weak king a treaty to work with us!" the Russek soldier bellowed. He pointed at the royal family now lined up beside him. "He refused the treaty. Now he pays the price."

One of the soldiers grabbed the queen's hair, dragging her forward. The queen screamed through her gag, kicking her legs. Horror filled Harley. She opened her mouth to yell at him to let her aunt go, but again, no words escaped her mouth. The soldier shoved the queen down until she was bent over the tower wall. Another soldier neared, an axe in hand.

Harley started running, waving her arms, trying to get the executioner's attention. She had to stop him from killing her aunt. Strong arms wrapped around her torso, pinning her in place. She shouted, but a hand covered her mouth.

"Shut up or you're next," a fellow Melenian hissed in her ear.

The executioner lifted the axe. The crude weapon seemed to pause in the air above the queen's neck, before slicing down, chopping the queen's head off. Blood gushed from the body, flowing down the side of the castle like a banner. Another soldier grabbed her severed head, raising it for all to see the queen's face distorted with shock.

The executioner shoved the body over the wall, and it plummeted two stories to the ground below, landing with a sickening *thud*.

A ringing sounded in Harley's head, and her entire body became numb. This had to be a nightmare. This could not be happening.

A Russek soldier brought Hollis forward. He didn't even try to fight.

Harley's legs gave out, but she remained standing since the man still held her upright. She could do nothing but watch as the soldier pushed Hollis down against the wall. "Fight," she begged, the word muffled by the hand covering her mouth. "Fight!"

The executioner raised the axe again. Blackness hovered at the corners of her vision and she squeezed her eyes shut, unable to watch. The sickening sound of metal clanking against stone echoed. Then a moment later, the *thunk* of a body hitting the ground. Harley opened her eyes and vomited. The man holding her shoved her away. She stumbled to her knees, her body violently shaking with shock.

Her cousin, Oriana, was next. Even with the gag on, Oriana's scream pierced the air. The Russek picked Oriana up, laying her on the wall so she was forced to see the executioner standing above her. Her body thrashed as the axe flew down. Gagging, Harley grabbed the dirt, trying to wake up from this nightmare.

The Russek barbarians cheered. She couldn't watch as Oakley and then Oliver were similarly killed.

They saved the king for last. Perhaps so he'd be forced to watch his entire family be murdered. It seemed as if time slowed as the king was stripped of his clothing. He kicked the soldier next to him, refusing to go down without a fight. The soldier withdrew his sword, slicing the king's leg, blood gushing out. Three soldiers pounced on the king, dragging him to the wall where they held his bucking body in place. Smiling, the executioner swung twice before the head was fully severed from the body. The front of the castle was blackened with blood.

"Your king is dead!" a Russek soldier exclaimed. "Melenia is no more!"

It felt as if something in Harley splintered into pieces. Mixed with undiluted horror was pure, violent rage at the injustice of what had happened. Her family dead. Her kingdom taken. Her heart broken.

Six Russek soldiers stepped forward, each jamming a spear into the tower wall normally reserved for banners. Then the executioner skewered a head to the top of each one. The Russeks whooped with frenzied excitement. Harley couldn't even look at the faces of her loved ones—each permanently contorted in fury, anger, terror, pain. She felt all of it mirrored inside of her.

"Now we take the rest of the kingdom!" a Russek soldier cried out. "Put down your weapons and join us or die!"

CHAPTER THREE

Chaos erupted as arrows rained down and people shouted, running away from the castle. Russeks advanced toward the Melenia soldiers, swords clashing as the barbarians began slicing through them as if they were stocks of wheat. Blood flowed on the ground like water after a downpour.

Harley considered remaining there. It wouldn't take long before a Russek rammed his sword into her. Then she, too, would be dead, unable to feel the pain from the losses of her loved ones. However, if she allowed herself to die, her brother would be utterly disappointed in her for giving up. More so, no one else would seek revenge for Hollis's death.

Her brother's death would not be in vain.

Determination brewing within, Harley scrambled to her feet, forcing herself to run for the nearby cornfield. Someone barreled into her, knocking her off balance and sending her flying to the ground. Rough hands grabbed her body, flipping her onto her back.

A Russek soldier pinned her arms down. He leered at her, his face covered with sweat and blood. "Didn't know there were any women left," he said. "We took care of all the ones inside. Now it's your turn." His knee shoved her legs apart.

Crude realization dawned on Harley. This man didn't want to simply kill her—he intended to violate her first. She screamed, hoping one of her fellow Melenians would assist her.

People ran by, yelling and fighting, but no one stopped to help her.

"No!" She shoved back with all her might.

His smile widened. "It's more fun when you resist." Using one hand, he clutched her wrists together above her head, his other hand yanking her dress up.

Thrashing wildly, she tried to break his hold on her, refusing to die like this.

The man flew forward, landing on top of her. With her arms no longer pinned down, she shoved at him, trying to get free.

In an instant, the weight was gone as someone pulled the man's body off of her. She sucked in a huge breath, staring up into a stranger's eyes. He flung a bow over his shoulder and reached a hand down. She didn't hesitate to take it. Clutching it, she let him help her to her feet.

While pushing her dress down over her legs, she glanced at her attacker, slack on the ground, an arrow protruding from his back.

"He's dead," the stranger confirmed. "Let's go." He started running, joining two other men, both armed.

Harley ran after them, not knowing what else to do. While the three men didn't wear the uniform of a Melenia soldier, they clearly weren't servants since they expertly wielded weapons. They weren't from Russek because they were too skinny, didn't bear war tattoos, and didn't sport furs. They had to be off-duty Melenia soldiers.

Bloodcurdling cries for help rang out behind Harley as she sprinted after them into the cornfield. With tears filling her eyes and pouring down her cheeks, she forced one foot in front of the other. Her brother would want her to do whatever was necessary to survive.

And survive she would.

They didn't stop until nightfall. Harley had no idea which direction they were going. Her stomach cramped from physical exertion, a lack of food, and the horror of what she'd seen. Heads. On spikes. And destruction everywhere. Panting, she bent over, trying to catch her breath.

"They're already here, too," one of the men said.

They'd stopped just outside a small farming village. Which one, Harley had no idea.

"We should rest," another said. "And we need food." He rubbed his face. "What now, Ledger?"

The two men turned to the stranger who'd saved Harley.

"Since they seem to be stationed along the Landania border, we need to head west."

Harley peered at Ledger.

His shaggy blond hair clung to his face, coated in sweat and dirt. He looked at her, and their eyes locked. "Who are you?"

She straightened. "I'm..." Tired, horrified, on the verge of collapse. "I'm the king's niece," she revealed. "My name is Harley."

Ledger whistled. "You're probably the only noble who made it out alive." His speech confirmed he was from Melenia, not

Russek. However, she couldn't determine his position based upon his nondescript clothing. His youthful face indicated he was around twenty.

One of the other men folded his thick muscled arms. "I'm Rayne. My father is a member of the king's royal guard." He closed his eyes. "Was. My father was...the Russeks murdered him." His slicked back hair highlighted the short beard on his face, putting his age around twenty-five.

Rayne had said his father was a member of the king's royal guard—which meant he worked with Hollis. Tears filled Harley's eyes remembering the gory image of her brother's head being skewered on a spike. Her stomach rolled with nausea, and she shoved the memory away. She couldn't think about it. Right now, all her focus needed to be on surviving.

"I'm a guard at the front gate," Rayne continued. "When Russek showed up, they started killing us. I was sent to warn the royal family. Someone hit me on the back of the head, so I didn't make it very far. I was left for dead."

She looked at Rayne. "My husband was on duty at the front gate. Do you know what happened to him?"

"They killed everyone," Rayne said softly. "I'm sorry."

She'd figured as much. Not that she cared since she didn't love Lyle. The loss of her relatives was another matter entirely. And her brother. It felt like a knife had been plunged into her heart.

"I'm Milard," the third man said. Like the other two, he had blond hair. However, his stringy hair reached his shoulders, his square face revealing his age closer to thirty.

Ledger clutched his bow, a mixture of anger, hurt, and sadness flitting across his face as he did so. "Milard and I are soldiers in the king's army. We're responsible for patrolling the castle. We weren't on duty during the takeover. Instead of helping our fellow soldiers, we were sleeping. Our shift was supposed to start at sunrise. We woke up when we heard people screaming. We barely managed to escape. More than half our unit was butchered like pigs."

Milard patted Ledger's shoulder. "No one blames you for what happened."

Ledger nodded, shrugging him off. "Now that we're far enough away from the castle, I want to find a safe place to sleep for a few hours. Then, when I can think clearly, we can figure out what to do."

She nodded. They'd all lost friends and loved ones today.

Harley peeled her crusted eyelids open. Everything hurt. Her body, her heart. She sat up, surveying the scene before her. Milard and Ledger sat next to a fire, the smoke concealed by the low hanging branches above.

"Where's Rayne?" she asked, yawning.

"He went to the nearby town to see the state of things," Milard answered.

"We've decided to continue west," Ledger added, poking the fire with a stick. "We're trying to get as far away from the castle as possible. Once we have a better idea of what's going on, we'll come up with a plan."

Milard snorted. "And by plan he means whether Melenia is truly lost to Russek or if we can raise an army to fight and take it back."

"Who would rule? There aren't any surviving royals," Ledger pointed out.

Harley sat up straighter. "That's not true."

Ledger pursed his lips. "I thought you knew," he said gently. "The entire royal family was executed."

"Did you see it?" she asked, scooting closer to the fire.

He nodded.

"Didn't you notice Prince Owen was not present?"

"I'd heard rumors he went on a secret mission to another kingdom," Milard said. "I assumed he'd returned." He scratched his head. "Four siblings were executed."

Harley wiped the tears already flowing again, surprised she had any left. "My brother, Hollis, wasn't on duty during the invasion." If Owen had been home, would Hollis be alive?

"Hollis?" Ledger asked. "As in Lord Hollis of the king's royal guard?"

She nodded. "We were at the party together, standing on the dais, when Prince Kerdan arrived. Hollis told me to hide in the secret passageways. No one noticed me slip away. That's how I escaped." She wiped her face with her sleeve, still unable to believe her brother had been brutally executed. The air became difficult to breathe. Her heart physically hurt.

"Put your head between your knees," Milard said. "It'll help."

She did as he suggested. The wretched feeling in her stomach intensified, but her breathing steadied. "I can't believe any of this is happening." She kept expecting to wake up from this nightmare. Maybe she'd been thrown from her horse on the way to the castle and was suffering from an injury. Because this...this couldn't be real.

"She's not looking good," Milard mumbled to Ledger.

"Please don't leave me here," she said. She didn't think she could fend for herself. Especially since she was a woman. The way that man had almost violated her was still fresh in her mind. Looking at her wrists, she saw bruises had already formed where he'd held her. She'd been too weak to fight him off. Growing up, she'd begged her father to teach her to fight. He'd refused, saying a woman's place was in the home, not wielding a sword. If he'd taught her, she could have saved herself.

"We're not going to leave you," Ledger assured her, tossing the stick in the fire. "You're the only one who knows Prince Owen is alive. Where can we find him?"

Owen was now the king of Melenia—a position her cousin wouldn't want. Not only would he be devastated to learn of his family's death, but he wasn't prepared to sit on the throne. Since he had three older siblings, he'd spent his days doing as he pleased. Oftentimes, he'd sneak and train with the soldiers, or hide in the king's office where'd he'd eavesdrop on his father's meetings. The king had indulged him instead of preparing him for a life embedded in politics. Harley cleared her throat. "Commander Beck and a large portion of our soldiers are with Owen," she said, recalling what Lyle had told her. "Once they return, it might be enough to retake the kingdom." Maybe. If there was anything left to salvage.

"Can you get a letter to Owen?"

She tried remembering where he'd gone. "He sailed to a kingdom across the sea." That much she knew. And her aunt had said something about illicit trading going on. "We have to go to Kreng. If there's a way to get a letter to my cousin, it'll be from there."

"Kreng?" Ledger said. "We're not supposed to step foot in that city. Even though it's in Melenia, we don't control it."

She was well aware of the particulars. Her uncle had frequently complained about the prosperous city. "If we want to save Melenia, that's where we need to go." Illicit trade only took place from one port—Kreng. And if they were trading with the kingdom across the sea, surely someone in the city would be able to dispatch a letter to Owen.

"It'll be in their best interest to cooperate with us," Milard pointed out. "We'll warn them of the invasion. Gain their trust. Maybe we can work together."

"And pray they don't run us through with a sword," Ledger mumbled.

Rayne joined them, carrying two skinned rabbits. "We can't stay here," he whispered. "Two miles to the east, Russek troops are moving south." Rayne skewered the rabbits on a stick, putting them over the fire to cook.

Rubbing her face, she wondered if her parents were alive. If Russek was pushing south toward Landania, her town had probably been overrun. Did her parents manage to make it out safely? Or had she lost everyone she loved?

Harley inched closer to the fire, wanting to warm her freezing hands. When she reached forward, she noticed the bruises on her wrists again. She shivered, remembering her first time with Lyle. After their wedding ceremony, he'd taken her to his house. Instead of entering through the front door, he'd led her in the back, which went to the kitchen. There, he explained that he expected her to prepare three hot meals a day for him. Then he shoved her onto the table where he pinned her wrists behind her back. He said he didn't want to see her ugly face as he rammed himself inside of her. She remembered telling herself it was better to be on her stomach where she couldn't see him, either. Once he'd finished, he'd ordered her to cook supper. Given her station in life, she'd never cooked anything before and had no idea what to do. She remembered sitting on the floor, crying, nasty bruises forming on her wrists.

"Are you okay?" Ledger asked, startling Harley.

Shoving the memories aside, she forced a smile on her face.

"I want to thank you for killing that Russek soldier earlier today." She'd been through enough with Lyle and didn't need to be abused by another man.

He nodded. "We were running by. I heard you scream. I shot him before I even realized what he was doing."

"He didn't." Not that she needed to explain anything to him; however, she wanted him to know that he'd not only saved her life, but he'd prevented her from being violated. "You stopped him in time," she clarified.

The three men all focused on the fire, each probably lost in memories of what they saw and experienced at the castle.

"I wish we could have helped others," Ledger muttered.

Milard peered over at Harley. "I'm sorry for your loss. My father was killed at the castle. It was a quick death. Nothing like what you witnessed with your brother and the royal family."

She couldn't think about them being tortured and executed. There were only so many horrific things she could handle. And the last twenty-four hours had provided her with more than enough to last a lifetime.

"Let's just get to Kreng quickly," she said. Having something to focus on gave her purpose and kept her mind from dwelling on the evilness she'd encountered. In order to make Hollis's death, along with the deaths of her aunt, uncle, and cousins, mean something, she had to rid the kingdom of Russek. And she needed to find Owen so he could retake the throne.

Ledger withdrew his sword, placing it over the fire. Milard and Rayne did the same, looking at her, expectation written across their faces.

Harley raised her eyebrows in question. "I'm sorry," she said, "I don't know what this means."

"We're making a vow," Ledger explained. "Do you have a weapon?"

When she shook her head, Rayne reached into his boot, withdrawing a dagger and handing it to her.

She took the weapon, sticking it over the fire as the others had done. Hers wasn't long enough to reach the tips of their swords, so she placed her tip against Rayne's blade.

"We vow here and now," Ledger said, "to seek vengeance for the murders and destruction committed by the hands of Russek soldiers. We will not rest until King Owen is on the throne and Melenia is once again under our control."

Everyone grunted in agreement, then removed their swords from the licking flames. Harley went to give the weapon back to Rayne.

"Keep it," he said, waving his hand at her. "You need something to defend yourself with."

"Speaking of defending myself," she said, "can you teach me how to use this thing?" She didn't even know how to hold it properly. Whenever she'd asked Lyle, he'd insisted a woman had no business touching a weapon.

The three men sitting alongside her all smiled. But it was Ledger who said, "We'll protect you. I promise."

That was when Harley realized her old life was truly gone, and nothing would be like it was before.

CHAPTER FOUR

ACKLEY

*A*ckley leaned over the railing of the ship. The ocean water slammed against the side of it as they sailed closer to Melenia. It had been almost two weeks and his stomach still felt like a raging storm. The first day aboard, he'd understood it. Expected it. But the entire miserable trip?

"Your sister asked me to come and check on you," Gytha said from behind him.

He peered over his shoulder, glaring at the warrior woman. From the moment she climbed on board, she'd had her sea legs, not sick at all. He resented her for it. As usual, Gytha's thick black hair had been pulled back into her signature braid, accentuating the angles of her high cheekbones and tanned skin. The muscles in her arms were well defined—especially for a woman. If he had to choose one word to describe her, it would be formidable.

"Just so you know, we're almost there." She stood alongside

him. There had always been an easy companionship between them. "Then you can stop heaving up your insides. Maybe regain your weight." She chuckled. "This must kill you—being the weakest one on the ship."

Ackley took a deep breath, trying not to let her comment sting. She was right, though. Being sick the entire two weeks across the Wendan Ocean proved him incompatible with the sea. And here he'd always thought he could overcome anything. The realization that there were some things he could not master only infuriated him all the more.

Maybe if the water didn't move so much, he wouldn't feel so awful. At least they were supposed to reach landfall tomorrow. He'd been diligently counting down the days until his head would stop being a bowl of mushed oatmeal and his stomach wouldn't expel the food he attempted to consume.

"You missed the meeting," Gytha said, gazing out at the bright sun gleaming over the water. "Owen is wondering if you should appoint someone else to be in charge of the Marsden soldiers."

Even though she hadn't asked it as a question, Ackley knew she was there seeking his decision. He rubbed his sunburnt face. He'd planned on leading the Marsden soldiers when they stepped foot on Melenia soil. However, in his current state, he didn't know if he could. It may take him a day or two until he felt better. And then there was the part about him needing to regain his strength. He hadn't been able to workout once since boarding this blasted vessel. Given that they had no idea what they'd face in Melenia, he hesitated, wondering if there be an immediate fight.

Ackley flexed his hand, his fingers shaking. He wouldn't be useless in a scuffle, but he definitely wouldn't be at his best. A full-blown battle was another matter entirely. "I'll consider it." There were several men who could do the job, but he didn't want to cede control right away.

He glanced at Gytha's face. Fierce determination shone in her eyes. It was one of the things he admired most about her. "Can I ask a favor of you?"

"Of course."

Focusing on the ocean again, he said, "I want you to watch out for my sister."

"It would be my honor."

He'd come on this trip for two reasons—one being to protect his sister. Now, he didn't trust his skills given his current state. Gytha was one of the most adept warriors he knew. When he'd first met her, he hadn't expected her to wield a sword with such strength and precision. When he sparred with her, he didn't have to rein himself in. It was one of the reasons she was a captain in the Marsden army and one of the king's most trusted soldiers. The other reason Ackley had ventured on this journey, he hadn't yet thought about. He'd deal with *her* later. For now, ignoring the woman he left back in Marsden was easier than facing the fact that she'd just married another man. He blinked, attempting to banish all thoughts of her from his mind.

"Speaking of your sister, here she is now." Gytha straightened. "I will leave the two of you alone."

Idina came alongside Ackley, her bright red hair flowing wildly in the wind. "How are you, of all people, still sick?" She wrinkled her nose in disgust.

He shrugged. He excelled in everything he did. Except sailing, apparently.

She looked sidelong at him. "When we arrive tomorrow, I'll need my brother in top shape."

"I'll be fine." He had no idea how he'd make the journey home. The likelihood of him ever stepping foot on a ship again wasn't promising.

Idina lowered her voice and mumbled, "Owen is concerned."

That made the two of them. Since his sister liked to overthink and overanalyze everything, he said, "Last time I checked, there were less than a dozen Marsdens sick. That means there will be more than enough healthy soldiers to march with Melenia's and take control of the kingdom." The letter Owen had received from Melenia stated that Russek invaded during a birthday celebration and took over, killing the entire royal family. With so little information, they had no idea if any Melenia soldiers, besides the ones onboard, were left to fight. Owen assumed the worst—that most soldiers had been killed during the invasion.

"We hope." She gripped the rail, digging her fingers in. "We have no idea what we're walking into."

At least they had the element of surprise on their side. "I assume we'll be one of the last ships entering port?" He hoped there wasn't a battle right away. Since the royal residence was located in the northeastern portion of the kingdom, he didn't see a reason for the Russeks to have soldiers stationed along the coast. Especially since no one knew where Owen had been.

Owen's mother, the late queen of Melenia, had sent him along with Commander Beck and five hundred Melenia soldiers to Marsden. Ackley rubbed his face. The entire thing had been a whole mess he didn't want to rehash. At least Owen had prevented Commander Beck from taking control of Marsden. Instead, Owen decided to trust Ackley, siding with him and striking a deal with King Dexter of Marsden. Part of that deal was Owen's engagement to Princess Idina, Dexter's cousin. The two kings hoped to have peace and trade between their kingdoms. Another part of the deal was Marsden soldiers coming with Owen to support him in his quest to take back his kingdom. Ackley had volunteered to go.

Owen had turned out to be a good guy. Too bad that while he was in Marsden, Russek invaded his kingdom, slaughtered the royal family, and took over.

"Owen wants to disembark in a cove where there's no port. Which means we'll be taking those smaller boats to shore." She nodded at the tiny boats attached to the ship.

Ackley rolled his eyes. This kept getting better and better.

Idina rubbed his back. "I've never seen you like this. I'm worried."

"I'll be fine."

"You haven't been to a single meeting." She glanced at the soldiers on the top deck, not far away. "We need you."

He couldn't be below deck—not even to sleep. It only made him feel worse. So here he stayed, day and night. He hadn't even changed his clothes. Every day for the past two weeks had been a struggle. The constant movement, the up and down...he leaned over the side, dry heaving.

"You're utterly useless," Idina muttered.

"Now's not the time." He couldn't stand to hear her telling him how incompetent he was at the moment. He wasn't used to this sort of feeling and didn't care for it.

"At first I thought you were moping over Reid. Now I understand how sick you are." She sighed. "Well, I hope you feel better. The last thing you need is to be run through with a sword when you step foot on land." With that, she turned and strode away, her dress wrapping around her legs from the vicious wind.

Reid. Ackley pinched the bridge of his nose. He couldn't think about her right now.

Soldiers ran around the deck in a flurry of activity. Sails were raised and lowered. The ship slowed. And finally, *finally*, the anchor was dropped.

Gytha approached Ackley. "The other ships report no one is in view of the shore."

That was good. Hopefully there wouldn't be a battle right away.

"A unit has been sent to investigate. We're to wait here until they return." She scanned him as he sat against a crate, the skin on his face peeling from his nasty sunburn. "You look awful."

"Thanks," he said, forcing a smile on his lips. "Just what every guy wants to hear."

She squatted next to him, her right hand patting his knee. "I will stay at Idina's side." She nodded as if the idea were her own.

Until Idina was officially married to Owen, she was Ackley's responsibility. And even then, Ackley doubted he'd just walk away and leave her alone. The need to protect her was second nature. Even though Idina was intelligent and headstrong, she was still a woman and his sister.

Gytha stood. "You're supposed to prepare to board a boat for shore."

He had no idea what that entailed. Since he'd been lying half-dead on the deck for most of the journey, he'd learned nothing about the ship or sailing. He hadn't even learned anything about those here with him. Before they'd boarded,

Owen had mixed the Melenia and Marsden soldiers in order for them to get to know one another better since they'd be fighting side by side.

As Gytha went to the other end of the ship, joining Idina, Ackley wondered how Owen was holding up. Owen was close to Ackley's age and far too young to be shouldering the responsibilities of a kingdom. Ackley knew what it was like to have a parent and sibling murdered. Thankfully Ackley's mother, his sister Idina, and his brother Gordon were still alive. Owen had no one. The letter he received stated that the royal family had been slaughtered by Russek. It didn't offer any other details. Ackley didn't think Owen would want them anyway.

Ackley didn't know much about Russek, other than it bordered Melenia. King Dexter of Marsden had sent seven hundred soldiers with Owen to help reclaim the kingdom. Once Owen was established as the king and wed to Idina, Ackley would return home with the Marsden soldiers.

Not that there was much to return home to. He supposed he should go back and take over the Knights of the Realm. However, he'd left it in capable hands while he was gone. Some time away would do him good.

Owen approached. "Scouts report no one in sight." His right hand gripped the hilt of his sword and he took a deep breath. "We're going on shore. We'll stay in the valley until everyone has regained their land legs."

"Land legs?" Ackley really should have asked questions about traveling via a ship across the ocean before he boarded. It would have saved him these past two weeks of torture.

"It'll take a day or two to adjust to land. I don't want everyone marching toward the castle until we're ready. If we're attacked, or cross paths with Russek, we need to be able to defend ourselves."

Ackley nodded. He had no idea what the plan was since he'd been barfing his guts up instead of attending any of the meetings. "We're heading straight to the castle?" Shouldn't they figure out where Russek's main troops were located? Then ambush them until they could easily retake the castle?

"Eventually." Owen glanced about before squatting eye level with Ackley. "As soon as you're able, I need you to go on a mission for me."

For the first time in two weeks, Ackley became intrigued. "I'm listening."

"There's a coastal city to the south, only a couple days' journey away. I need for you to go there and find out if it's been taken. And then I need you to locate my cousin."

Ackley raised his eyebrows, trying to understand why Owen would want to seek his cousin out when he needed to focus on regaining the throne.

Owen lowered his voice. "The correspondence I received informing me of my family's demise came from this city and was written by my cousin."

"And?"

"My cousin should be dead." Owen pursed his lips. "She would have been at my sister's birthday party when the takeover happened. Which means she managed to escape. She may be the only living relative I have."

"Are you afraid she'll challenge you for the throne?" There was something Owen wasn't telling him.

"No." He scratched his forehead. "It's complicated."

"If I'm going to find your cousin, I need to know." He wasn't going to walk into the situation blindly.

"This city, Kreng, it's not part of Melenia. Meaning, we

47

were never able to gain control of it. We reached a treaty with the people there and allow them to function independently of the crown. They have their own army. My family isn't allowed to step foot in the city."

"Then why would your cousin go there?"

"An excellent question. It is, however, the only city that could have dispatched a letter to me."

Ackley considered what Owen had said. "Do you trust your cousin?"

"I do."

"Do you think she is in Kreng of her own free will?" Or had someone kidnapped her, dragging her there in order to lure Owen to Kreng so he could be murdered?

"I certainly hope so. I also pray she has remained a free citizen."

"Are you afraid that those ruling Kreng may have taken her hostage?" Ackley asked, getting to what he suspected was the heart of the matter.

Owen stood. "While we've gotten along peacefully for decades, they may be holding her captive to use as a bargaining chip with Russek. It's what I would do to keep an enemy off my land."

Knowing that this mission would require someone of Ackley's skillset and that this cousin could be Owen's sole remaining family member, he had little choice. "I'll find her for you." It was the least he could do for Owen. Especially since Owen had helped Ackley recover Idina when she'd been kidnapped.

The lines around Owen's eyes relaxed. "Disembarking will begin shortly."

That was the best thing Ackley had heard in a long time. The sooner he got off this blasted ship, the better.

Ackley cursed. As he stood on the shore, he could swear the ground moved up and down, just as the ocean did.

Gytha patted his back. "They say it only lasts a day or two."

He knew it would take a couple of days to feel normal. What he didn't expect was to not have a reprieve—no matter how small that might be.

She jerked her head to the north. "Let's go."

Reluctantly, Ackley followed her, hoping he didn't topple over like a drunk fool. The half circle cove was carved into a mountainside. The narrow beach wasn't large enough for the hundreds of men still making their way to shore. Where the ones who'd already disembarked went, he didn't know. At the northern end, there appeared to be a cave cut into the rocks. Gytha headed straight for it, entering the darkness without hesitation. Ackley followed, but his vision struggled to adjust to the solid black around him after spending so many days in the bright sunlight. After a hundred feet, the tunnel opened to a large grassy area surrounded by steep mountains.

"We're setting up camp here." Gytha motioned to the soldiers already busy erecting tents.

Ackley squinted, scanning the mountaintops. "Isn't this too exposed?"

"Owen insisted it's safe." She folded her arms. "This was all decided at our meetings."

Of which he hadn't attended. He pressed his palm against his forehead, willing his queasy stomach to settle into something more manageable. Maybe eating would help now that he had two legs firmly planted on the ground.

"Your tent is over there. I suggest you go and rest. You look

like death. Now if you'll excuse me, I need to help Idina."
Gytha bowed, then left.

Ackley focused on the tent she'd pointed out. Maybe if he
rested a bit, the ground would stop moving. Forcing one foot in
front of the other, he went to his tent. Once inside, he
stretched out on the bedroll and pinched his eyes shut. He
hated relying on others to make sure the area was secure, the
tents erected, and people had been put on watch. However, he
was useless in his current state. And maybe, just maybe, a
couple hours of rest would get him back to some semblance of
normalcy.

He drifted in and out of sleep for the next several hours,
knowing Gytha would get him if trouble arose. When the dim
light of dawn cut through the entrance of his tent, he sat up. A
bowl of some sort of soup had been placed just inside the tent
flap. Needing to regain his strength, he made himself eat the
cold soup. It wasn't that bad. For the first time in two weeks,
his stomach didn't cramp with the need to expel its contents.
He stood and stretched. And then he gagged. Not from the
food or the feeling of going up and down, but from the awful
stench radiating from his body and clothes. He needed a bath.
Desperately. How had he not noticed how awful he smelled
until now? His belongings were stashed in one of the corners.
After he bathed, he'd change.

Exiting the tent, he scanned the area. Hundreds of tents
were set up in the grassy valley. Next to his were two larger
ones; most likely Owen's and Idina's. Gytha was probably
stationed inside with his sister.

Movement caught his attention. To the north, three soldiers
began climbing the steep mountain. It appeared steps had been
carved into the rocky side. Wanting to find out where they
were going and what lay beyond the surrounding mountains,

Ackley ran over, climbing the steps after them. In order to curb the sensation that the steps were moving like water, he kept one hand on the rocky wall next to him. He wasn't used to having any sort of a physical limitation that kept him from doing what needed to be done. At least the perception of swaying had lessened significantly from yesterday. Hopefully by tomorrow, the world around him would remain steady.

At the top, the three soldiers spread out, relieving the others to take up watch. Ackley joined them and scanned the surrounding area. While he'd initially had concerns with Owen choosing to set up camp in a valley surrounded by mountains, he now understood his worry had been for nothing. The other side of the steep mountain was rugged and impossible to traverse. One of the soldiers explained that the only way in or out of this secluded valley was through a tunnel. And if anyone tried to go that way, the narrow entrance would serve as a bottleneck, prohibiting large groups from getting in. An additional half dozen soldiers were on duty there.

Not seeing a single city or dwelling in sight, Ackley thanked the soldiers and headed back down the steep steps. At the bottom, he inquired about a place to bathe and was directed to the cove where they'd come on shore yesterday. Apparently, there was a freshwater area to clean up in. After a thorough bath, exhaustion consumed him. He made his way back to his tent and climbed inside. Tomorrow, everything would stop swaying and he'd feel better. Tomorrow, he'd be back to normal. Himself. Tomorrow...

Ackley woke up. The fabric of his tent remained in one place, unmoving. He breathed a sigh of relief. For the first time in weeks, the world around him didn't sway. After dressing, he exited the tent and headed for the larger one with the flag atop it, assuming he would find Owen in there.

A soldier standing guard granted him entrance. Ackley stepped inside and spotted the new king hunched over a table covered with maps.

When Ackley approached, Owen glanced up. "Nice to see you up and about instead of sprawled out half-dead somewhere."

"It was all an act so I didn't have to work on the ship," Ackley said with a sly smile.

Owen folded his arms, considering him. "You're a prince. I sincerely doubt I could make you do anything you didn't want to do."

Ackley laughed. "True." He came around the side of the table so he could see the map of Melenia better. "What's the plan?"

"The army will remain here while I send out scouts. Once they inspect the nearby cities and report back to me, I'll decide how to proceed." He folded his hands behind his back, his blue eyes focused on the map. "Since most everyone will remain here, doing nothing, it's the perfect opportunity for you to head south to Kreng. You leave as soon as you're ready."

Ackley noted the way Owen's back arched, the line across his forehead, and that his right foot hadn't stopped tapping. "You seem unusually tense."

Owen nodded. "As the fourth child, I didn't train in battle strategy, moving an army across a kingdom, or politics." He closed his eyes. "I was never meant to have the throne." He opened his eyes and glanced at Ackley.

Ackley shrugged. "My father never knew what to do with me

either." As the third born son, there had been no need for Ackley to learn those things. His father had wanted him to go into finance. Since he found the study of numbers so boring, he'd pretended he couldn't add or subtract. Thankfully, his father had let him learn sword work instead. And then there was the matter of Anna stepping in and recruiting him as a knight.

"Don't forget that my sister can help you," Ackley said. "You don't have to carry the burden alone." Idina had an uncanny knack for spotting patterns and understanding people's motivations. Ackley scanned the map, searching for Kreng. It was just south of their current location. It should only take him a day or two to reach it. "There are also several good, qualified men here who can give you counsel. Utilize them. Don't try and do it all on your own."

"It would be nice to have a commander."

Ackley agreed. However, since Commander Beck had turned out to be a traitor, it was best the man was dead. "You should probably appoint a new one."

"I know." Owen rubbed his face. "There's so much to do."

"What do you want the scouts to discover?"

"I need to find out how ravaged the kingdom is. How many towns have been destroyed? Where are the Russek soldiers located?" He swallowed, anger clouding his eyes. "I swear I'll kill King Drenton and his son, Prince Kerdan. I won't rest until I've run my sword through both of them."

Ackley nodded, wondering if either the king or prince were here leading their men, or if they remained safely holed up in Russek.

"Before I can focus on revenge, I need to know if my cousin is alive and well."

"I'll leave right away for Kreng. I'll find her. I promise."

"I'd like to request something of you." Owen sat on the edge of the table.

"Something besides me going on a mission to rescue your cousin?" He smiled sardonically. Not that he minded doing this errand for Owen. In fact, he'd much prefer to go rescue a damsel in distress than sit around here for several days.

"Please be kind to her. I don't know what she's been through."

"Of course I'll be kind." He wasn't a monster.

"Maybe I didn't say that right," Owen muttered. "I want you to treat her as you would your own sister. Be friendly, nice, and accommodating. If that's even possible."

Ackley snorted. Instead of replying, he studied the map, contemplating how he would make his way to Kreng since he'd need to avoid major roads. "When I get to the city, I'll need to be able to identify your cousin."

Owen nodded, his shoulders rising and falling. "Her name is Harley. She's eighteen years old. She has long blonde hair and blue eyes."

Ackley gripped Owen's shoulder in reassurance. "I'll find her. I promise." After all, this was what he'd been trained to do. If Harley was in Kreng, it was only a matter of time until he discovered her whereabouts.

"There's one more thing you should know. The only way to reach Kreng is by water."

"Water?" Ackley repeated, wanting to make sure he'd heard correctly.

Owen nodded. "The city is well protected."

Ackley would swim there before he'd step foot in another boat. "Good to know. It shouldn't take me more than a week to get there, locate her, and return here." Hopefully Harley wasn't dead. That would certainly complicate matters.

"My cousin could be in prison," Owen reminded him. "It might take you longer than a week if that's the case."

Ackley's lips curved into a smile. "You forget, I'm an expert locksmith. Prison or not, I'll rescue your cousin." He headed toward the exit.

"Will you be taking anyone with you? Gytha seems the most logical choice."

"I want Gytha to remain here as Idina's personal guard." As a woman, she could be inside the tent at night with Idina.

Owen smiled. "I'll make sure your sister is well protected. I'm entrusting you with my cousin, you can offer me the same courtesy with your sister. After all, she will be my wife shortly."

Ackley had seen Owen wield a sword and knew he was well trained. Even though he might not know how to lead an army—or kingdom for that matter—he certainly knew how to fight and take care of himself. And the match between Owen and Idina wasn't just political. Since the moment Owen met Idina, he'd been taken with her. Any time she snapped at him, he only fell deeper for her. Rationally, Ackley knew Owen would protect Idina. But they were in an unstable kingdom. And this was Ackley's only sister they were talking about.

Instead of arguing or voicing his concerns, he simply nodded and headed back to his tent to gather supplies. He wouldn't need much. Just some food and his weapons. Traveling alone would allow him to move faster. And once he reached Kreng, he would be able to discover the information he sought without a clumsy soldier tagging along. He'd gotten a good look at the map and knew the terrain and where he needed to go.

After shoving everything in his traveling bag, he exited his tent, coming face to face with Idina. "Is something the matter?"

She folded her arms and raised her eyebrows. "You're not going anywhere alone. It's too dangerous."

Not in the mood to verbally spar with his sister, he leaned down and kissed her cheek. "Of course not. I don't even know my way around this kingdom." He shouldered his bag.

"Please be careful."

He knew what she wasn't saying. That they'd lost too much already—their father, their brother. "I will. But you have to promise me you won't go anywhere without Gytha."

Her eyes searched his. "Take Gytha with you."

"I'll take a Melenia soldier." He couldn't believe he was lying to his own sister, but he had to go alone. He needed to clear his head.

Gytha approached the two of them. "You look better." She sounded mildly disappointed.

"Don't let my sister out of your sight."

"I won't." She jerked her chin toward him. "But before you leave, I want to see you throw that dagger in your boot. How about you hit the wood peg holding up the right side of the tent over there." She pointed behind him.

What an insult—he could hit that blindfolded.

"Don't look at me like that," Gytha chided him. "You've been unwell for a couple of weeks. I doubt your strength has returned. Maybe you should see before you find yourself in a fight for your life."

"I concur," Idina said, leaving no room for discussion.

Since these two insufferable women would persist until he complied, he dropped his bag on the ground, withdrew his dagger, and bowed with a flourish. Idina simply blinked, clearly not amused. He sighed. The target was eighteen feet away and slightly to the right, the two-inch circular peg at a downward angle. A simple throw. The familiar feel of the hilt in his palm calmed his mind and forced it to focus. He threw the dagger. It sailed through the air, landing with a satisfying *thump*.

Ackley stood there, staring at the dagger embedded in the ground just below the peg. He blinked. If that were a person, being off by that much could mean the difference between life and death.

"You'll get your steady arm back in another day or two," Gytha said, her voice low so no one would overhear.

Ackley ran his hands through his hair, unable to remember the last time he'd missed a target like that. His hands only shook slightly. However, his stomach felt queasy and the ground seemed to be swaying again, though not nearly as bad as before. He should have taken those things into account. Walking over, he withdrew his dagger. Not wanting to practice there in front of everyone, he slid the weapon back in his boot. Alone in the forest, he would get his aim back—even if it killed him.

After slinging his bag over his shoulder, he turned to face Gytha. "Protect Idina."

"King Owen has assigned a dozen men for her protection. She doesn't need me. You do. I'm coming with you."

Stubborn was another word he'd use to describe Gytha. And right. Not wanting his pride or foolishness to guide him to a bad decision, he simply nodded and started walking toward the path cut into the mountain. A few minutes later, he heard the crunch of boots on dirt as Gytha caught up with him. Considering that it only took her a handful of minutes, she must have still had her belongings packed and ready to go. He half wondered if this had been her plan all along. No matter. Even though he wanted to travel alone, having a skilled fighter with him was a good idea. Especially if he had to break Owen's cousin out of prison.

At least the world seemed still again. It was only when he turned quickly or bent over that his sense of the ground beneath him swayed. By the time he reached the other side of the mountain, his legs ached from the lack of activity over the past couple of weeks. He welcomed the pain.

CHAPTER FIVE

ACKLEY

*A*ckley and Gytha traveled all day with little conversation. While Ackley itched to practice after being sick on the ship for two weeks, he decided traveling as far as he could was a better use of his time. Besides, the idea of embarrassing himself in front of Gytha wasn't something he cared to do.

"Are you going to stop and make camp?" Gytha snapped, her steely voice cutting through the darkening sky. "Or do you plan on walking all night?"

"If you can't keep up, you can head back to Owen and the others." He didn't need a nursemaid.

"I can keep up just fine," she huffed. "It's you I'm worried about."

He was finally able to walk in a straight line, the ground only occasionally seemed to sway, everything he'd eaten today had stayed down, and his strength was gradually returning. Instead of saying any of that, he glanced over his shoulder and smirked. "There's a town not far from here. I plan on stopping just before we reach it." Close, but not too close.

They'd been traveling on a dirt road lined with knee-high brown weeds on both sides. The ocean remained to Ackley's right, though not in sight. He could smell it taunting him of what he'd been through and would have to go through again in order to return home. A few trees shone in the distance. "Let's head over there." They would provide some cover for the night.

As they wove between the thick weeds, Gytha cursed. "The ones with the orange stuff on them are sharp." Blood trickled from her palm.

Ackley's focus wasn't on the shrubs but on the surrounding area, searching for any signs of life. While he hadn't spotted any movement, that didn't mean someone wasn't hiding nearby.

They reached the handful of trees.

"At least it's clear of weeds here," Gytha commented, tossing her bag on the ground and stretching.

Ackley placed his bag beside hers. "Do you want to hunt or set up camp?"

Gytha raised her eyebrows. "You think there's anything living around here that's suitable for consumption?"

He'd spotted a few quails. However, he didn't have his bow with him. "I'm sure there's a rabbit or squirrel." While he hadn't seen any movement that indicated a person was nearby, he'd heard plenty of smaller creatures scuttling about.

"I'll find something," Gytha mumbled. She withdrew a dagger. "Can't have you getting dizzy and lost on me." The corners of her lips curled into a sly smile, baiting him.

In no mood to spar with Gytha—verbally or physically—he ignored her and started gathering wood to make a fire.

Ackley awoke with a start. Rubbing his eyes, he sat up. Darkness blanketed the land, and thousands of stars dotted the sky. After making the fire, he must have fallen asleep.

Gytha was sitting against a tree trunk, a knife in hand. "I was just about to wake you for your watch," she said. "Your food is over there." She pointed to his right, then sheathed her weapon. After lying on the ground, she turned, setting her head on her bag with her back to him.

Ackley picked up his food and took a bite, finding the rabbit meat cooked but cold. While eating, he scanned the area. Everything remained quiet. No wind blew, making the air oddly still. He guessed it to be just after midnight.

Sitting there, he watched time pass as the stars slowly disappeared and dawn approached. When he stood, the ground beneath him remained solid and unrelenting. Ackley stretched his arms and neck, pleased the world seemed static once again. He focused on the nearest tree trunk, picking two targets. Then he withdrew a dagger, the weight of it in his palm reassuring. Quick as lightning, he raised his arm and threw the weapon. Before it even hit its mark, he withdrew another dagger, launching it at the second target. Both struck true. Relief filled him. His hands were steady, the daggers exactly where he'd intended. He went over and reclaimed his weapons.

"Do you want to spar?" Gytha asked around a yawn.

"We need to get going." Grabbing his bag, he slung it over his shoulder. "I want to pass by the town before it gets too light out." As far as sparring, they could practice tonight, once he was certain she wouldn't knock him on his arse. Gytha never held back. Another meal or two would do him good before he fought the warrior woman.

Once they made their way back to the dirt road, they continued south.

"When do you plan on telling me what we're doing?" Gytha asked, walking two feet behind him.

He waved her forward. Once they were side by side, he lowered his voice and said, "Owen asked me to find his cousin."

"Now?" she asked incredulously.

"She could be his only living family member."

"She?" They walked in silence for a moment. "Are you sure she's a cousin and not a lover?"

Ackley chuckled. "Yes." He saw the way Owen looked at Idina. From the moment they'd met, Owen had been smitten with her.

"Why didn't he send one of his soldiers?"

"There's a treaty that states Melenia soldiers are not permitted to enter the city of Kreng."

Gytha's eyes widened. "I assume we're going to Kreng?"

"We are."

Another reason he liked Gytha, she didn't have to overanalyze everything like his sister did.

A pungent odor hung in the air. "Do you smell that?" he asked.

"What is it?" Gytha wrinkled her nose.

"Ash." He knew the stench well. After Reid's castle had burned to the ground, he'd had the smell stuck in his head for weeks.

Gytha withdrew her short sword as they crested the small rise, coming to a stop at the sight before them. The skeleton of a village was all that remained.

"I guess it's safe to say Russek passed through here." Ackley folded his arms, not wanting to go any closer. The stone well in the center was the only thing left untouched. All of the structures were charred rubble.

"This looks like a simple farming village," Gytha muttered, nodding to the crops on the eastern side. "Not a military outpost."

Along the southern perimeter, spikes had been placed in the ground. On top of each spike were the remains of a human skull. Owen had warned Ackley that the Russek warriors were vicious. But this…murdering innocent people. He shook his head. "No one's here. Let's continue on." He hoped Kreng wasn't decimated as well. For Russek to have come this far west, well, the chances of any town remaining were slim.

Once Owen reclaimed his kingdom from Russek, would anything be left? Or would Owen have a ravaged land with no farmers to work it? Ackley didn't know if he could leave his sister here to such a bleak future.

"Why would they bother with a small village?" Gytha asked. "It makes no sense."

The day he learned Eldon, his half brother, had murdered his father, he'd stopped trying to make sense of things. Sometimes people did terrible deeds. Trying to figure out why only led to more problems. "We have a mission," he reminded her. "Let's focus on that."

The dirt road turned decidedly inland. The city Ackley needed to reach was along the coast, due south. Assuming he'd read the map correctly. Trusting he had, he headed that way, thankful Gytha didn't question him.

After another three or so miles, they came to a river. Not having any time to waste locating an alternate path, Ackley removed his shirt and pants, rolled them up, and tucked them in his bag.

"What are you doing?" Gytha demanded.

"I thought I'd wash my clothes," he said sarcastically. "Maybe sunbathe." He tied the top of his bag closed. Satisfied nothing would fall out, he took a few steps back from the edge of the river. Then he ran and hurled his bag to the other side. It just made it. Now he had to cross. Even though he could swim, the strength of the current concerned him since the water appeared to be rushing by fairly quickly. The bottom of the river looked rocky, and he'd have to be careful not to lose his footing.

Without waiting for Gytha, he stepped into the brisk water. The pull of the current caused his right foot to slip, so he widened his stance. Swimming would be safer than trying to traverse the rocky river. He angled his body toward the shore on the opposite side and took another step. The water reached his knees. Another careful step and the water went up to his waist. Deep enough to swim. He pushed off, keeping his body angled toward the other side as he swam with the current. Three feet from the shore, he dug his heels in, slowing his speed until he regained his footing. A few rocks sliced his skin, but not badly. After climbing out of the water and onto the shore, he headed to where he'd thrown his bag.

Gytha crossed the river the same way Ackley had, joining him a few minutes later. Her wet body shook from the crisp air.

They quickly dressed, then continued south. About a mile later, Ackley stopped, observing the area around them. On the horizon, the sun touched the water, about to set, casting an orange glow over the land.

"What is it?" Gytha whispered, her hand on her sword.

Up until this point, they'd been traveling alongside brown knee-high grass. Here, the grass only went to his ankles. And it smelled different, too. The tang of salt from the sea and the aroma of dry vegetation had been replaced with a mixture of spices and smoke.

"Ackley?"

"The city," he murmured. "It's here."

Gytha scanned the area. "Here where?" she asked, turning in a slow circle.

Given the late hour, Ackley contemplated the pros and cons of locating the city before dark. They could sleep out here in the open, under the stars, and find the city in the morning. Or they could try and find it now, not knowing where they'd sleep once they found it. He tilted his head to the side, cracking his neck. With the city nearby, he had to be concerned with sentries patrolling the area.

"Hide your hair," he instructed Gytha. "This kingdom is more closely aligned to northern Marsden than the Axian you grew up in. Here, women wear dresses and are subservient to men."

Gytha snorted but didn't argue. She wound her braid around her head, then covered it with a cap. "Now what?"

"Kreng trades with Marsden," he thought out loud. "Which means they have a port." He headed to the edge of the land, facing the ocean. The ground dropped straight down to the unrelenting water, fifty feet below. Even though he couldn't see the waves crashing against the cliffside, he could hear them. Which meant the land he was standing on jutted out slightly more than the lower portion. Kneeling, he laid on his stomach, then scooted toward the edge of the cliff.

"What are you doing?" Gytha hissed, grabbing his ankles to prevent him from falling over the side.

He tried not to bristle at her touch—she was just being helpful. But he didn't need help. He never needed help. He was fully capable of doing this on his own. Swallowing the retort on the edge of his tongue, he said, "There's something down there." He was certain of it.

Peering over the side, he saw buildings carved into the face of the rocky cliff, a port, and people milling about. He scooted back, amazed that an entire city could be hidden like that. "The question is, how do we get down there?" As far as he could see, he couldn't tell if Russek occupied the city or not. If he had to guess, he didn't think so, since nothing appeared burned and there was life. Most likely, Russek didn't know about this city so they went right on by it.

"There must be a hidden path or entrance somewhere," Gytha said, searching the area.

If they had a rope, Ackley could rappel down. He recalled Owen saying something about the only way in was by water.

"Do you think there are any sentries on duty?" Gytha asked. "Maybe you could wave until one of them sees you?"

"That's an absurd suggestion." The sentries would probably shoot first and ask questions later. Ackley would much rather enter the city without anyone knowing he was there. In order to do what needed to be done, stealth was key.

She shrugged. "It was just a thought. I don't hear you coming up with any ideas."

Doing as Gytha suggested put them at the mercy of their captors. It would be better to infiltrate the city, learn the state of things, and then proceed from there. "Can you climb?"

Gytha raised her eyebrows. "You want me to climb, using only my hands and feet, down the side of a cliff with the raging ocean below? Are you mad?"

Well, when she put it that way, the idea didn't sound as good. "We passed a river about a mile back."

"So?"

"Owen told me we could reach the city by water." Maybe the river led to the city.

"He probably meant we had to charter a boat or something. This is why you should've brought someone from Melenia along." Gytha walked to the edge, peering over it. "I'm sure they have some sort of patrol. We've probably already been spotted."

Ackley had no intention of sitting there and waiting for someone to stumble upon them. "All the more reason to get moving." Without waiting for a response, he headed north, back toward the river.

Gytha mumbled several curse words before trekking after Ackley. Thankfully, she didn't argue with him.

At the river, he followed it to the edge of the land where it plummeted fifty feet into the ocean below. Peering over the side, Ackley examined the waterfall. Next to it, a rope had been nailed into the cliff about a foot below from where he stood. Squatting, he reached down, tugging on it. The rope held firm.

He removed his bag, hiding it near a boulder about ten feet from the edge. It would be easier to climb without it. "I'll go first." Turning his back to the ocean, Ackley winked at Gytha, then climbed over the edge. With his hands firmly wrapped around the rope and his feet against the rocky cliff, he slowly lowered his body. The mist from the waterfall coated his hair and clothes. Thankfully, the rope felt rough instead of slick. About half way down the cliff, he came to a slight ledge, a cave next to it. The rope only had another yard or so to it, so Ackley planted both feet on the ledge before releasing the rope. He took a step into the cave and waited for Gytha to join him.

Leaning against the side, he folded his arms and stared out at the ocean, watching as the sun slipped behind the water. The sky turned a brilliant shade of reddish orange, reminding him of a painting his mother kept in her bedchamber.

Gytha landed on the ledge. Ackley clutched onto her arm, yanking her into the cave. Panting, she cursed.

"You've been spending too much time with soldiers." He released her, then headed deeper into the cave.

"What's that supposed to mean?"

"Your language. Most women don't swear."

She shoved his back. "I'm not most women."

"No, you most certainly are not." The cave narrowed. "I think this is a tunnel." It probably led straight to Kreng.

"A boat would have been easier."

"Did you see a boat? Because I don't recall seeing one." Keeping his right hand on the rocky interior, he made his way along the tunnel and into complete darkness. The air remained fresh, indicating this led to an opening.

After about ten minutes, a pale light could be seen up ahead. Slowing his pace, Ackley listened for signs that sentries guarded the exit. Not hearing anything, he came to the end of the tunnel and stopped. Straight ahead, the ocean extended for miles. The sky had turned gray. Peering out of the tunnel, he noticed the rocky cliff to his left curved inward. That had to be where the city was located.

"It's only ten feet from here to the water," Gytha mused.

"The ocean is too rough to try and swim from here to the city. We'd be smashed against the rocks." Reaching down, his fingers came across another rope. Lying on his stomach, he studied it. The rope went straight down into the water. "It's high tide."

"What do you want to do?" Gytha started pacing.

"Owen said the only way in is through the water."

"And?" She paused to look at him, her eyebrows raised in question.

"I'm going to follow the rope and see what happens."

"Didn't you just say it wasn't safe to swim?"

"I'm not swimming," he assured her. "I'm simply following the rope."

"And if it doesn't go anywhere?"

"I can hold my breath for a while. If I don't find a way out, I'll come back up."

Gytha shook her head. "If you don't return, do you want me to follow you?"

He shrugged. "Only if you want to. Otherwise, remain here. Once I find Owen's cousin, I'll return."

She smiled. "And miss all the fun? I don't think so."

For the second time that day, Ackley found himself climbing over the side of a cliff, though this wasn't nearly as high as the previous one. The sky continued to darken around him. The rough water below smashed against the rocky cliffside, spraying him. Wrapping his arm around the rope, he prayed his body didn't get slammed into the rocks. He couldn't afford to be knocked unconscious. Once the water reached his waist, he sucked in as much air as he could, then quickly descended under the water.

The swell pushed him forward. Instead of being tossed against something hard as he'd feared, his body was carried through the water, his hands sliding along the rope which was now above him. In the darkness, he couldn't see where he was going, but it felt as if he'd entered an underwater tunnel. The rope suddenly ended. Feeling above him, his hands came across the end of a rocky passageway. Not having much air left, he let go of the rope, kicking until his head shot above the water. Ackley sucked in a welcome breath and looked around. He found himself in a small cave.

He swam to the edge, then climbed out, observing the sight before him. Through an opening in the cave, he saw a moon shaped cove. Buildings had been carved into the face of the cliff. Light shone from hundreds of open windows as candles burned inside, revealing people moving about. He blinked. It was unlike anything he'd ever seen before.

Gytha joined him. "Now what?" she whispered, water dripping from her hair. She withdrew her cap from under her waistband, wrung it out, then put it on.

He'd lost his own hat in the water somewhere. "Once we're not soaking wet, we'll enter the city." The wind blew, making him cold, but he welcomed the feeling. It would help keep him alert and awake. He observed the buildings, trying to get a feel for the people inside. Were they dressed differently? Did they speak another language? Owen had a thick accent, but Ackley understood him without much trouble.

"How are we going to find Owen's cousin?" Gytha sat a few feet away, leaning against the wall of the cave.

Ackley had been contemplating the quickest way to locate her. It would be so much easier to slink around the city without having Gytha as his shadow. However, she'd proven to be capable and hadn't slowed him down. Maybe he could use her. An idea formed.

"Every time you get that look on your face," Gytha muttered, "I know I'm not going to like whatever it is you have to say."

Tilting his head in her direction, his lips curved into a smile. She most definitely wouldn't like what he was about to suggest.

CHAPTER SIX

HARLEY

"Harley," Ledger called from the hallway. He knocked before opening the door a couple of inches.

"Go away," Harley mumbled. "I just came off my shift and need to sleep." What could he possibly have to say that couldn't wait until after she got up? She groaned in frustration.

"Rayne spotted ships off the coast."

That was about the only thing worthy of rousing her. She blinked and peered over at the doorway. Since her room didn't have a window, she couldn't see Ledger's face. All she could make out was the silhouette of his body from the candles burning in the hallway at the inn. She sat up, waving him inside. "Do you think it could be my cousin?" For the first time in weeks, a glimmer of hope surfaced. She lit the candle next to her bed.

Ledger stepped into her room, closing the door behind him. "It's either him or more Russek soldiers. In either case, we need to discover who it is."

"Where were they spotted?"

"Heading slightly north of here. There's an old military cove. If it's your cousin, that's probably where he went." He folded his arms, leaning against the door.

"What's the plan?" she rubbed her eyes. Exhaustion consumed her. She'd worked all day cleaning the rooms and serving in the tavern. In exchange for a room, she'd agreed to help around the inn. The arrangement had turned into her practically being the only servant in the place. But at least it provided her a roof over her head. Ledger, Rayne, and Milard were working in the barn in exchange for sleeping in it with the animals—which she refused to do.

"Rayne and Milard already left to investigate."

"What about you?"

Ledger rubbed his forehead. "I'm going to meet with the commander of the soldiers here in Kreng. I'm still trying to convince them to support your cousin."

For some reason, Ledger always referred to Owen as *her cousin*. She supposed calling him King Owen offered too much hope. And hope was in short supply these days.

"I'm surprised you stayed behind." She knew Ledger had already spoken to the commander on multiple occasions. Every time he was told the same thing—Kreng wanted to remain sovereign. The commander claimed that if he supported Owen, then Kreng would be involved in Melenia's politics. While Harley understood where he was coming from, she didn't think he fully comprehended the ruthlessness of Russek. Kreng wasn't safe while Russek occupied Melenia.

"We considered it. But we didn't think it wise to leave you here alone."

The simple statement warmed her. "Thank you for always watching out for me." Especially since he didn't have to.

"I'd want someone to do the same for my sister."

Harley knew he was worried about his mother and sister. After safely delivering Harley to Kreng, he'd insisted on staying at her side instead of going to check on his family. While the people here had welcomed them in, she felt as if she were being watched with suspicion. Since Ledger had warned them of a possible invasion, they'd allowed him to assist the soldiers here. He'd sent out scouts to do reconnaissance and made sure no Russek soldiers came too close to the city. Ledger had learned that Kreng had two hundred active soldiers and about five hundred citizens who could be called on if needed. Numbers like that could help Owen retake the kingdom. The problem seemed to be that no one here was interested in helping Melenia.

Ledger reached for the door handle. "We should know something in a couple of days. Be prepared to leave at a moment's notice."

Harley nodded. The four of them had a boat stashed nearby in case Russek descended upon the city. "If it's Owen?"

"We'll leave immediately to join him."

Anticipation filled her along with a mixture of unbearable sadness and hope. Harley longed to see her cousin. However, the grief they'd have to face at losing their loved ones would be difficult. But at the same time, Owen was Melenia's only hope. He was the one person who could rid the kingdom of Russek and take up the crown as the rightful king of Melenia. Harley also had every intention of helping Owen seek retribution against Russek. Together they would destroy the brutal kingdom.

It had been four days and still no word came. Harley thought she would have heard from Rayne and Milard by now. She chewed on her lip, hoping the delay wasn't because more Russek soldiers had arrived.

Harley entered the tavern, searching for the innkeeper. As she suspected, he was sitting at the bar nursing a cup of ale. If he paid half as much attention to the inn as he did to his alcohol, the inn would be far more profitable.

"I finished cleaning the rooms," she informed him. It was nearly time for supper, and she was famished. "Am I permitted to stay here another night?" She hated having to ask him every single evening if she'd worked enough to warrant a room.

The innkeeper turned his head toward her. "I need your help here at the tavern tonight."

She'd worked at the tavern almost every night this week. "I'm tired from cleaning all day."

"Laci just left," he said, facing his drink again. "One of her kids is sick or something. Until she's back, I need you here."

Harley considered her options. If she left, the innkeeper couldn't do anything to her. But then she'd have nowhere to sleep since she didn't have any money. The innkeeper fed her three meals a day and gave her a room for the night in exchange for her help. Working a few more hours at the tavern would be worth it for a warm bed.

Without answering, she headed to the kitchen and snatched a slice of bread, shoving it in her mouth. The cook had also made stew for the patrons. After grabbing an apron, she went back out to the tavern. Most of the tables were already full with people eating and talking. She adjusted the apron around her brown wool dress. It wouldn't be bad if the material wasn't so rough and scratchy. But it was all she'd been given—a commoner's dress. Until now, she'd never realized what not

74

having money meant. All the times she'd seen people back home in Penlar begging for food, she'd never understood, never imagined what they were going through.

Shaking her head, she went over to a table where a young man had just sat down. "Can I get you a bowl of stew?" Harley pasted a smile on her face.

The man's head tilted to the side and his eyes scanned her body, reminding her of Lyle's assessing gaze. She shivered, immediately on edge.

"Yeah," he answered. "And I also want a cup of ale."

"Of course." Harley waited until she was in the kitchen before rolling her eyes. Did a man ever come in to the tavern just to eat? Why did they all have to drink? Drinking impaired judgement. After grabbing a bowl of stew and a cup of ale, she went back out to the tavern. When she set the items on the table, the man's hand shot out, latching onto her arm. She yelped in surprise, though no one noticed in the loud room.

He pulled her closer to him. "How much?" The man's breath reeked of stale ale. How many drinks did he have before coming to the tavern?

She tried putting some distance between them, but he didn't loosen his grip on her arm. "For the stew and ale that'll be three quelps."

"Not for the food. For you."

Looking the man directly in the eyes, she said, "I'm not for sale." She tried not to cower, but this man reminded her of Lyle.

A slow smile spread across his face. "Everyone has a price."

Her body started shaking from both rage and fear. "Release me."

"Aren't you filling in for Laci?" he asked. "She charges ten riglars. I'll pay you nine." He yanked her closer to him, knocking her off balance. "You're a bit too skinny for my taste."

Panic filled her. She needed to get away from this man. If the innkeeper wasn't so immersed in his drink, perhaps he'd see this customer being a bit too forceful with her. "Please," she begged. "You're hurting me." Tears filled her eyes.

The man flew forward, his head landing in his bowl. Hot stew splattered over the front of Harley's apron. He released her and she jumped back, shocked. Holding the man's head down was a woman wearing pants with a cap covering most of her hair. Harley gawked.

"Why don't you pick on someone your own size?" the woman said. She let up a bit so he could remove his face from the bowl.

He cursed, stew sliding down his forehead and cheeks.

The woman chuckled. "Not so bold now, are you?" She shoved his face against the table, pinning it there. The man reached back, grabbing onto the woman's tunic. She elbowed him, and he released her. "You're pathetic," she spat. "That all you got?"

When she let go, he jumped to his feet, throwing a punch at her. She twisted, and his fist missed her face. He went for her again. She smiled and stepped to the side as his hand flew right by her. Rage twisted his features. He screamed and launched himself at her, knocking her to the floor.

Harley could have sworn she heard the woman laughing.

The innkeeper ran over, yanking them apart. "I'm tossing the two of you in the barn until someone can come sort this out. I won't have any fighting at my establishment. This is a respectable place." He dragged them from the tavern, not bothering to see if Harley was okay from the ordeal.

Harley removed her stew-splattered apron, about to head to

the kitchen, when her skin prickled. Glancing behind her, she spotted a man sitting at a table in the corner of the room, his eyes trained on her. Two cups of ale were on his table, even though he was alone. The chair next to him was askew as if someone had been there only moments before. Had she just robbed this man of his companion?

Wanting to thank him for the woman's help, Harley crossed the room, heading straight toward him. He tilted his head down, his face now cast in shadows. The innkeeper really needed to add a few more sconces to brighten up the place. She stopped a foot from the table. "Pardon me, but is the woman who assisted me your wife?"

"Wife?" he asked, a slight accent to the word.

She nodded, wishing he'd look up so she could see his face. "If so, please thank her for me. I'd also like to apologize for her predicament."

The man's pointer finger traced the rim of his cup. "If anything, you did us a favor. That was easier than I expected." As he spoke, his accent faded away.

Harley still couldn't believe the woman had been dressed in pants and that she'd antagonized a man. She'd never seen anything like it before.

"If you could point me in the direction of where my *wife* is being held, I'd appreciate it." He stood, his face still tilted downward, hidden by the shadows of the room, as if he knew just the right angle to make sure she didn't get a good look at him.

Both cups were filled to the brim, though Harley got the impression the man had been sitting there for some time since she hadn't served him.

"Your wife was taken around back to the barn. She will be held there until the watchmen arrive to escort her to prison."

Clutching the apron, she felt awful the woman was going to be arrested for helping her. "If you like, I can speak on your wife's behalf."

The man was about to toss a coin on the table when he paused, considering her. "Can I ask you a question?"

"Of course." She set the apron on the table and gave the man her full attention.

He set the coin down with a soft *clink*. "Have you worked here long?"

"No. I've only been here a few weeks." He must have been able to tell she was inexperienced. The other women who worked there wore scandalous dresses and flirted with the patrons. She never did so and couldn't feel at ease in an establishment such as this. Someone of her social standing didn't frequent taverns.

"I'll take you up on your offer of speaking on my wife's behalf. Can you escort me to the barn where she's being held?"

"I would be happy to." She led him out of the tavern and to the narrow street out back. The barn was up ahead on the left.

"Do you think it wise to bring me through a dark, deserted alleyway?" the man asked, his voice low, matching the night. "If I wished to hurt you, no one would be nearby to help."

Now that he'd pointed it out, yes, it seemed ill-advised to do such a thing. Realizing her err in judgement, she stopped and confronted the man, wishing she could see his face. He remained in the shadows, as if he were one himself. Goosebumps covered her skin, and she shivered, though it wasn't cold out. "Your wife came to my aid." Her voice was barely above a whisper. "I doubt she would do such a thing if her husband were of questionable character."

A low chuckle escaped his lips. "You're not a tavern worker, that much is obvious from your speech. And the woman isn't my wife, she's just a friend."

She blinked, unsure what he was implying.

He took a step closer to her. "I suspect your penmanship is impeccable, you normally wear fancy dresses, and you are usually the one being served."

She swallowed, suddenly feeling like she was ensnared in a carefully set trap. "Who are you?"

He took another step closer, invading her personal space. "You're not from around here, are you, Harley?"

Her eyes widened, and she stepped back, away from him. How could he possibly know her name?

He took another measured step closer to her. She sucked in a breath, about to scream for help, when she realized he'd moved into the light cast by a nearby window. Momentarily stunned, she stood there staring, unable to look away. The man's face was more youthful than she'd expected. He had to be only a couple of years older than her. His dark hair hung loose around his angular face, framing his brown eyes. Standing a solid foot above her, he was taller than she'd first realized.

He raised a single eyebrow, awaiting her response.

Unable to utter a single word, she simply shook her head. She'd never been tongue-tied around a man before. What was wrong with her? Of course, she'd never met someone like him —equal parts alluring and dangerous.

"Your name is Harley, isn't it?"

She nodded.

The man's face instantaneously softened, and he smiled. "Your cousin, Owen, sent me. Now let's go and get my friend before she's hauled off to prison, though that's why we came into the tavern in the first place. Seems you saved us quite a bit of time. I'm Ackley, by the way. And the woman—her name is Gytha." Sliding his hands into his pockets, he sauntered toward the barn, not even bothering to see if she followed.

Now that the shock of the man's beauty had worn off, the news he'd sprung on her made her feel as if she'd stumbled into a frozen pond. Owen sent him? Did that mean her cousin was here in Melenia? She hurried after Ackley who stood at the entrance to the barn.

When she joined him, she saw Gytha's wrists had been tied together and she was sitting on a bale of hay. The man who'd attacked Harley was similarly situated. The innkeeper presided over both of them.

"I sent one of the stable boys to fetch the watchmen," the innkeeper said when he noticed Harley.

Before she could respond, Ackley said, "I have what we came here for."

"That was fast," Gytha mumbled, eyeing Harley. In the dim light of the barn, the woman looked more warrior than savior. Gytha lifted her arms, the rope dangling from her wrists.

"Hey now," the innkeeper protested. "How'd you get free?"

"You don't tie knots very well," Gytha said, jumping to her feet. She strode toward Ackley. "Let's get out of here."

"You created a disturbance in my tavern," the innkeeper said. "You fought with another patron."

"She did nothing wrong," Harley stated. "She only helped me when no one else would. You will let her go."

"I can't do that," he responded, folding his arms in protest. "The law is the law."

Ackley sighed. "Fine." Quick as lightning, he spun and kicked the innkeeper's head, knocking him to the ground.

Harley yelped in surprise. "What did you do that for?"

Kneeling next to the innkeeper, she checked to see if he was still breathing. His chest rose and fell. He was alive.

"Let's go," Ackley said. "We don't have any time to waste."

Harley stood and observed Ackley and Gytha. They both had dark hair indicating they weren't from this kingdom. So who were they, and why had Owen sent them instead of a fellow Melenian to retrieve her?

As if sensing her confusion, Ackley told her, "I'll answer all your questions on our way." Then he grabbed her wrist and pulled her from the barn.

Out in the alley, Harley struggled to break free.

"I'm sorry," Ackley said, releasing her. "I just didn't want you to say Owen's name in front of anyone." His brows pinched together as he watched her, making her feel oddly exposed before him.

She rubbed her wrists, attempting to ignore the memory of the soldier who'd tried raping her. And Lyle. Oftentimes he held her wrists together so she couldn't push him away.

"We need to get moving," Gytha said. "The watchmen will be here shortly."

"I can't leave." Not after everything Ledger had done for her. If she disappeared, he'd be worried sick. Plus, he was a Melenia soldier. They needed to stick together.

"I promised Owen I would find you." Ackley kept scanning the alleyway, as if he expected Russek soldiers would descend upon them at any moment.

She folded her arms and raised her chin in the air. "I didn't say I wouldn't go with you. I simply said that I can't leave right this minute. There's someone I need to speak with before we go."

"The innkeeper is starting to rouse," Gytha said, sounding irritated. "We don't have time for this."

Ackley groaned. "Just so you know, Owen insisted I treat you like my own sister." He reached down, slinging an arm around Harley's waist, then flinging her over his shoulder as if she were a sack of flour.

"Put me down!" she squealed. There was no way Owen would tell someone so brusque to treat her so informally. She pounded against Ackley's back. How dare he behave this way?

"That's one way to handle Owen's pampered cousin," Gytha said with a chuckle.

Pampered? Harley had been working at the inn and tavern for the past few weeks. She most certainly wasn't pampered. There was nothing funny about this situation. And to think, Harley had appreciated Gytha's help only minutes before. Well, she didn't like the woman anymore. How could she be privy to such outlandish behavior?

Hanging upside down, bouncing as Ackley had the nerve to jog, Harley had no idea which way they were going. She pounded her fists against his back.

"Stop hitting me," Ackley demanded. "You don't need to be so difficult. I'm trying to help you. Unless you don't want to see your cousin?" His voice turned softer, almost accusing at that question.

Letting her arms go slack, she replied, "No, I do wish to see Owen. But as I mentioned previously, I need to tell the soldier who helped me escape what's going on. I hardly think that's too much to ask." Her head began to pound from bouncing upside down.

"I've been wondering how you made it here," Ackley said. "There's no way you could have managed on your own."

"Where's the soldier at?" Gytha asked. "I can go and get him."

She was about to answer when Ackley came to an abrupt

halt. Harley peered around him, trying to see what had caused him to stop.

Gytha withdrew a dagger, stepping in front of Ackley and blocking Harley's upside-down view.

"Put Lady Harley down," Ledger's furious voice demanded.

Ackley chuckled, the sound laced with menace, making the hair on Harley's arms rise. She wanted to cower. How did her cousin come to know this man? Luckily Ledger was a skilled fighter, trained by the king's best men. He would be able to best Ackley and free Harley from her current predicament.

"Who are you?" Gytha asked, almost sounding bored.

"That's none of your business," Ledger replied, a hint of affront seeping through. "Now don't make me repeat myself." The sound of steel sliced through the air.

Realizing that this could turn nasty and someone could get hurt, Harley cried out, "Put your weapons away." The last thing she needed was to be run through with a sword simply because she was being carried over Ackley's shoulder. "And set me on my feet so we can discuss this civilly."

"Maybe I don't want to be civil," Ackley said, his voice low and sultry.

Harley shivered. His grip around her thighs tightened, making her heart beat faster.

"I can't place your accent," Ledger stated. "Which means you're not from around here."

"That is correct," Ackley said. "Now if you'll excuse us, we have somewhere to be."

Knowing Ledger wouldn't back down, Harley intervened. "Apparently my cousin sent these two to fetch me. The woman, Gytha, just saved me from an unpleasant encounter inside the tavern. They don't mean me any harm—even though I am being treated atrociously at the moment."

"Your cousin is here?" Ledger asked, his voice losing its hard edge.

"According to these two individuals." Perhaps that was why Rayne and Milard hadn't returned yet. If Owen sent Ackley and Gytha to retrieve her, then when Rayne and Milard showed up, he probably insisted they remain there, assuming Ackley would be successful in his endeavor.

"And you intend to take Lady Harley to King Owen?" Ledger asked.

Harley stilled. *King Owen.* She wasn't used to people addressing her cousin that way. The formal title felt odd. All her life, he'd been Prince Owen. With three older siblings, no one ever thought he'd inherit the throne. The role he now had to fill was an enormous undertaking and would require support. She would help him in whatever capacity she could.

"That's the plan," Gytha said. "Her cousin asked us to retrieve her. Are you the soldier who's been helping her?"

"I am," Ledger replied.

"Then you're welcome to join us," Ackley said. "Let's go. The sooner we're out of here, the better." He started walking. Lowering his voice, he said, "Owen won't be pleased you're dallying with a common foot soldier."

"Excuse me?" Harley said, sure she'd heard him wrong.

"It's obvious the guy's in love with you. You shouldn't encourage him."

Harley patted Ackley's back. "You can set me down now." Ledger was not in love with her. They'd simply been through a lot together and had formed a friendship.

"We need to move quickly before the watchmen catch up with us."

"I'm perfectly capable of walking." She wasn't an imbecile.

Ackley swung her upright, setting her on her feet. "All I'm

saying is that if you were my sister, I wouldn't approve. I think I know Owen well enough to know he'll probably want to end that guy for taking your innocence."

Harley had known Ackley for less than an hour, and already she couldn't stand him. Furious, she took a step closer, and slapped him.

CHAPTER SEVEN

ACKLEY

*A*ckley blinked, momentarily stunned. Harley had slapped him. Not that it hurt—he barely felt it. He just didn't anticipate her standing up to him. Until that point, he'd thought of her as a weak, timid little thing. Not bold enough to slap a man she'd recently met. Lifting a single eyebrow, he stared down at her, trying to intimidate her. Only, he found his confidence shaken. How could *he* possibly be intimidated by *her*?

A light blush spread across her cheeks from the cool night air. Her blonde hair stuck out in several directions from him having held her upside down. For a split second, he imagined her legs wrapped around his waist while he ran his hands through her wild hair, enjoying a jaunt in the sack with her. But then he remembered she was Owen's cousin. And a pampered, entitled, weak woman at that. He just hadn't expected her to be so attractive. Her eyes narrowed, and her hands balled into fists as her chest rose and fell, fury emanating from her entire body.

Forcing himself to look away from her heaving chest, he met her eyes and said, "That was a very stupid thing you did."

"Likewise. Don't ever treat me so disrespectfully again." She put her hands on her hips. "There is nothing going on between me and Ledger."

Ackley folded his arms, assessing Harley. While she certainly looked slight at five feet three inches and a hundred and ten pounds, her striking blue eyes hinted at underlying intelligence and something else he couldn't pinpoint yet.

"Where's Gytha and Ledger?" she asked.

Sliding his causal demeanor back into place, he glanced behind him. Gytha came lumbering along with Ledger slung over her shoulder. "What happened?"

Gytha rolled her eyes. "He tripped and smacked his head."

"Is he all right?" Harley asked.

"He's fine. He's already starting to rouse."

Ledger moaned.

Ackley chuckled. "The lout knocked himself out?" He laughed again. "You sure know how to pick them." He smirked.

"I don't need this," Harley stated. "I've dealt with enough men like you that I won't stand for it any longer. You and Gytha can return to Owen. I will remain here with Ledger. Once he is capable of walking, we'll travel to the cove and meet up with everyone there. For now, it's best we part ways."

Idina would chastise him to no end if he didn't return with Harley. Especially if it was his fault for toying with her. He needed to rectify this situation—quickly. "Lady Harley," he said in an overly formal voice. "Would you be so kind as to accompany me along this delightful alleyway?" If she wanted fluff and someone who exuded court etiquette, he would give it to her. The last thing he needed was her storming off. And one thing was certain—he would not leave without her.

Her shoulders rose and fell as she took a deep breath, trying to regain her composure. "Are you mocking me?" Her voice was crisp and refined.

He smiled. "I would never dream of mocking someone so graceful and lovely as you." Of course he was making fun of her. She made it way too easy to do so.

"We're going to have company," Gytha mumbled, adjusting Ledger on her shoulder. "I hear men shouting not far away."

In order to exit the city, they needed to make their way to the bottom level. Ackley quickly thought over the path they needed to take. Never in his life had he seen a city built into the side of a cliff like this one. Kreng had to be fifty stories tall with hundreds of staircases and ladders connecting each level. They were currently on the tenth level—where all taverns and inns were located.

Ledger groaned. Good, they needed him awake so he could walk. Having Gytha carry him was not ideal.

"Fifteen feet and closing," Gytha muttered.

From the sound of the approaching footsteps, Ackley counted four people. One heavier man, two of average weight, and one lighter fellow. Would it be easier to dispose of the four men? Or should they hide and evade them? He glanced sidelong at Harley, trying to figure out how quickly she could run. However, it wouldn't matter with Ledger semi-unconscious.

Ackley sighed, then stretched his neck from side to side. "The three of you stay here."

Gytha slid Ledger onto the ground near Harley's feet. "I don't get to partake in the fun?"

"Next time. I promise." He winked before turning to face the four approaching men.

Since the alleyway was dark and narrow, he'd have to be careful not to cause too much of a raucous and rouse the people staying at the nearby inns. While most windows appeared dark, he had no doubt eyes lurked behind some of them. The last thing he wanted was attention. The less people who knew what they were doing and where they were going, the better.

Four men came within view. "What'd you do to the innkeeper?" the heavier one on the left asked.

Not wanting to bother with small talk, Ackley withdrew his dagger. He needed to lure them in closer in order to knock each one out.

"Authorities have been contacted," the skinnier man said. "We don't want any trouble."

"Then perhaps you should turn around and leave me and my companions alone." Ackley palmed his dagger, making sure they saw it. When they made no move to leave, he took a few steps toward them until they were only three feet apart. After envisioning each move he'd make, he struck. Spinning, he kicked the guy on the right, easily knocking him down. The man on the left rushed at Ackley. Ackley twisted and slammed the hilt of his dagger against the back of the large man's head. He collapsed. One man took off running. Only one opponent left. Ackley flung his elbow up, smashing the guy's nose. He flopped to the ground.

Ackley hadn't even broken a sweat. Normally, he didn't fight untrained civilians. However, this situation couldn't be helped.

He returned to his companions. "We need to get out of here before more men come looking for us."

"Did you kill them?" Harley demanded.

"No." He wasn't a monster. "They'll all be fine."

Ledger stood, swaying slightly. Harley wrapped her arm around his waist, steadying him.

"Can you walk?" Ackley asked.

Ledger nodded.

"Good. Let's go."

The four of them made their way to the ladders where they descended to one of the lower levels. When a group of people came into view up ahead, Ackley turned down a dark alley to avoid being seen.

"Where are we going?" Harley asked, glancing behind them.

"I'm trying to keep us hidden."

"I don't understand why. Just tell the authorities Owen is here and we need to be on our way."

"Kreng isn't part of Melenia." Didn't she know this?

"Your point?"

"They could keep you here," Ledger answered. "Use you as a bargaining chip with King Owen. Or they could turn you over to Russek in exchange for leaving the city alone. Either way, it's something we can't risk."

"Oh."

"Also, no one knows King Owen is here," Gytha added.

"It would be prudent to keep Owen's presence hidden for now," Ackley said. "It'll give us the element of surprise when we attack Russek." He didn't know why he bothered explaining any of this to Harley. Clearly, she had no military knowledge. Owen had said she was sheltered. But this level of naivety was downright appalling—even for a woman.

They descended to the bottom level where most of the stores were located. As they made their way to the northern end of the city, dozens of people milled about. Ackley hadn't expected so many people to be out at this late hour.

Wanting to blend in, he caught Gytha's attention, then tilted his head toward Ledger. Gytha nodded in acknowledgment before cozying up to Ledger and slowing their pace. Ackley slid his arm around Harley, pulling her in close. Instead of melting against his body as he expected, she stiffened.

A group of men headed their way. Harley was not playing the part. She probably had never been properly courted by a man and had no idea how to act with one.

"Relax," Ackley murmured. "We want anyone who sees us to think we're a couple out for a nightly stroll."

"Why do we have to be a couple?"

"So no one will suspect us. Authorities are looking for four people. That's why we split up."

She didn't look his way as she said, "We can be a couple without you touching me so intimately."

A chuckle escaped his lips. "I hardly think this is intimate."

Harley stopped walking. When she looked up at him, her blue eyes beckoned him to lean in closer. For some strange reason, his breathing sped up. He brushed her hair over her right shoulder, fully exposing her ear. "Now this is slightly more intimate," he whispered, his nose gliding along the side of her soft neck, breathing her in.

Harley shivered.

The group neared, so Ackley maneuvered his body, gently pressing her against the side of the nearest building. He tilted his head as if about to kiss her, blocking her face from those passing by. Her body stiffened, and panic flashed in her eyes. He remained that way—inches from her—without his lips touching hers.

As the group passed, Ackley kept part of his attention on the men and the rest on the beautiful, but frightened, woman before him. Sweat coated her forehead even though the night air had a cold bite to it, her skin seemed unusually white, and her entire body shook. He raised his eyebrows, hoping she'd offer some sort of explanation. She averted her eyes.

Now that the men had passed, Ackley took a step back, putting some space between them. Only one conclusion could be deduced from her behavior—she'd been harmed in some way, probably during the takeover. While he wanted to discover to what extent, this was neither the time nor the place to do so. He was there to escort her to her cousin. Owen could speak with her about what took place. If she provided names, Ackley would hunt down those responsible for hurting her and dispose of them with pleasure.

He wished he hadn't upset her—it wasn't his intention to do so. While he had enjoyed goading her, he didn't mean to cause her any distress. "I'm sorry." Running his hand under his chin, he watched Harley gain control over her emotions.

Her eyes cleared, her body stopped shaking, and she lifted her chin with an air of confidence. Without uttering a word, she turned and hurried after Ledger and Gytha, who'd reached the end of the alleyway.

Following behind her at a safe distance, Ackley remembered when his sister had been abducted from the castle. He'd intended to murder—slowly, painfully, and quite thoroughly—the men who'd taken her. Owen had been the one to accompany him to retrieve Idina. Thankfully, she hadn't been harmed. If she had, Ackley didn't think he would have ever recovered. Banishing those thoughts, he scanned the area, checking for anything out of place. He had a job to do.

The four of them regrouped, heading toward the cove.

Gytha and Ledger were speaking to one another in hushed whispers, Gytha repeatedly glancing over her shoulder at Ackley, making him wonder what the two of them were up to.

They came to the end of a street, the ocean straight ahead of them.

Ledger peered around the corner. "Everything looks normal."

Harley hovered close behind Ledger, her arms folded across her chest, the wind tossing her long blonde hair. Even wearing the drab brown clothing, she was quite stunning.

"The cave we need to reach is to the north of here," Ackley said.

"I've been explaining to Gytha that there's an easier way out of here," Ledger said.

"Great. Lead the way." Ackley assumed there had to be more than one route in and out of a city this large.

Gytha snorted. "You won't like it. The three of us can go the easier way. You can go back the way we came in."

Ackley narrowed his eyes, considering her remarks.

"Don't be ridiculous," Harley said, blowing warmth into her hands. "He'll go with us. There's enough room."

Dread coursed through Ackley. "Room in what?"

"The boat we have stashed," Harley answered. "It's just over there. A lot of the locals own one for sea transportation. We made sure to acquire a small boat when we arrived so we could leave quickly if the need arose."

"How is taking a small boat out into the open ocean late at night any safer?" Ackley tried hiding his rising panic. If he stepped foot in a boat, he would be useless. And he had no desire to feel that way—especially in front of other people. It would make Ledger's embarrassing fall look like nothing if Ackley was heaving up his insides.

93

"The tide is in," Ledger explained. "The waves are calm. We'll head straight out past the cove, then turn and go north, parallel to the cliffs. When we reach the waterfall, there's a cave big enough for the boat to dock in. From there, all we have to do is climb up a small rise. Even a child can do it."

Ackley wanted to punch Ledger. Instead, he shrugged, trying to act nonchalant. "I'll meet the three of you at the top of the waterfall." Without waiting for a response, he stepped out of the alley and headed away from them. He'd sworn to never get in a boat until his trip home. Just the thought of being out on the water made his stomach queasy.

"We need you," Ledger called out after him. "I can't row the boat by myself."

Gytha snorted. "I can row. How hard can it be?"

"But you're a woman."

Now things were getting interesting. Chuckling, Ackley turned, hoping to catch Gytha's fist smashing into Ledger's stubby nose. While her hands were balled into fists, they still remained at her sides. She wouldn't last more than a minute.

"I have two arms just like you." She took a step closer to Ledger. She was an inch taller than the man and probably weighed about the same. "Are you implying that my arms do not function simply because I am a woman?"

"Well, no," Ledger stuttered. "But rowing requires strength which you don't have since you're a woman."

"Since I'm a weak woman, this shouldn't hurt." She swung her fist, punching him in the stomach.

He grunted and hunched forward, trying to catch his breath, his face turning a deep shade of red. It was a beautiful sight to see.

"Why are you bent over? I'm a woman and, according to

94

you, not very strong." Gytha folded her arms, waiting for his response.

"Stop," Harley demanded. "The both of you are acting like children." She wrapped her arm around Ledger, comforting him like a mother would.

Ackley snorted at the irony. Before he had a chance to come up with a snarky reply, movement to his left caught his attention. Three stories up, a group of people carrying torches were shouting and climbing down the ladders to the lower levels.

"We're about to get company. Move. Now." He turned and started jogging toward the cave.

"We'll never make it without you," Ledger said, his voice a little higher pitched than previously.

Judging by how quickly the mob was descending, Ackley estimated they had less than five minutes to make their escape. While he could easily reach the cave in time, navigating through the dark water during high tide would be difficult. And even if he could accomplish such a feat, he doubted Gytha would fare so easily with Harley and Ledger.

"I'll manage," Gytha said, as if reading his thoughts.

He knew she'd manage. But would that be good enough? Probably not. He squeezed his eyes together and cursed. Once the decision was made, there was no point in second guessing it. "Let's go." Grabbing Ledger by the shoulder, he hurried him along.

Without questioning him, Gytha took Harley's arm and followed close behind.

"Where to?" Ackley demanded, scanning the area for potential threats.

"Sharp right." Ledger was walking straighter now. "The boats are in the northern cliffside."

When they got closer, Ackley saw hundreds of boats stashed in the actual cliff. It appeared as if someone had taken a shovel and carved out spaces for each boat in the rocks. Some spaces had two boats jammed in.

Ledger jogged along the cliffside, counting.

At this point, Ackley didn't care which boat they used so long as they took one and got the heck out of there.

"Here." Climbing up to the third row, Ledger yanked on the end of a boat, sliding it out of its space.

Ackley helped him, grabbing hold of the other side. The two men carried the boat toward the water. Examining it, unease filled Ackley. The rickety thing didn't look like it would float. Had Ledger built it himself? The wood boards appeared hastily slapped together. This was a bad idea. They reached the water just as the mob descended to the ground level.

"Lower the boat into the ocean," Ledger commanded as he rushed into the water. "Help the two ladies in."

Ackley almost asked who the second lady was when he realized Ledger was referring to Gytha. Gytha wasn't a lady, but he knew better than to say anything. He didn't need the warrior woman's wrath right now.

Gytha deftly jumped in, then reached out to help Harley. While no waves crashed against them, the water—which was now up to Ackley's knees—did have a strong pull to it. Harley fell in the boat, unable to climb in with her heavy wet dress clinging to her legs. Ledger swung in next, grabbing one of the two oars.

Voices rang out not far behind Ackley. Gritting his teeth, he jumped in the boat and grabbed the other oar. He and Ledger began rowing in sync. No one spoke as they headed west, trying to get out of sight from the mob that had reached the shoreline.

"As soon as we're out of the cove," Ledger said, "turn north."

Ackley didn't want to look back. He suspected people were already getting into boats and heading out after them. Thankfully it was nighttime, and they could hide easier in the dark than in the daylight. "Do you think those people know what direction we're headed?" If they did, perhaps they should take a different route.

"Yes," Ledger said between strokes. "But there's no other way."

"It's fine," Gytha said. "We'll outpace them. Row faster." She reached into the water and started paddling with her hands. She whacked Harley. "Help. You row over there."

With shaking arms, Harley stuck her hands in the water and paddled, though it didn't help much.

They rounded the cliff, out of sight of the city and prying eyes. Ackley kept his feet planted against the bench seat in front of him as he rowed. Now that they were traveling north, he felt the rocking of the water as it tilted the boat from side to side. Vomit rose in his mouth.

"Keep it steady," Ledger barked.

Sweat dripped down Ackley's forehead and cheeks—not from exertion but from the back and forth, the up and down. "Where's the blasted cave?" he said through gritted teeth.

"Not much farther," Ledger huffed. "Let's move in closer to the cliff so we don't miss it."

In the dark, it was difficult to see how quickly they were approaching the cliff, and Ackley had no desire to smash into it.

"I hear the waterfall," Gytha said, still paddling with her hands.

"Head straight for it," Ledger commanded. "The cave is just past it."

Nausea rolled through Ackley. Leaning over the side of the boat, he vomited. The oar slipped through his hand. Not wanting to lose it, he grabbed it before it disappeared under the water. Knowing that all three people in the boat were staring at him, he refused to face them. Instead, he reached down, splashing water on his forehead and neck. He needed to pull it together. Otherwise, he'd lose all credibility with his companions.

"Are you okay?" Harley asked gently.

"I'm fine," he snapped, not liking that she saw this side of him. Something that made him vulnerable. Weak.

"I see the cave," Gytha said, capturing everyone's attention. "It's to the left of the waterfall."

Situating himself back on the bench seat, Ackley clutched the oar and began rowing again. The faster he rowed, the sooner they'd reach the cave and he could get out of this blasted boat.

Since Ledger had his back to the cliff, Ackley made sure to steer them toward the cave's entrance. The closer they got, the more concerned he became. "So this cave," he said, already suspecting the answer but not quite believing it, "are we just going to...row into it?" In the dead of night? Without a torch?

"Yes," Ledger answered. "When we go in, the boat will hit bottom. Once it's secure, we'll climb out. We should have no trouble even at night."

Ackley sincerely doubted that.

"A light is rounding the cove," Gytha said, panic laced in her voice. "We need to get in that cave. Fast."

"Almost there," Ackley said, huffing.

While he steered the boat, the strong swell made it difficult to stay on course. Fighting the water, he used his strength to row hard and fast, aiming for the dark entrance to the cave. As they neared it, the water became even more turbulent.

Shoving his oar forward, he pulled it back, again and again. His shoulders burned. The swell increased, sending the boat up and down. His head pounded, and his stomach cramped. He wouldn't last much longer. They were just about to reach the entrance.

"Steady," Ledger said.

Ackley lifted his oar, reached forward with it, and accidentally clipped Harley's outstretched arm when the boat dipped down.

She yelped and tumbled out of the boat and into the dark ocean below.

CHAPTER EIGHT

HARLEY

Frigid water and sheer darkness enveloped Harley. The heaviness of her wet dress weighed her down, making it difficult to kick her legs. Unable to resurface, panic consumed her. She was going to die. No, she chided herself, she would not die here tonight. After surviving the takeover and witnessing her brother's murder, she would find a way to survive. She needed to avenge Hollis's death and make Russek pay for what they did. She had too much to accomplish to drown now.

Frantically reaching out, she sought the boat. If she could find it, she could hang on. If that didn't work, she'd attempt to remove her dress, freeing herself from it.

Strong fingers gripped her right wrist, yanking her head above water. She heaved in large gulps of air, her lungs stinging. Ackley and Gytha hauled her over the side and into the boat. Voices shouted around her, but she couldn't focus on any of them as she collapsed on the floor of the boat, coughing. She rolled over and expelled some of the water she'd inadvertently consumed during her near drowning. Gytha hit her back, yelling something in her ear. Harley clutched the bench seat, trying to calm her shaking body, stinging lungs, and ragged breathing. She was alive.

The boat slammed into something, startling her. Complete darkness—similar to underwater—surrounded her.

"I'll get out first," Ledger said, his voice somewhat panicked. "Ackley, use your oar to keep us from being pulled back out." The boat shifted. "It's only knee deep." There were some splashing noises. "I've got a hold on the boat. Everyone out."

"I can't see a thing," Gytha muttered. "Where do we go?" The boat shifted again.

"I don't know," Ledger snapped. "Figure it out."

"Well now," Gytha said, her voice singsong. "I'm just a frail little woman. I don't know if I can do anything without a man."

"You're right," Ledger said. "I'm sorry I was curt with you. I will escort you from the cave momentarily."

"Oh bloody hell," Ackley muttered, the boat shifting again. "She was joking." Slim fingers curled around Harley's waist. "Come on," he said, his voice close to her ear. He lifted her out of the boat, then swung her up into his arms, carrying her onto the shore.

Unable to see in the dark cave, Harley clung to Ackley's shirt, feeling his solid strength beneath. She was alive.

"The stairs are narrow," Ledger said. "Go slowly."

"I can see a faint light from the moon and stars," Gytha said. "There must be an exit at the top."

"There is," Ledger replied.

Ackley carried Harley out of the cave. She didn't protest because she wasn't sure she could climb the stairs in her heavy, wet dress.

"Are you okay?" Ackley asked softly.

He probably felt guilty for almost drowning her. "I'm alive." And right now, that was all that mattered.

"I'm sorry I knocked you in the water. It was an accident."

"Since you saved me, I forgive you." They exited the cave. The cool night chilled Harley's dress, making her shiver.

"Can you walk?" Ackley asked.

Before Harley could answer, Gytha approached them. "I can carry her if you're still seasick."

She'd forgotten Ackley had vomited during the boat ride. "I can walk," she insisted. There was no need for other people to coddle her.

Ackley gently set her on her feet. Her wet dress clung to her legs.

"I know you're cold," Gytha said, "but we must keep moving. It's not safe to stay here tonight."

Harley understood; however, exhaustion consumed her. She could barely feel her fingers, toes, and ears.

"There's a village not far from here," Ackley said. "It's mostly destroyed. If we can make it there, it'll provide enough cover for us to have a fire."

Harley liked the sound of that. She almost sighed at the mere mention of warmth. "Will you be able to make it there?" she asked Ackley, wondering if he was still ill. Although she didn't know him well, she could have sworn his eyes flashed with annoyance.

"Now that we're on land, I can assure you, I'm fine." He walked away from her, heading toward the river.

"What are you doing?" He was going the wrong direction.

"I left my bag on the other side of the river. I'm going to retrieve it. The three of you can head north. I'll catch up with you in a bit." He sat on the ground, removing his boots and socks.

"You're going to cross the river in the dark?" Harley asked.

"It can't be any worse than rowing a boat in the ocean at night." He stood and untied his pants. "I suggest you hurry along unless you want to see me naked."

She turned away from him, most definitely not wanting to see him without his clothes on. Regardless, she didn't think crossing the river at night was a smart idea. However, Ackley clearly didn't care what she thought.

"I'll lead the way," Ledger said. "I know where we are and where we're going."

Harley followed him, Gytha behind her. If Gytha wasn't worried about her friend, then Harley shouldn't be concerned about him, either.

The three of them headed north. After a mile or so, Ackley caught up to them. He handed Gytha her bag. She opened it and pulled out a tunic, giving it to Harley.

Harley took the blessedly dry material and slid it over her head and onto her body.

No one spoke as they made their way north.

A few times, Ackley broke away from their group and doubled back, making sure they weren't being followed. After another mile, Harley started shivering so badly, her teeth chattered. She wished she could remove her soaking wet dress that clung to her legs. And maybe if her hair wasn't dripping down the sides of her face, she wouldn't be quite so chilly. Even if they managed to get a fire going, it would take a good amount of time before she was fully dry. Wrapping her arms around her torso, she glanced at the moon. It had to be after midnight. What she wouldn't give for a warm bed right now.

Ledger stopped. "The village should be right around here." He put his hands on his hips, turning in a slow circle.

"With the buildings burned to the ground, it may be harder to spot at night," Gytha pointed out.

Ledger nodded and resumed walking.

"I suggest heading to the east," Ackley said. He traveled at the back, behind Gytha.

Given what Harley had seen of Ackley so far, he had to either be some sort of mercenary or soldier. Regardless of his profession, he'd have to have a good sense of direction since he'd found her in Kreng. Still, Ledger was a soldier born and raised here. He should know the land better than a foreigner.

After a few minutes, Ledger headed eastward. A quarter of a mile later, he announced that he saw the burned village in the distance. Once they reached it, Ackley stepped around Ledger, leading them to one of the larger homes that had part of a single stone wall still standing. He and Gytha cleared a space for the four of them to sleep for the night. While they did that, Ledger gathered wood for a fire.

Unable to feel her fingers or toes, Harley sunk to the ground, trembling. The smell of burnt wood hung in the air along with another smell she couldn't pinpoint. Death perhaps. Thankfully, the darkness concealed what she suspected to be charred bones scattered about. Tears filled her eyes. Everything was a mess. Her beloved kingdom was in disarray, her family slaughtered, and her life forever changed. She wished Russek hadn't invaded Melenia, bringing so much death and destruction.

Ledger dropped some wood on the ground, then turned and left to find some more. As Ackley stacked it, Gytha sat next to him.

"Are you going to offer Harley the extra set of dry clothes in your bag?"

"They won't fit her." He continued stacking the wood, not once looking her way.

"I only had the one extra tunic, and I already gave it to her. It's probably wet by now. She'll need to remove all her wet clothes and put something dry on."

He continued stacking the wood, not responding.

"Ackley." Gytha placed her hand on his forearm. "What's the matter?"

"Nothing," he snapped.

"Fine. Be that way. But when I see your sister, I'm going to tell her what an arse you've been."

Harley pretended not to be listening in on their conversation. Pulling her legs to her chest, she thought about what Ackley's sister must be like. She was probably similar to Gytha. A fierce fighter who could take care of herself. Jealousy filled her. She wished she could fight and defend herself.

"What do you want from me?" Ackley asked, putting the last log in place.

"Your clothes."

He chuckled, the sound low and sultry. "You didn't get a good look at me back at the river, so you want me to take my clothes off here for you?"

Gytha smacked him. "You're so full of yourself." She shook her head. "Do you want to go a round with me right now? I wouldn't mind walloping your arse."

"While I'd like to spar with you, I am going to do a perimeter check, then take up watch. I need to make sure no one is following us."

"Just get the fire started before you leave. I want to get Harley warmed up."

By the time Ledger returned with another stack of wood, Ackley had the fire going. Without a word to Ledger, Ackley stood and walked away from them, disappearing into the shadows of the night.

"Now that the fire is going, you need to take your clothes off," Gytha said as she sat next to Harley. "That way they'll dry faster and you can warm yourself up." She opened Ackley's bag, pulling out dry clothes.

"Won't he mind?" Harley asked.

"No, he won't." Gytha looked at Ledger, waiting.

"Oh, I'll uh...I'll go over there so I can't see you," he stuttered, pointing to a pile of rubble. "If you need me, just shout."

"He could have just turned his back," Gytha said, shaking her head in disapproval.

What about Ackley? Was he far enough away so he wouldn't catch a glimpse of her? Harley removed her boots and socks, setting them by the fire to dry. Then she took off Gytha's borrowed tunic, handing it to her. After wearing it over her dress, it had become soaking wet. She peeled off her dress and undergarments. She slid on Ackley's tunic, the warm fabric engulfing her. Then she pulled on his pants. They were huge, but she didn't care. If anything, the long material covered her bare feet.

Already feeling better, she scooted closer to the fire, holding her slightly purple hands out. The heat stung.

"Are you okay?" Gytha asked, staring into the flames.

"Feeling is already starting to return to my fingers and toes."

"No." The warrior woman shook her head. "I meant, how are you feeling? A lot has happened. You look like you're about to fall apart. I'd like to keep you together until we reach your cousin."

She hadn't expected Gytha to care. "I'm fine." She would survive. Even if she lost a toe or two, she was alive, and that was all that mattered.

Gytha chuckled. "You're not what I expected."

She didn't know how to respond to that. "What did you picture?"

"I'm not sure, but not you. You actually remind me a lot of Owen."

"I'll take that as a compliment." Since her cousin was close with Hollis, she'd spent a lot of time with him and knew him well. He was an honorable man.

"Good, because it is one." She picked up a stick, poking one of the logs so it moved into the flames a bit more. "Do you have any questions for me?"

Harley studied the warrior woman. "Questions?"

She nodded. "Like how your cousin is doing."

"I assumed he's okay. Otherwise, you would have said something." So much had been going on that Harley hadn't considered Owen not being well.

"He's fine. He had some trouble in Marsden—that's where Ackley and I are from. One of his own men, Commander Beck, tried killing him and taking control of Melenia's soldiers."

Panic filled Harley. Her father-in-law had tried killing Owen? "Are you certain it was Commander Beck?"

Gytha nodded. "When Owen received word your kingdom had been overthrown, he struck an alliance with our king. Ackley and I came here with Owen, along with a few hundred Marsden soldiers. We are here to help you retake Melenia."

Not only was Owen here, but he'd returned with extra soldiers. For the first time in weeks, hope took root.

"I'm telling you this so you understand that Ackley and I

are here to help. We're on your side. Even if he seems a little standoffish, Ackley's a good man."

"I'm glad you're here." As for Ackley, she didn't care if he was a good man or not. All she cared about was that he was on her side. The more people fighting against Russek, the better.

"I need to get some sleep so I can relieve Ackley in a few hours." Gytha laid next to the fire, across from Harley.

Harley stretched out on her side. "Have you known Ackley long?" The two of them seemed rather close, and she wondered if they were romantically involved with one another.

"No. But he's one of the most skilled fighters I've ever known. Of course, he'd have to be to be a knight."

"What's a knight? A man who fights for the king?"

"More along the lines of an assassin."

Her cousin had sent an assassin to fetch her? "What about you? Are you an assassin?"

"No. I'm a captain in the king's army. I fight. Ackley can fight, but he also gathers information and can kill a man in a crowded room without anyone seeing. I admire him. If you're going to be in a scuffle, Ackley's the man you want guarding your back."

It was hard to think of an assassin being a good man. Her uncle chose not only skilled fighters to be part of his guard, but men of nobility and honor. Not assassins. She should have known Ackley was skilled in the art of killing. He'd fought those men back in Kreng as if toying with them. A snake to mice. It had been so simple for him to incapacitate four men in under a minute. She shivered. He could have just as easily killed them. "Are there other women soldiers where you're from?"

"During our journey here, Owen told me a little bit about your kingdom." She rolled onto her back, staring up at the sky as she spoke. "Your kingdom does things differently from mine. I'm from Axian, which is the southern part of Marsden. There, women are equal to men."

An intriguing notion. Women fighting alongside men. "Are female soldiers allowed to marry?"

Gytha chuckled. "Yes, but I'm not married if that's what you're asking."

"I think I'd like to visit your kingdom one day."

Harley opened her eyes. The sky had just begun to lighten. A thick fog coated the land, hiding most of the charred rubble. Directly in front of her, Ackley lay sleeping. Harley's back remained warm; the fire still smoldering. Near her feet, Ledger slept, snoring lightly. She didn't see Gytha anywhere. The warrior woman was probably on watch.

Not wanting to sit and wake everyone, she decided to remain there. Since meeting Ackley, this was the first time she'd had the opportunity to study him in detail. His dark hair clearly indicated he wasn't from around here. While the color was fascinating, she found his eyebrows and eyelashes truly striking. Black, like the night sky when no moon or stars shone. His face had odd patches of lighter spots, and she wondered if he'd had a nasty sunburn he was still recovering from. A few freckles dotted his nose and forehead. His hands were calloused—more so than either her brother or Lyle's. A testament to his profession.

When she looked from his hands to his face again, his eyes were open, staring directly at her.

"Don't move," he mouthed.

Fear slid over her like a blanket. This man in front of her

was an assassin and could kill her before she'd even have time to blink. However, she didn't think he intended to harm her in any way.

"There's a rat sniffing your hair," he whispered.

She screamed, flailing her arms around her head, trying to scare the rat away.

Ackley flung his arm around her, yanking her toward him while simultaneously sliding a dagger from his sleeve, throwing it just above where her head had been. He flipped her on top of him.

"Stop moving," Ackley demanded.

She froze, her face right in front of his, their noses almost touching. Her hair slid around their heads, shielding them in. "Did you kill it?" she whispered.

"I don't know. I can't see it with your hair all over the place." His chest rose and fell.

"Why is your hand on my…bottom?"

"I told you not to move," he answered. "You moved. I grabbed you in the wrong spot."

"So it's my fault your hand is still on me?" With the entire front side of her body crushed against his, she felt something hard press into her.

Ackley's eyes flashed with panic. "You weigh more than you look." He lifted his hand from her rear end, then shoved her off of him.

She scrambled to her knees as Gytha came sprinting toward them, sword in hand.

Right where Harley's head had been, a rat lay prostrate, a dagger embedded in its body. She shivered, hoping the rat hadn't been in her hair. "Did you plan to kill that thing with me just lying there?" He could have had her move before he started throwing weapons at her head.

He propped his body up on his elbows. "I considered it. Then I decided to roll you out of the way so you didn't freak out." He shrugged. "Looks like you're freaking out anyway." He sat up and rubbed his face.

"Let me get this straight," Gytha said, sheathing her sword. "All of this commotion is over a rat?"

"A very large rat." Harley pointed at the rodent.

Gytha shook her head. "Ledger, now that you're awake, come with me to find something for us to eat. There's farmland to the east of here."

Yawning, Ledger stretched. "Sure." He stood. "Harley, want to come with us?"

"She'll remain here," Ackley said, not giving her a chance to answer for herself.

Once Ledger and Gytha were far enough away, Harley glared at Ackley. "I am perfectly capable of speaking on my behalf. You are not my keeper, and you do not make decisions for me."

"Are you done throwing your temper tantrum?" He knelt and tossed a few more logs on the dying fire, stoking it to life again.

"I'm not throwing a tantrum." If anyone was being unreasonable, it was Ackley. He didn't own her. "Are you going to do something with that rat?" She didn't want to see its body.

He tossed it in the fire. "Better?"

"Much." She shivered from the mere idea of the rat being close to her while she slept.

"I want my clothes back." Ackley sat next to the fire. "Now."

She blinked, processing what he'd said. A smug smile slid across his face, as if he enjoyed irritating her. Well, she would not give him the satisfaction. Her dress was not only dry but toasty from the fire. Grabbing it, she went on the other side of the wall. After removing Ackley's clothes, she put her dress on.

Before rejoining him, she needed to cool her temper. He could have just told her there was a rat, and she could have slid away. He didn't have to throw a dagger at her head. And he most certainly didn't have to pull her body on top of his. He was a soldier, an assassin. And she a lady. If anything, he owed her an apology for his behavior. The part about his hand placement or feeling his hardness must have been a reaction to the situation. An accident. Nothing to bother thinking about.

Rolling her shoulders back, she stood tall and rounded the corner. She handed him his neatly folded clothes. "Thank you for letting me borrow them."

He raised a single eyebrow as he took the clothes. The simple gesture made her stomach do a little flip. She hated when men knew they were handsome and used it to their advantage. Pretending he had no effect on her, she sat by the fire again. If she were to ever be with another man, it would be someone sensitive, kind, considerate. The opposite of Ackley.

"While we're waiting for Gytha and Ledger to return," he said, eyeing her over the fire. "I have a few questions for you."

She didn't respond because she owed him nothing. There was no reason to be civil to this man. Especially considering where he'd accidentally touched her.

"Owen is trying to learn the state of the kingdom. What towns Russek has gained control of, where their troops are, that sort of thing. Did you learn anything while in Kreng?"

Surprise washed through her. While she owed Ackley nothing, she did want to help Owen. "I didn't. Ledger was the one working with the commander in Kreng." But he hadn't told her much of what they'd learned. As a woman, she hadn't thought it her place to question him.

"Hopefully Ledger can convey to Owen any pertinent information."

She played with the hem of her dress, trying to think if Ledger had once told her anything useful that he'd discovered. He'd said things about keeping Russek away, but not much beyond that. "During the takeover, I did overhear something of importance." Someone besides her should know, just in case. "There is a traitor. Someone inside the castle aided Russek and helped them get past our defenses."

"Do you know who it is?"

"No. I only know about him because I overheard him speaking with Prince Soma of Russek. Soma was there to assassinate his stepbrother, Prince Kerdan, who planned the entire invasion. He said once Kerdan was assassinated, the Melenia royal family would be killed. So I warned Kerdan."

Ackley's eyes widened in surprise. "You warned the Russek prince?"

Although he'd asked it as a question, it sounded more like an accusation. "Yes. He was the only one keeping my family alive." She quickly told him all that had happened, starting with the birthday celebration when Kerdan entered, her lighting the signal fire, Kerdan giving her the key before she was attacked and locked up, and ending with her fleeing for her life with Ledger, Milard, and Rayne. She did skimp on the details of her family's beheading and the attempted rape.

Instead of asking questions as she thought he would do, Ackley withdrew into himself, not speaking. Even when Gytha and Ledger returned with apples, nuts, and berries, he didn't converse. As Harley ate, she watched him. His keen eyes remained alert, and she got the impression he was working through something.

After they ate, they headed north, traveling all day. When it became clear they wouldn't arrive at the cove before dark, they set up camp for the night, sleeping under the stars. Harley had a hard time falling asleep, afraid a rat would crawl on her.

The next morning, they set out early. Just before noon, they reached a tunnel that cut straight through a mountain. Ackley explained that the tunnel led to where Owen and the soldiers had set up camp. A handful of sentries stood guard. When they saw Ackley, they immediately granted them passage.

As Harley traveled through the dark tunnel, she could almost feel the mountain pressing down on her and the dampness of the land seeping through.

"It's not much longer," Ackley said, as if he'd known she was starting to panic with the thought of being crushed alive or suffocating.

"Is that the exit up ahead?" She could just make out a hint of light.

"It is," he answered. "Almost there."

The closer they got to the light, the faster Harley walked. "I want to see Owen right away."

"Of course," Ackley said. "I'll take you straight there."

Harley stepped out of the tunnel and observed the sight before her. Bright green grass covered the valley; dark green and brown trees blanketed the surrounding mountains. In the middle of it all, hundreds of tan tents stood erect in neat rows. Dozens of soldiers rushed to and fro. Emotion overwhelmed her. Her lip quivered, tears filled her eyes, and joy flared in her heart. Owen was here.

"This way," Ackley said, gently gripping her elbow. He led

her through the camp, heading toward the largest tent with a flag atop it.

When they reached the tent, two sentries in full uniform stood guard. Seeing the familiar crest of the royal family on their chests made her swell with pride. This was her kingdom, and Owen was her cousin. Together, they would seek retribution. Without waiting to be granted entrance, Harley burst inside.

Owen stood at a table, several soldiers surrounding it, all of them studying a map. When Owen glanced up and saw her, he closed his eyes, his shoulders rising and falling in apparent relief. He opened his eyes and ordered everyone out. As the soldiers exited, Harley realized Ackley, Gytha, and Ledger had remained outside the tent.

Finally alone, Harley ran to Owen, throwing her arms around him. He held her tightly, kissing her head. His chest shook, and she realized they were both crying.

CHAPTER NINE

ACKLEY

*A*ckley watched Harley enter the tent, unable to figure out why the woman made him feel off-kilter. She was beautiful, to be sure. But she was a lady. She probably sat around knitting and drinking tea all day. He almost snorted just thinking about how she reacted when he told her there was a rat near her head. Typical woman. Of course, his body had reacted like a typical man's. He'd have to make sure that didn't happen again, which shouldn't be a problem. He doubted their paths would cross often.

Idina joined him. "I heard you'd arrived." She looked him over. "You appear to be in one piece and nothing seems to be wrong with your legs."

He lifted a single eyebrow. "You doubted my ability to fetch a young woman and return here unharmed?" His sister knew what he was capable of since she helped run their network of spies back in Marsden. She'd sent him on missions far more dangerous. There was no need to be concerned now simply because they were in a foreign kingdom.

"I'm trying to figure out why you're standing outside of Owen's tent instead of coming to see me." Folding her arms, she tapped her foot in agitation.

He smiled. "I was going to find you after I finished here." Once he spoke to Owen. Which reminded him that Ledger and Gytha were with him and he hadn't bothered with introductions. But Ledger was only a soldier and once he gave his report, he'd be absorbed into the army.

"Is Owen's cousin in there with him right now?" Idina asked, pointing at the tent.

"She is."

"Excellent. I'm eager to meet her." Idina pushed the flap aside and hurried into the tent.

He was about to tell her to wait since he didn't know how the reunion was going, but Idina rushed in before he could stop her. Not only had Harley been through a terrible ordeal at the castle during the takeover, but she hadn't had an easy go of it since. Owen probably wanted to know everything, and Ackley thought the two of them should have some time alone to discuss the details. Plus, Harley looked like a total disaster at the moment. Since she'd fallen into the ocean, her hair was a tangled mess. She also had soot on her face from sleeping in the burned village. The ugly brown commoner dress didn't help matters either. Which was why Ackley didn't understand his physical attraction to her given her current state. But it didn't matter—she wasn't his type, and he had no intention of tying himself to another person. Ever. He enjoyed his freedom.

Mumbled voices came from inside the tent. A moment later, Idina opened the flap and waved the three of them inside.

"We have a lot to discuss," Owen said by way of greeting, his arm wrapped around Harley. "First, I want to thank Ledger for aiding in my cousin's escape. Your father was a good man and will be missed."

Ledger bowed his head, his chest heaving up and down. Hopefully, Ledger would channel that hurt and devastation into being battle ready. The more soldiers they had in the right frame of mind, the better.

"Ledger, if you and Captain Gytha would get my generals, I'd appreciate it."

"Of course, Your Majesty." Ledger bowed, then left the tent with Gytha following close behind.

"*Your Majesty* sounds like your father," Harley said.

"I agree. I hope I can be half the leader he was."

"I have no doubt you'll be that and more."

Owen squeezed his cousin. "Now that it's just the four of us, there are a few things you need to know before the others join us." Owen released Harley, looking her square in the face. "Besides my being engaged to Princess Idina, you need to know that your father-in-law betrayed us. He tried to assassinate me and was killed for it."

Ackley blinked, understanding but not truly believing what he'd just heard. "Commander Beck is Lady Harley's father-in-law?" He wanted to be certain.

"Yes," Owen answered. "Though I never liked the guy." He shrugged sheepishly. "Sorry, Harley."

She shook her head. "I never cared for him either." Her attention went to her hands now clasped together.

The news rattled Ackley. Commander Beck had been instrumental in trying to take over Marsden. He was a devious man who deserved to die. But that wasn't what had him so shaken. It was the father-in-law part. That meant Harley was married. He rarely made errors in his judgment of others, and he didn't know how he could have been so wrong about this young woman before him. "Where's your husband?" he inquired. Had her husband traveled to Marsden along with Commander Beck? Did she have children? He wiped his hand off against his thigh—the hand that had accidentally grabbed her arse.

"Dead," Harley answered. The corners of her lips rose slightly. "Lyle died during the takeover. I am a widow."

"I'm so sorry," Idina said, her voice soft and comforting.

Harley's eyes hardened. "There's nothing to be sorry for. It was an arranged marriage, and I didn't particularly care for Lyle. He was his father's son."

Her words hung heavy in the air. Harley had not only been through a bloody takeover, but she'd lost her husband. And her husband had been a man she didn't care for. Another reason Ackley refused to wed—he didn't want to be forced to marry someone he didn't love strictly for political gains. If that were the case, he would only despise the woman for tying him down.

"Regardless," Idina said, "Prince Ackley and I offer our condolences."

Harley's face paled. "*Prince* Ackley?" She glanced at him, her eyes widening in horror.

"Yes, I'm here with my brother. I thought you knew that was Ackley?" Idina waved a hand in his direction, annoyance written across her face. And a promise to yell at him later for this. He withheld his amusement for self-preservation.

Harley shook her head. "Forgive me. I was not aware I traveled with a prince since neither he nor his companion identified him as one." She looked at Owen, as if pleading for help.

Ackley wasn't one of those stuffy royals who insisted on formality. Still, he knew how strange it was for someone in his position to go off on a clandestine assignment. Of course, that was what Owen had been doing in Marsden, so maybe it wasn't all that unusual for a son who wasn't first or second in line for the throne to do such things. He shrugged. Being a prince was simply a title; it didn't define who he was.

Ledger and Gytha entered the tent with a handful of soldiers who must be Owen's newly appointed generals. At least Owen had started to surround himself with people he trusted and who could help him. Ackley took note of each man, wanting to speak with them privately later in order to assess each one.

"I'll go now that your generals are here," Harley said.

"I want you to stay," Owen insisted. "I'm sure you have vital information to share."

She looked at her cousin as if he had two heads.

"Princess Idina has shown me there are other ways to do things," he added.

Idina smiled, pride radiating from her. Ackley couldn't help but think how lucky his sister was to have someone who not only loved her but valued her opinion. Owen came from a society that didn't have women in positions of authority. However, after meeting Idina, he had no qualms about listening to and trusting her. She was a shrewd planner, and he'd be a fool not to take advantage of her knowledge.

Once everyone was standing around the table, Owen began. "We've learned a lot over the course of the past few days." He placed the map of the kingdom on top of the other papers strewn on the table. "My spies have returned with information. The most important of which is Russek has withdrawn from Melenia."

"Withdrawn?" Ackley said. If the war was already over and he'd suffered those two weeks on that blasted ship needlessly, he'd punch something.

"That is the word from the few citizens my spies managed to come across. There is vast destruction across the kingdom. Most towns and villages are burned, and there aren't many survivors. But from those they spoke to, they all said Russek suddenly up and left."

"If Russek has withdrawn, then is there no war to be fought?" Ackley asked. "You are king, and your throne is secure?"

"Not even close," Idina said. "You didn't hear the second part yet." She folded her arms and looked at Owen.

"It seems someone is sitting on my throne." Owen drummed his knuckles on the table. "Someone other than me."

"Is it someone from Russek?" one of the generals asked.

"According to my spies, it is a Melenia soldier. One of my own has betrayed my family."

Silence filled the tent.

"Are you sure?" Ledger asked. "I was there, and I don't recall seeing a Melenia soldier aiding Russek."

"Maybe the soldier took the throne out of necessity?" one of the generals suggested. "If he thought the entire royal family murdered and Russek withdrew, then he saw the need for a ruler?"

Owen shook his head. "I wish that was the case, but it's not. We have a traitor to kill."

"How do you know?" Gytha asked.

One of the generals shifted on his feet, appearing uneasy with Gytha questioning the king so directly. Thankfully, he didn't ask why Owen allowed women to be present during this meeting. Where Ackley came from in northern Marsden, it was just as backward. However, in southern Marsden, where he met Gytha, women were treated equally. Owen seemed to be readily embracing that ideology.

"Lady Harley, didn't you say you overheard the traitor?" Ackley inquired. She was there during the takeover and had a lot of vital information to share. She just needed to be bolder and speak freely.

"Yes," she replied, not looking at any of the generals as she spoke. "I overheard one of our own plotting against the royal family."

"Do you have any idea who it is?" Owen asked.

"No. He spoke softly, and I did not get a look at his face."

"Your spies haven't been able to discover who it is?" Idina asked.

"Not yet. All we know is that a Melenia soldier declared himself king while Russek was still occupying the land. He worked with the Russek soldiers until they up and left, saying Prince Kerdan demanded all troops return home immediately."

"Prince Kerdan withdrew the troops?" Harley blurted out, surprise showing on her face.

Given what she'd revealed to him, Ackley wondered whose side Kerdan was really on. It seemed this information warranted a visit to the Russek prince. Unfortunately, Owen wouldn't condone Ackley traipsing off for a couple of weeks simply to gather information. He'd have to think on the matter more. Maybe he could send a few of his men to set up a meeting. Owen wouldn't have to know about it.

"That's what my spies reported." Owen scratched the back of his neck.

"What's our plan?" Ackley glanced at the map, noticing three lines marked from their camp to the royal castle, each line taking a different route. "With Russek gone, I assume your objective has changed?" Technically, Owen didn't need Marsden's soldiers any longer.

"I must still reclaim my throne." Owen straightened. "The traitorous king has taken up residence in my castle. I need to know if he has Melenia soldiers with him. If so, are they loyal to him? Regardless, we should have the numbers to take the castle back and dethrone the traitor." He flexed his hand.

So now instead of fighting a neighboring kingdom's army, Melenia was fighting against its own—or what was left of it. Ackley didn't think it would be as easy as Owen made it seem. However, Ackley would remain here with his Marsden soldiers until his sister's position in Melenia was secure.

"Are you certain you want to return there?" Harley asked, her voice soft and delicate, capturing everyone's astute attention. Her gaze remained on Owen. "After the royal family and my brother were murdered, they killed everyone. The royal castle is filled with death. You could build a new home."

"The castle is my home, and I will reclaim it," Owen said gently.

"Once you retake your throne," Harley said, fierce determination lighting up her eyes, "promise me you will make Russek pay."

Owen took her hand, squeezing it. "I promise."

Rubbing his chin, Ackley tried to fathom why a kingdom would invade another kingdom, slaughter so many, and then just leave. He needed to learn more about Russek and the state of this continent before he could make an accurate assumption.

"Do we know why they invaded in the first place?" He addressed his question to Harley since she'd mentioned something about Kerdan wanting the king to sign a treaty.

"They wanted soldiers," she answered. "But King Coden refused."

Ackley tapped the map where the kingdom of Russek was labeled. "I think we're overlooking one additional thing that needs to be considered."

"What's that?" one of the generals inquired.

Taking note of how Russek bordered Melenia, he replied, "If Russek came here for soldiers, did they get them? If so, what do they need them for?" In other words, was there something larger brewing on the continent? "I'm also concerned with Russek's sudden withdrawal. Does it have to do with this traitorous king, or is something else going on here on the mainland?" There, he'd said it. What he feared—a war was coming. If his past had taught him anything, it was that his gut was usually right.

Everyone stared at the map, as if it would provide the answer.

Harley cleared her throat. "When Prince Kerdan asked for soldiers, King Coden said he refused to align with Russek because he didn't want to go against Emperion."

"For good reason," one of the generals said. "Emperion is the largest and strongest kingdom on the mainland. To go against them is suicide."

Another thing Ackley had learned through the years was that power changed people and made them do stupid things. This traitor obviously sought power. What was the price he'd paid for it?

"These are all excellent points that need to be considered," Owen said. "Since there are so many of us, traveling to the castle will take a couple of weeks. We can work out these details along the way. For now, I want everyone to prepare to leave tomorrow at first light. My generals are dismissed; everyone else, please stay."

Studying the map, Ackley wondered which route they'd take and why. "You're going to keep the army together and not split us up?"

"Correct." After the generals exited the tent, Owen peered at Harley. "I can escort you to your parents' home on our way."

"If it's even still there."

"Let's hope so. Penlar is in a pretty remote location. Think about it. Once you've decided, let me know."

"I want to stay with you. I want retribution." Her eyes glistened with unshed tears.

Owen's hands balled into fists. "I promise we will avenge their deaths. My parents, brothers, sister, and your brother."

"I want all those responsible to pay," Harley whispered. "King Drenton, Prince Soma, the Melenia soldier who betrayed us. I want them all to suffer." She glanced at Ackley as if he alone could accomplish this.

"They will," Owen answered. "I won't rest until they're dead—every single one of them."

"Good." Harley nodded.

Ackley had thought there would be an all-out war when they arrived in Melenia. Instead, this was sounding more and more like a huge mess that wouldn't be sorted out easily. It wasn't that he minded being there and helping Owen. It was that he feared for what his sister was getting into. If Melenia wasn't strong and capable, Idina would be a sitting duck on the throne. And that was something he wouldn't stand for.

It was time for him to get to work. He needed to send out

his men to glean information. And right now, information was key.

⁂

Ackley stepped out of the small lagoon and dried off. He hadn't bathed in days and the clean water felt refreshing, though it was a bit warm for his taste. After dressing, he stretched out on the ground, staring up into the sky. The sun had set and pale pink clouds drifted over the ocean.

"I thought I'd find you here," Idina said by way of greeting.

He peered over his shoulder at her approaching form. "You're alone?" Gytha or someone else should be guarding her.

"Don't give me that look." She sat beside him. "I needed a moment to myself. And, to be honest, I wanted a couple of minutes alone with my brother. Ever since we left Marsden, I've had people hovering around me. It's exhausting."

He chuckled, knowing exactly what she meant. "Better get used to it." As queen of Melenia, she would rarely have time to herself. At least out here in the cove, it was secluded and safe. Gytha was probably waiting for Idina back in the tunnel that led to the valley where everyone was staying.

Idina adjusted her dress around her legs.

"I'm sure someone has a pair of pants you can borrow." It would be much easier for her to travel in even though he knew she'd never agree.

She scoffed at him. "I am perfectly capable of riding a horse or walking in a dress, thank you very much. While I understand that we are in a state of unrest, with the possibility of fighting breaking out at any minute, there is no need to sacrifice my clothing. I can still look good while leading my soon-to-be people."

He smiled. Idina always had a thing for pretty dresses. He especially liked the fact that she looked and acted like a proper lady, but was cunning and ruthless underneath. An upbringing he and his brother, Gordon, had seen to. Ironic, considering women in northern Marsden were considered less than men. It was something their father had believed and lived by. It was something Ackley never thought, regardless of what was shoved down his throat. To survive, his sister had learned to show one side to the world while keeping the other side hidden from those who would not understand. He wondered if other women were the same. Reid certainly was. Which led him to wonder about Harley. Was there more to her than what she showed him?

"What's the matter?" Idina asked. "You have that look on your face again."

"What look?" He didn't realize he had a look.

"The one you get when you're trying to work through something. It's this funny little mark on your forehead." She reached over and traced a line on his forehead as if to prove the point.

He batted her hand away, then laced his fingers together behind his head, observing the darkening sky. "It's nothing important." He shouldn't even be thinking about Harley. Instead, he needed to focus on making sure Owen didn't find out about the man he'd sent to Russek to make contact with Kerdan. Technically, as a prince, he had the right to set up a meeting with Kerdan. However, since he wanted to discuss the takeover, specifically Harley's involvement in it, he thought it best not to mention it to Owen. Not only that, but Owen probably wouldn't appreciate Ackley doing something behind his back.

"How did your assignment go?"

"It was uneventful." Since his sister was going to marry Owen, and he was going to leave her here, he needed to make sure this continent was stable. If Melenia was invaded again, his sister would be the one slaughtered. And that was something he couldn't live with. So really, he had a duty to meet with Kerdan, learn as much as he could about the mainland, and embed his own spies throughout Melenia. Anything less than that would be negligence.

"Harley seems nice." Idina picked a blade of grass, twirling it between her fingers. "What do you think of her?"

"I didn't really form an opinion. She didn't talk much." His sister rarely asked questions just to ask them, so he began wondering what she was getting at.

"No, I would imagine not. She just lost her brother, husband, aunt, uncle, and three cousins. I can't even begin to fathom what she's been through."

"She seems young to be married." Being the king's niece would make her valuable, though. Which brought Ackley back to thinking about Harley being married to Commander Beck's son.

"She's eighteen." Idina shrugged since that was a reasonable age to marry. Especially considering she was only seventeen.

Still, Harley felt younger than Idina. Gazing up at the sky, Ackley estimated it would take the man he'd sent to Russek about two weeks to establish contact with Kerdan and report back. That gave him two weeks to figure out how to get Owen to send him on another mission.

Idina twisted the blade of grass. "So...Harley..."

"Why do you keep bringing her up?" He eyed her sidelong.

"She's Owen's cousin."

"And?"

"I'd like to have someone I can rely on."

"You have Gytha."

"I meant someone here in Melenia. The problem is, I can't decide what sort of person Harley is. Which is unusual. Normally, I can read someone. But she's been through so much she's closed off right now." Idina tossed the blade of grass on the ground, then stretched her arms out behind her, leaning slightly backward. "I figured you'd have a read on her. You spent a couple of days with her, and you're good at this sort of thing."

"She'd make a fine companion at court, but I don't know about having her in your inner circle."

"Why is that?"

"I don't know how politically savvy she is," he mused, trying to work through what was bothering him. Since Commander Beck was her father-in-law, and he'd turned out to be a traitor, Ackley had to examine the possibility that Harley's husband had been involved in the commander's activities. Harley very well could have overheard important conversations between father and son. Or, worse, she could have been an unwilling participant. Which led him to speculate if she could be trusted.

An involuntary sigh slipped out. He hadn't intended on bothering with Owen's cousin. However, if his sister needed someone she could trust, someone from Melenia who could advise her accordingly, it was his duty to assess Harley. He'd have to decide if she could be trusted. Because if she couldn't, he'd have to get rid of her before she harmed Idina.

The following morning, the entire army set out, leaving the valley. They traveled all day, not covering much ground since they moved at an ant's pace, driving Ackley mad. He wished they had horses.

The Melenia and Marsden soldiers remained mixed together. However, Ackley pulled a dozen Marsdens to stay at Idina's side, putting Gytha in charge of them. With his sister well protected, he was able to walk with different soldiers, listening in on conversations, trying to learn as much as he could about Melenia and its people. He checked in with Idina every so often. Harley didn't leave Owen's side, seemingly uncomfortable traveling with so many men.

When they stopped around midday to eat, Ackley found his sister sitting alongside Harley and Gytha.

"Should I feel honored that you're here with me instead of rubbing elbows with your soldiers?" Idina glared at Ackley.

He hadn't thought his sister would be upset he didn't walk with her. "I assumed you and Lady Harley could use the time to get to know one another." Lowering his voice, he asked, "Was Lady Harley so droll you almost fell asleep?" He peered at Harley to see if she was listening in on the conversation.

Harley scowled at Ackley, confirming she'd heard him. He chuckled.

Gytha shook her head.

Owen joined them. "What did you do, Ackley?" he asked as he sat across from Idina. "Why are all the ladies looking at you like that?" He took a bite of his food. "It seems like they all want to kill you."

"My brother, as always, is just being his charming self."

Harley finished eating, setting her bowl aside.

Ackley withdrew a game from his bag, placing it before him

and setting up the pieces. "Lady Harley, join me in a game of War."

She peered at the board and pieces. "I don't know how to play."

"It's easy." It would prove to be an excellent way to assess her, since he suspected her to be more shrewd and intelligent than she let on. "I'll teach you."

Harley glanced at Owen who was engaged in conversation with Idina. "All right."

Ackley quickly explained the game. Each person started with nine pieces on opposite ends of the board. The board was divided into squares, for a total of eighty-one. The goal was to get your pieces to the opposite end of the board. If you landed on an opponent's piece, you claimed that piece and it went out of play. The person who had all of their remaining pieces to the other end first, won.

Harley's eyes narrowed as she studied the board. After a minute she said, "Who goes first?"

"You."

She nodded and made her first move.

Ackley noticed she started with no clear plan in place. She'd move random pieces, watching to see how he responded. After five minutes, he realized she'd shifted strategies and was now mirroring his moves. There were several ways to win. But he didn't care to win. He wanted to assess her. He switched tactics and started moving his pieces to the middle of the board. Fifteen minutes in, Harley sat there staring at the game.

"Are you going to move?" Ackley asked. "It's your turn."

She absently nodded. A minute later, she started making moves on her own, no longer mirroring him. She now shifted most of her pieces together toward the middle. Twenty minutes in, she started sacrificing her pieces. Thirty minutes in, she had two pieces left. One piece slid into the square on his side.

Ackley had about half his pieces on her side. Harley hadn't taken any of his pieces, but he'd taken seven of hers. She pushed the one piece toward him, wanting to sacrifice it. If he took it, she'd win, so he refused to touch it. She chewed on her bottom lip, narrowing her eyes. He kept moving his pieces toward her side. If she didn't start taking his pieces, he'd win. Harley moved that one piece back to her own side, where it had started, instead of moving it toward his side. If she moved it to his side, once her last piece was in, she'd win. So why was she moving it back to where it had started?

Ackley let it play out. Once it reached the square at her side, she looked at him. He realized the only way for him to win was to take that piece so his own piece could go there. The second he did, the game would end in a tie because they would be simultaneous winners. He'd never seen anyone force his hand like that before.

"Why?" he asked. She could have just slid that piece to his side and won.

"Why not?" she countered.

"You could have won much sooner," he pointed out.

"I didn't think the point was simply to win or lose. Isn't this about strategy?"

"It is." He had to hide his smile.

"Sometimes, if you look at things differently or take another approach, there is a way for everyone to win. There doesn't have to be a loser." She stood. "Thank you for the game." She turned and walked away.

Ackley watched her go. She'd confirmed his suspicions. It would be a waste to have Idina use Harley as a confidant. There was a better, more appropriate, position for someone like her.

That night, once camp had been erected, Ackley joined Owen in his tent.

"I know," Owen said by way of greeting. "You don't need to complain to me." Owen was stretched out on a bedroll in the corner of his tent, maps strewn about next to him. A single candle lit the space.

"Maybe there's something we can do to quicken the pace." Ackley sat on the ground, contemplating their options.

"Unfortunately, there isn't. But there is something you can do."

He had Ackley's attention. "Do tell."

Owen sat up on his bedroll and reached into his bag. Pulling out a flask, he uncorked it and took a swig. He held it out to Ackley.

Ackley shook his head. He never drank.

After putting the cork back in, Owen tapped his finger against the flask. "You, of all people, must suspect what's at play here."

One of the problems with coming to another kingdom like this was that Ackley didn't know the politics or the players and felt half blind. Instead of saying any of that, he settled with, "Enlighten me."

"You know the saying keep your friends close and your enemies closer?"

Ackley had never been one for friends.

"You're one of the Knights of the Realm," Owen said, a slight tilt to his words most likely caused by the alcohol. "You have to know what I'm up against."

Ackley still wasn't following.

"My cousin," Owen prompted.

Ah, Harley. The sole survivor. Even though Ackley had questioned her about the takeover, he still wondered how she'd managed to survive when her brother, husband, and family hadn't. "You don't trust her?"

"I trust her. It's everyone else I don't trust."

"Are you referring to the minor detail about her being married to Commander Beck's son?"

A smile slid across Owen's face. "That would be the one." He pointed the flask at Ackley. "I knew you'd get it."

"We know Commander Beck was a traitor, but what about his son?" He'd tried coaxing information about the man out of Harley. However, she hadn't wanted to talk about him at all. There was definitely something amiss there.

"I don't know. Lyle didn't live at the castle, and I barely knew him." Owen put the flask away. "But that wasn't who I was referring to."

"Who else don't you trust?"

He rubbed his tired face. "I don't know if Harley's parents...arranged anything with Commander Beck."

"Harley's mother is the queen's sister?"

Owen nodded.

Then getting rid of the royal family did nothing for Harley since she was not in line for the throne. That simple fact cast doubt on Harley's parents being involved. On the other hand, Commander Beck was a power-hungry man who thrived on violence. Even though he hadn't been present during the takeover, it didn't mean he wasn't involved in it.

"I need to discover my aunt and uncle's loyalties. If I send one of my men, they'll learn nothing. I need to send Harley."

"You need to send Harley to test her parents?"

"Exactly. But Harley can't know what you're doing."

"I'm doing?" If he wanted Ackley to accompany Harley to

Penlar, this would work out exceptionally well. It felt as if he were being handed a gift.

"Yes. You will go with her to assess them."

"I'm not sure Harley will like that idea." She seemed intent on staying with Owen and not stepping foot in Penlar. "I can go without her." He could speak to her parents and glean information; he didn't need Harley for that.

"Just tell Harley you're checking to see if her parents are alive."

"She'll want to know why me and not someone from Melenia."

"Good point." He tapped his hand on his thigh. "I'll tell her I only trust you to protect her. It's true you know."

"And if her parents are dead?"

"If there's anything left of their house, search it. But if they're alive, I need to know if they made any sort of deal with Commander Beck."

While Ackley certainly understood why Beck would have wanted his son married to the only niece of the king, he didn't know why Harley's parents would agree to it. What did they gain from marrying their daughter off to the commander's son? He stood to go. "What about on your father's side of the family? Does the king have any brothers who might want the throne?"

"No. He was an only child."

"And you're certain you trust Harley?"

"Yes, why do you ask?"

Because she was the sole survivor and far more savvy than she let on. "Have you considered that her loyalties may have changed once she married?"

"They haven't."

"How can you be certain?"

"You trust your sister, don't you?"

Ackley nodded.

"I trust my cousin like you trust your sister."

For Ackley, it wasn't that simple. He didn't trust easily—even when it came to family. A result of being betrayed by Eldon, his own brother. However, he had come to respect Owen, so he didn't argue any further. He would go with Harley, not because Owen wanted him to analyze her parents, but because he had plans of his own.

CHAPTER TEN

HARLEY

Tossing and turning, Harley couldn't fall asleep. Every time she closed her eyes, she saw Lyle leering at her, teasing her, telling her how worthless she was. Then his face was replaced with the Russek soldier who'd tried to rape her. Frustrated, she sat up. Idina and Gytha were in the tent with her, both of them sleeping. Harley stood and wrapped one of her blankets around her body. Knowing there would be a soldier standing guard outside the tent, she lifted the edge near her bedroll, crawling underneath it.

She stood between her and Owen's tent, listening. Not hearing any voices, she moved to the back and headed away from the tents. She walked with purpose, hoping no one stopped her. If anyone did, she would say she had to relieve herself. At the edge of camp, she went straight, not wanting to get lost. When she was far enough away, she sat in the thick grass, it coming up to her chest.

So much had happened in such a short amount of time that she was having trouble processing it all. She didn't know how she felt. Her heart hurt, that much she knew. Rage also filled her at the injustice of it all. Helplessness also kept wedging its way in. Her life had been flipped upside down, and she didn't know who she was any longer. When Owen had offered to take her to her parents, she'd balked at the idea. To have their deaths confirmed would sap the last of her strength. To entertain the idea that they were alive required too much hope. Now she understood why Ledger hadn't wanted to go and see if his mother and sister were alive. Sometimes not knowing was better than dealing with reality. There was another emotion that kept working its way in—guilt. Guilt that she lived. Guilt that she was happy her husband had died.

"What are you doing out here all alone?" Ackley asked, startling her. He sat next to her, waiting for an answer.

She was tired of always doing what others wanted and expected of her. A tear slid down her cheek, so she wiped it away. Lyle always asked her questions like that. When he found her reading a book one day, he'd asked her why she bothered reading. When she said she enjoyed it, he ripped it from her hands and tossed it in the hearth, claiming a woman had no business reading. After that, she hid her books and only let him see her do useful activities such as knitting. Strange she thought of that now.

"I saw you leave your tent, so I followed you."

Under the dark night sky, she couldn't make out his features. It reminded her of the first time she'd met him when he'd purposely remained in the shadows. "I couldn't sleep, Your Highness." Maybe if she gave him an answer, he'd leave her alone.

"It's just Ackley."

She still couldn't believe she'd slapped him the night they met. Even though he'd completely deserved it, he was a prince and could have her thrown in the dungeon for doing such a thing. She found it intriguing that he hadn't revealed his title to her that night, nor did he want her using it now. "Tell me, Ackley, how are you both a prince and an assassin?"

"Right now, I'm only an assassin. And I want you to tell me what you're doing out here."

Goosebumps covered her skin. She thought he came after her because she was a woman all alone. Now she was starting to suspect it was for another reason—he didn't trust her any more than she trusted him. He probably didn't trust anyone. Although, he appeared close with his sister and Owen clearly liked him. Other than Gytha, the soldiers seemed half in awe and half scared of him. Exhaustion overcame her, and she answered truthfully. "When I close my eyes, I see monsters." She couldn't believe she just admitted that to Ackley.

They sat in silence for several minutes, neither speaking.

Then Ackley mumbled, "I have the same problem."

"Since you're an assassin, I would imagine so."

"I spoke with Milard and Rayne. They said they escaped with you. That Ledger shot a man and saved your life."

She shivered, wishing Ackley would leave her alone.

"I'm surprised more of you didn't escape," he continued.

He didn't understand what it was like. The chaos of that day. The blood that had coated her feet.

"I'm surprised that Ledger, Milard, and Rayne were running away instead of standing with their units."

"They weren't on duty." They'd barely escaped. The Russeks had been slaughtering the Melenia soldiers as if they were nothing.

"Where I come from, a soldier takes an oath to protect his king and kingdom."

"They protected me."

"You're nothing to the crown."

While his words stung, they were true. "Why are you telling me this?" She wished he'd get to the point.

"I'm just trying to understand what happened that day."

"There's no understanding it. It was senseless. Power hungry men destroyed hundreds, if not thousands, of lives." She couldn't stop thinking about Lyle. He'd married her so he could become the captain of Penlar. She was a means to an end. Because he wanted power. Was that all men cared for? Power over others?

"There are ways to stop people like that."

He'd said it so softly, Harley almost missed it. "What do you mean?"

He shrugged. "Like you so eloquently expressed in our game of War, war should be avoided at all costs. There are always ways around a battle."

She eyed him sidelong. He'd purposefully stated earlier that he was an assassin right now, not a prince. If she only considered what he said as if he were an assassin and nothing more, it changed things. "Where you come from, are there knights who are women?" She found the idea of a woman assassin intriguing. Her heart pounded, waiting for his answer.

"Yes."

Again, when he spoke, his voice was soft and inviting. As if he wanted to lure her in and gain her trust. She needed to be careful with him—he was not to be trusted.

"It's late," he said. "You should get to bed. Owen wants to leave at first light."

She understood a dismissal when she heard one. Nodding, she stood and traipsed back to her tent, ideas and possibilities swirling inside her head.

Days of endless walking passed. Harley only caught glimpses of Ackley, never having the chance to talk with him. It always seemed he was busy speaking with soldiers, ordering men about, and just disappearing for hours. A little over a week into their journey, word came through the ranks that they were about to pass a village. Harley tensed, fearing this one would be burned like the others.

The quiet murmuring that had been going on amongst the soldiers ceased, and a hush descended. A rancid smell permeated the air along with a buzzing sound. The first thing Harley saw were spikes sticking up out of the ground. Skewered on each one was a single decaying head. She tried not to notice the smaller heads belonging to children.

Several soldiers broke rank and vomited.

Most of the buildings had been burned, but not all of them.

"I'm going to send soldiers to investigate," Owen said. "Remain with Gytha." He looked at Harley and Idina. Both nodded. He jogged up ahead and started barking out orders.

"If there were any survivors, I think we would have seen them," Idina whispered.

"I agree." Regardless, she was glad Owen was checking, just to be sure.

They continued on, not stopping until sunset. Harley and Idina helped Gytha erect their tent. Once they finished, the three of them went to get supper.

Harley grabbed a bowl of stew and followed Gytha to a fallen log. She sat down, Gytha and Idina on either side of her.

"How close are we to the castle?" Gytha asked.

"We're a little more than half way." They'd be passing by Penlar soon. Harley shoved that thought from her head, not wanting to think about the fate of her parents.

"I don't know about you," Idina muttered, "but I'm not hungry." She pushed the food around in her bowl.

"We'll have our revenge," Harley commented. "As soon as Owen reclaims the throne, we'll go after Russek and make them pay for what they've done."

Idina set her bowl down. "That's what I'm worried about. Do you think it's wise for us to attack Russek? Do we even have enough soldiers for such an assault?" She folded her hands together, placing her elbows on her knees. "I see the devastation here. These Russek barbarians kill without mercy, slaughtering innocent women and children. If they fight without rules, if they are this vicious, how can Owen stand against them?" Her lip quivered.

"I think the real question is, how can he not? If he does nothing, he will be condoning this behavior. He has to stand up for what's right—even if that means going to war." Her brother's death would not be in vain. Men who sought power, and greedy people like Lyle, who took what they wanted without asking, couldn't win. Something she'd heard Ackley say wedged its way in. He'd said war should be avoided and that there were ways to seek revenge without going to war. She rubbed her temples, confusion setting in.

Idina placed her hand on Harley's forearm. "I'm afraid that because you and Owen lost everything, your judgement may be clouded by anger. Russek left Melenia. Isn't that enough?"

"How can you even ask that?" Tears welled in her eyes.

"Let me counter your question with one of my own. How can you risk waking a sleeping bear?"

"All bears eventually wake," Ackley said from behind them, startling Harley. She hadn't heard anyone approach. "Russek came once. If Owen doesn't strike back, they'll come again."

Idina swung around to face her brother. "How can you say that?"

"As the saying goes, if the hunt is good, the hunter will return."

Harley couldn't believe Ackley was siding with her on this.

"There can be diplomatic relations between kingdoms," Idina pointed out.

"Perhaps." Ackley shrugged. "Perhaps not. We don't have enough information to determine that."

Shaking her head, Idina said, "I'm not in the mood to argue with you tonight. All I wanted to point out is that maybe our focus shouldn't be on revenge. That's all."

"I know war and the taking of another's life should never be done without considering all options," Ackley replied.

Idina snorted. "Funny coming from you."

"Because it's late, I'm going to ignore that comment. I need a moment of Lady Harley's time." He finally looked her way.

Harley nodded and stood, following him away from everyone and deeper into the woods. She was about to insist they not go any farther when he stopped and faced her.

"Owen asked me for a favor." Ackley shoved his hands in his pockets, looking at the tree beside him and not at Harley.

She waited for him to explain.

"Since some of the larger towns have been spared, he wants to know if his aunt and uncle are alive."

Harley's parents. She'd been trying hard not to consider the possibility of them being alive. To think it only to discover them dead would be unbearable.

"I'm going to find out for him."

Her cousin could send anyone to find out if Penlar had been destroyed. So why did he choose to send Ackley?

"Since I don't know my way around this kingdom, Owen asked that you accompany me."

Liar. "You found me in Kreng just fine."

A ghost of a smile slid across his face and then disappeared.

"Why is my cousin really sending you?" she asked. "And why does he want me to go?" There had to be another reason. Maybe there was someone in Penlar Owen wanted assassinated, assuming Penlar was still standing. However, that didn't account for her part in this.

"If your parents are dead, Owen wants to make sure they're buried properly. He figured you wouldn't want an audience as you said your goodbyes, and he trusts me to keep you safe."

Safe with an assassin? She almost laughed out loud. Folding her arms across her chest, she started pacing, trying to decide if she was strong enough to return to Penlar. "Would we only be going to my parents' manor?" She didn't look at Ackley as she asked the question.

"Where else would we go?" His voice turned lower, softer, making her shiver. "To the house you shared with Lyle?"

Her body tensed just hearing Lyle's name. She glanced at Ackley, carefully watching her. He took a step closer, his penetrating eyes seeing more than she wanted him to. She froze, caught in his gaze. "Would we go there?" she whispered, not knowing if she could step foot in that house again. It had never been her home even though she'd lived there for a few months.

"It'll just be the two of us."

The air turned hot. The two of them. Alone. She rubbed her forehead. How would she travel with a prince and assassin she did not like or care for? And why did her stomach flip when he came near her? Why did her heart speed up? Her palms become sweaty? It had to be because he was an assassin; no other reason made sense.

Whenever Lyle had entered the room, dread and hatred coursed through her. She would have to calm her shaking body, pretending it was fright or desire and not anger.

"Well?" Ackley asked, raising a single eyebrow.

"If Owen wishes me to go, then I'll go."

"But do you wish to go?"

"No, I do not. But what choice do I have?"

"You always have a choice."

She knew that. But all choices came with consequences. Early on in her marriage, she'd learned to pick her battles. Considering the conversation she'd just had with Idina about Russek, she decided to go along with Owen in this matter. If he wanted her to go to Penlar, she would. But when it came to seeking revenge against those responsible for killing her brother, she would stop at nothing to see that through. Maybe traveling with an assassin, alone, would be useful. He'd sided with her, not Idina, regarding Russek. If Owen believed as Idina did, Harley would have to take matters in her own hands. A lethal assassin could come in handy. She just wished he wasn't so handsome; it would make being around him easier.

Peering up into his eyes, she said, "I'll accompany you to my parents' manor. But I will not step foot in Lyle's house. Are we clear?"

"You should be this decisive all the time. It suits you." With that, he turned and strode away, melting into the shadows of the forest.

Harley trekked along, bored from another day of walking. She hadn't realized how much longer it would take to reach the castle traveling with so many soldiers.

Owen and Idina were up ahead of Harley, Owen explaining how the kingdom was divided into provinces and which family controlled each one. Not in the mood for a history lesson, Harley had fallen back. Glancing around, she didn't see Ackley or Gytha nearby.

"Harley," Ledger said as he came to walk beside her. "How are you doing?"

"I'm fine." It was good to have a kind, friendly face around.

"I want to offer my services to you."

She had no idea what he was referring to.

"We'll be passing Penlar soon."

She was well aware of it and had been reliving her conversation with Ackley over and over again. There was more to it than Ackley was letting on, she was sure of it.

"I've heard from the scouts that not all cities are burned. If you want, I can escort you to Penlar to see? Perhaps your parents are alive?"

"Thank you for thinking of me. However, you don't need to escort me there."

"Don't you want to know?"

"I do."

"Then I'll take you."

She sighed. "Prince Ackley is taking me."

They walked in silence for a few minutes. Then Ledger asked, "Who's all going?"

"Just the prince and me."

"Do you think that wise?"

No, she did not. However, it wasn't up to her. Owen wished for her to go with Ackley, so she would. "It's already been decided."

"If something changes, let me know. My offer still stands."

"Thank you, Ledger. I appreciate it."

He gave a curt nod before falling back to walk with the unit he'd been assigned to.

They stopped at midday to rest and eat. Clouds rolled in, the temperature dropping. Harley hoped it didn't rain. After grabbing her food, she found a quiet spot away from most of the soldiers to eat her meal in peace. When she'd just about finished, she noticed Ackley exit from a cluster of trees not far away. She hadn't seen him all morning and wondered where he'd been and what he'd been up to.

Standing, she decided to confront him. If she was going to be traveling with him, she needed to be able to talk to him freely. As he headed to where the food was being distributed, she cut him off.

"Where were you?" she asked.

His eyes scanned her body for a long minute before responding. "I needed to speak to some of my soldiers."

She hadn't seen anyone else exit the forest with him. "Are you really here to help Owen?" Perhaps he had other plans and was only using Owen.

"My number one reason for being here is to ensure my sister's safety. Right now, that means making sure the kingdom is stabilized."

"Then why bother taking me to Penlar? I assume you'd want to remain at Idina's side."

He considered her a moment, then replied, "I trust Owen to protect Idina."

Given his desire to ensure his sister's safety, she couldn't understand why he'd leave her side to go with Harley to Penlar. The only information he would learn was whether her parents were alive or not. How would that knowledge benefit him? Her parents were in charge of the province of Penlar. They were the only nobles who hadn't been at her cousin's birthday celebration. In one fell swoop, Russek had managed to wipe out all of the people who could govern and lead the kingdom. It was a genius move by Russek.

Her heartbeat sped up as she started to look at the situation objectively. "Owen doesn't think my parents had something to do with the takeover, does he?" Because they didn't. She was certain of it.

"It is miraculous that you managed to survive. If Penlar is untouched and your parents are alive, it won't look good."

A chill slid over her skin as his words sunk in. No, it most certainly wouldn't look good if her parents were the only ones that managed to survive. And Owen was the one who asked Ackley to go and see for him. Bile rose in her throat. "If my parents are alive, do you have orders to kill me?"

A slow, devious smile crept across his face. "While I might have entertained such thoughts, Owen hasn't. He assured me *you* are loyal." His deep voice slid across the space between them, making her feel uneasy.

"And my parents?" she whispered, fear coating every word.

"I am here to do what needs to be done to ensure Melenia's survival."

Unable to look away from Ackley's intense gaze, she knew,

right then and there, that if he thought she posed a threat to his sister, if he suspected she were involved in this takeover in any way, he would have no qualms about running a sword through her.

Judging by the cold gleam in his eyes, he knew she was aware of it.

Not able to form a coherent sentence, she nodded and hurried away.

The following morning, as Harley tied her boots, she heard a commotion coming from just outside her tent. She poked her head out to make sure everything was all right. When she did so, she saw a person dressed in civilian clothing requesting to speak with King Owen immediately. Only, no one seemed to know where Owen was.

Harley scrambled out of the tent just as Gytha approached with a bowl of oatmeal.

"What do you mean no one knows where King Owen is?" Gytha demanded.

The handful of men standing around all came to attention, facing her. "He left early this morning," one of the men answered.

Gytha shoved the bowl at Harley before crossing her arms and glaring at the men, each now quivering in his boots. "When did he leave?"

"Just before sunrise," one of them answered.

"How do you know?" Gytha asked, her voice hard as steel.

"I, uh, was on guard at the time. He told me to remain here."

Gytha peered inside Owen's tent. "Where's Prince Ackley?"

The soldiers glanced between themselves, shrugging.

Gytha sighed, shaking her head. "I suggest you find out where King Owen and Prince Ackley are. When you do, let them know a spy has returned with information."

Harley observed the man. She'd thought he was a regular person, not a soldier in the army. Looking closer, she saw about a week's worth of stubble on his face, dirt smeared on his forehead, and the thick smell of horse radiated from him. She wondered where he'd been and what he'd learned.

"How do you know King Owen and Prince Ackley are together?" one of the soldiers asked.

Gytha's eyes narrowed at the question, and one of the soldiers took a step back before mumbling, "We'll go and look for them." They hurried away.

Harley couldn't believe the men had listened to Gytha so readily.

Gytha placed her hand on the spy's shoulder, leading him to Owen's tent.

Harley turned to go back to her own tent when Gytha barked, "With me, Lady Harley."

She jumped and did as Gytha said.

Inside Owen's tent, the warrior woman pointed to the corner where a small stool and table were. "Eat, Lady Harley."

Sitting on a stool, she quietly ate her oatmeal. Owen's bedroll, bag, and maps were neatly stacked near the entrance of the tent, indicating he hadn't left on a whim.

Gytha folded her arms and stood in the corner opposite Harley, keeping a watchful eye on the spy the entire time.

Fifteen minutes later, Ackley and Owen entered the tent, not saying a word. Harley wanted to ask where they'd been, but she knew not to in front of the spy.

"Glad to see you're back in one piece," Owen said by way of

greeting. "What news do you have?" Taking a seat next to the spy, he handed him a flask of water.

Shocked she hadn't been asked to leave, Harley set her bowl aside. Her focus drifted over to Ackley, who faded into the shadows of the tent. If she hadn't seen him enter, she wouldn't know he was there.

"All villages along the border are burned. No survivors."

"What else?" Owen asked.

"I rode my horse to Landania and met with my contacts there. Word is that after Russek invaded Melenia, they began mounting an attack against Emperion. As a result, Kricok, Fia, and Landania all joined with Emperion."

"Willingly?" Owen asked.

"Yes. They signed a treaty and are part of Emperion now."

Owen whistled. Emperion was already the largest kingdom on the mainland. Now with three additional kingdoms under their command, they were without a doubt the most powerful as well. No one would be able to stand against them.

"Have there been any battles between Russek and Emperion?" Owen asked.

"Not yet. Russek kidnapped Princess Allyssa of Emperion. There are rumors she's been killed. Information is slow to come, but people are saying King Drenton of Russek is dead." He took a long drink from the flask, gulping the water down.

"I assume Emperion killed the Russek king for kidnapping their princess?"

He shook his head. "My sources say it was an inside job. Someone in Russek killed King Drenton. There are rumors it was Prince Kerdan. Others say Queen Jana. When the king died, Kerdan ordered all Russek soldiers out of Melenia and back to Russek. Since then, Kerdan and Jana have been battling for the throne."

"Anything else?"

"Emperion has soldiers stationed all along their border. They haven't attacked yet. Probably because Russek is facing a civil war."

Owen rubbed his forehead. After thanking the spy, he sent him to get something to eat.

Once the man left, Ackley stepped out of the shadows. "The question becomes, what happened to Prince Soma?" He withdrew his dagger, tossing and catching it by the handle. "You said he is Kerdan's stepbrother?" He looked to Harley for confirmation.

Suddenly feeling self-conscious, her palms became sweaty. "Yes. Kerdan is Drenton's son; Soma is Jana's son."

"So Russek intended to attack Emperion. They invaded Melenia for troops. Before they could attack, King Drenton was murdered." He tossed the dagger and caught it. "Jana and Kerdan are vying for the crown, both claiming the other killed the king." Toss, catch. "We happen to know that Soma tried killing Kerdan as well." He sheathed his dagger. "And I thought my family was bad. At least we don't have to deal with Russek right now." He pointed at Owen. "Reclaim your throne, then we'll worry about Russek. With a civil war brewing, you have time."

"What about revenge?" Harley asked. Owen had promised her.

"When the time is right, we'll strike." Owen stood.

"It's the perfect time to strike," Gytha said. "Russek is weak and won't expect us to attack right now."

"We can't attack until we know who's our enemy and who's our ally." Ackley waved for Gytha to join him as he headed toward the exit of the tent. "Russek is a neighboring kingdom. We don't want war to always be looming over our heads."

"Or we can let Emperion slaughter them." Gytha gripped the hilt of her sword as she followed Ackley.

"That's a possibility," Owen agreed.

Ackley paused at the tent flap. "There are other ways to handle this besides declaring war."

Harley wondered if he referred to assassinating their enemy. It was an intriguing idea that he'd hinted at before. Instead of war, a stealthy invasion to end those responsible for killing her family. That way hundreds of Melenia soldiers wouldn't have to die. Before lifting the tent flap, Ackley looked right at her and winked, as if he knew her thoughts.

Once Ackley and Gytha were gone, Harley shook her head, unable to believe she'd just agreed with Ackley—the assassin-prince.

Owen came over, sitting on a stool beside her. "Today we're going to pass by the road leading to Penlar. I've asked Ackley to escort you there to see if your parents are alive. I will continue on with the army. When you're done in Penlar, you can rejoin us."

Standing, she ran her hands down the front of her dress. "Don't you think someone from Melenia should take me?" she asked, giving him the opportunity to voice any of his concerns about her parents.

"I trust Ackley."

But not her or her parents. Forcing a smile on her lips, she said, "I'm surprised you're letting me travel alone with a man. Aren't you afraid people might get the wrong idea?"

"You're a widow. You have no virtue to protect."

While true, the simple statement felt like a slap in the face.

"I'm sorry," Owen stammered. "That came out wrong. What I meant to say is that Ackley is a prince, and he won't take advantage of you or the situation."

She almost laughed. Owen should be more concerned about her and Ackley trying to kill one another rather than anything romantic happening between them. They were about as different as night and day.

"If I don't get a chance to see you again before you depart, safe travels." He wrapped her in a hug. "Ackley is a good man, and he will protect you."

Harley wished she believed that.

CHAPTER ELEVEN

ACKLEY

*A*ckley and Harley had been traveling on the same dirt road all afternoon since breaking away from the army. The scenery gradually changed from dense forestry to low rolling hills, making Ackley feel exposed. Once in a while he thought he saw something in the distance, only to realize it was a burned house or village. At one point, he thought he saw a person on horseback. When he pointed it out to Harley, the rider was gone.

Harley led the way so he didn't have to worry about her lagging behind or falling without him knowing. Not once did she complain or ask to rest. He thought Harley would have at least tried to make small talk as they traveled. She was a woman after all. He hadn't been around one so silent before. Not even Gytha was this quiet. And it wasn't like Harley had problems talking to men. He saw her speaking with Ledger on several occasions. It was just Ackley then. Regardless, he liked knowing who he was working with. Surprises were never a good thing. And he found Harley a hard woman to read.

He considered saying something. Maybe if he spoke first, she would warm up to him and be more comfortable. However, since they'd be traveling together for several days, he decided not to force conversation. It would come. Eventually. Besides, he was never one to fill the silence just because. It would only come off as being inauthentic. And there was as much to be learned from the refusal to speak as there was from speaking.

That night, he found a cluster of boulders that provided some cover. They laid their bedrolls out, then ate a small meal. Since it was just the two of them, a fire was too dangerous to risk.

Harley snuggled under her blanket. Ackley wished he hadn't woken so early this morning to accompany Owen to that town. It would make staying up all night watching over Harley that much more difficult. But he hadn't wanted to miss the chance to meet with those civilians who used to work at the castle. He needed to hear their accounts of what happened during the takeover to see if it aligned with what Harley had said. While he hadn't found any inconsistencies, what these servants reported seeing was a hundred times worse than what Harley let on.

He glanced at Harley, finding her already asleep. Her mouth was slightly parted, her hair spread out around her head. She never wore it pulled back like Gytha. Since it was so thick and long, it seemed to always be a tangled mess. He suspected it wasn't normally that way. She was probably used to wearing fancy dresses and having her hair impeccably done. Traveling with an army didn't afford her those luxuries. But it did afford him the opportunity to watch her from afar.

Her behavior came across prim and proper, always the

perfect lady, even dressed as a commoner. However, there were moments when her eyes flashed with anger, hurt, and fire. It was in those moments that he believed he saw a glimpse into who she really was. The part of herself that didn't conform to society, so she kept it hidden from the world. What he wouldn't give to free that side of her.

The following day was much the same as the previous one. Harley didn't talk as she led the way to Penlar. When evening approached, they came to a fork in the road.

"It's getting late," Harley said, speaking for the first time. "Do you want to go straight to my parents' manor or find a place here to sleep for the night?"

They hadn't stopped for food the entire day. Ackley kept waiting for her to ask for a break, but she'd forged on without a word. "How far away is their home?" He scanned the horizon, not seeing any signs of a city nearby.

Peering over her shoulder at him, she raised her eyebrows. "It's not far from here. We'll be there before dark if that's what you're worried about." She smirked before taking the dirt road to the right. "What?" she asked. "No snarky remark about not being afraid of the dark? I just attacked your manhood. Aren't you going to defend it?"

He blinked, surprise rippling through him. She was toying with him. He didn't think it possible. For the first time since they'd met, Ackley felt as if Harley had the upper hand, and it left him unbalanced. He'd have to be careful with this woman. Especially since he noticed the way his breath quickened when she looked at him.

Harley stopped just ahead of him at the top of the rise. With her hands on her hips, she stood there waiting for him.

Ackley adjusted the bag on his back as he joined her, observing the view. Stretched out below, a sprawling city filled the landscape. It had to be several miles wide—by far the largest city he'd seen in Melenia. The buildings didn't appear destroyed nor did they have any evidence of being burned.

"Smoke is coming from the chimneys in several of the homes," Harley pointed out. "There must be people here."

Squinting, Ackley looked closer. People were out and about, walking along the streets. He eyed Harley, waiting for some sort of reaction from her.

Chewing on her bottom lip, she peered up at him. "Do you think Russek missed Penlar since it's so secluded?"

He shrugged. "It's possible." More likely, Harley's parents were involved in this mess somehow. So what did they have to gain from destroying the royal family? On the surface, nothing stood out, especially since Harley and her brother had been at the castle during the invasion. But one thing he'd learned was that anything was possible—especially when it came to people seeking and clinging to power. Even though Owen insisted Harley was loyal, Ackley had to at least consider the possibility that she was in league with her parents.

"All this time, I thought they were dead," she whispered. "I assumed I only had Owen." Tears filled her eyes. "They're alive." She smiled and headed along the pathway winding down the hill and into the city below. She had a bounce to her step Ackley hadn't seen before.

While Ackley knew there weren't any Russeks down there, he still felt exposed on this deserted road. Anyone in the city would see them coming. Maybe that was why the city had been designed this way. Regardless, he had that feeling he got when he was being watched. All senses on alert, he followed Harley, keenly aware of every sound he heard and movement he saw.

"My parents' estate is over there." She pointed up ahead of them and to the right. "All the farms are located on the northern side where the lake and forest are."

"And your house with Lyle?" He'd noticed she never used the word *home* when referring to it.

"It's on the south side, right where the city ends and the open land begins."

"On the opposite side of the city," he commented. "Did you want to get as far away from your parents as possible?" He said it like a joke but wondered if there were any truth to it.

"The captain in charge of Penlar is always stationed next to the garrison." Her words came out monotone, all emotion stripped from them.

Ackley wondered what sort of man had Harley's husband been. She was only eighteen, so he had to be at least ten years older than her to hold the position of a captain. Owen had mentioned he couldn't stand the guy, which meant Ackley probably wouldn't have liked him either. Harley said it was an arranged marriage and that she didn't care for the man. Ackley couldn't imagine being married to someone he didn't love and respect, let alone like.

They reached the first set of buildings. Most of the stores had dingy windows that were so dirty, he couldn't see through them. Many of the apartments didn't even have windows. People hurried from one place to another, dirt kicking up from the street. They kept their heads down, not acknowledging either Harley or Ackley as they passed.

"Is this city similar to other large cities in Melenia?" Ackley asked casually. What bothered him was how much this city looked like northern Marsden where poverty was rampant. It wasn't until he'd traveled to Axian, in southern Marsden, where he'd seen what wealth and prosperity really looked like.

"I wouldn't know," she answered, the words clipped and angry. "I've only ever been here and to the royal castle. Until the takeover."

A woman with a young child on her hip rushed by. When the woman glanced at Ackley, her eyes widened. She entered the store across the street, slamming the door behind her.

"I'm wondering if Russek passed through here," Ackley mused.

"Why do you say that?"

A man with a limp lumbered by, staying as far away from them as the street would allow. Up ahead, two kids in tattered clothes ran from one building to another. A man behind the nearby window pulled the curtain shut. "The people seem wary."

"They're always like this." Lowering her head, she hugged herself as if warding off the chill.

They turned and headed north, just about to exit the main portion of the city where most of the buildings were located.

"What sort of man was the late king?" Ackley hadn't considered him being mean or ruling with an iron fist since Owen didn't exhibit any of those traits.

Her brows pulled together. "He was my uncle. He loved his children and doted on them. I visited them often. He always made me feel welcome."

"How did he treat those outside his family?"

Her brows drew together. "I never saw him interacting with his subjects, if that's what you're asking. When he threw parties for the nobility, he always seemed to be the center of attention. They all acted as if they loved him."

He hadn't known Harley long, but he knew she chose her

words carefully. To say they *acted* as if they loved him spoke volumes. He could only deduce that King Coden was a fairly weak ruler. "And your parents? They're in charge of this province?"

"Yes." She hesitated as if she wanted to say more, but prevented herself from doing so.

"And?" he prompted.

"They're older and aren't as involved as they used to be. We've had some uprisings and things of that nature. But that's to be expected in a place as large as this. That's where Lyle came in. As captain of the soldiers stationed in Penlar, he made sure to keep the peace and arrest those who caused problems."

Now they were getting somewhere. "Who'll rule after your parents? Would it have been your brother?"

She shook her head. "He was a member of the king's personal guard. When he took up the position, he gave up his right to rule Penlar. The duty then fell to me."

"So both you and Lyle would have complete control over Penlar."

"I'd never thought about it before." Her hands started visibly shaking. "I don't know if I can do this."

"Do what?"

She clasped her hands together. "Tell my parents that their only son is dead. And it's my fault he died." A crow flew overhead, cawing.

Ackley's eyes narrowed. "Won't your parents be happy you're alive? After what's happened, they probably assume both you and your brother are dead."

"True." She adjusted her bag. "But my brother sacrificed himself by taking Owen's place so Russek would think they had the entire royal family. It afforded me the opportunity to escape. My parents won't understand that. They will only see it as my brother coddling me and insist it's my fault he died. In their minds, I should have sacrificed myself to save Hollis."

It was the first time she'd said her brother's name in his presence. The way it gently rolled off her tongue spoke volumes about the love she had for the brother she'd lost. "If your parents don't understand his sacrifice, that's their problem, not yours." Anger welled inside of him, and he had to tamp it down. He hated the way she always made him feel overprotective.

"This way." She turned down a road leading them away from the crowded, dense city buildings and to the large estates with acres of land. The sun had just set and darkness started to roll in, bringing with it a thick, low fog.

Ever since they'd reached the first set of buildings, Ackley had spotted five men tracking them. Now that they'd exited the city proper, those same men still followed about twenty yards behind. All five wore black pants and navy tunics, and each had a sword strapped to his waist. "What do the uniforms of this city's soldiers look like?"

"The tunics are dark blue and the pants are black. There's a small crest of the king's shield embroidered on the right shoulder. Why?" She started to turn around.

"Don't look back." He fake-sneezed, making sure Harley's focus remained in front of her. "There are five men behind us as you described. They probably want to make sure we're not up to any trouble." Not likely. Otherwise, they would have approached Ackley by now and confronted him.

"If soldiers are following us, they should recognize me."

Since Harley was dressed as a commoner, her hair in disarray, and her face free from dusting powder, Ackley doubted they would recognize her. Given her current state, they wouldn't believe a word she said. "How far until we reach your parents' estate?"

"It's the next one." She nodded at the private road thirty yards away.

Ackley had a knife in each boot, one small sword along his back, a dagger up each sleeve, and a sword hidden in his bedroll that was tucked inside the bag on his back. The soldiers maintained their distance, never getting any closer.

"Should I ask them what they want?" Harley inquired.

"No."

As they neared the turn-off to her parents' home, Ackley noted the large tree at the corner of the property—a perfect spot for someone to hide in. Someone with a bow. He would have to eliminate that person before taking out the soldiers behind him. Which meant he had a solid six seconds to strike the man in the tree, two seconds to throw his second dagger at one of the soldiers, then three seconds to withdraw his knives, throwing each of them. At that point, the last two men would be upon him. He could easily handle that many at once. The issue would be making sure Harley wasn't harmed or taken during the mild altercation.

Now for the real dilemma. Under normal circumstances, he'd kill these men without hesitation. However, this wasn't his kingdom, these men should be on their side, and Harley's low opinion of him being a brute assassin would be confirmed. Not that he cared what she thought of him, but he wasn't only a killer. And he only killed when necessary. That was what he needed to show her.

He would have to incapacitate the men instead of killing them then, which made his job infinitely more difficult. No matter. He thought through his plan one more time, imagining the hits, strikes, and moves he needed to make in order to injure without killing.

"When I tell you to," he whispered to Harley, "drop to the ground and remain there."

"Of course." She didn't even ask a single question or argue.

Sliding the daggers from his sleeves, he placed one in each palm, needing to throw them just the right way so the hilt would hit each man instead of the blade. "Now." Ackley threw his dagger at what he hoped was the archer's head. Then he whirled and flung his second dagger at the man on the far left. Withdrawing his two knives, he aimed for the foreheads of the two men in the middle, the hilts striking them. Three of his five pursuers were on the ground, moaning. He chanced a glance back. The archer had fallen from the tree and was holding his leg, his bow snapped in two.

The last two men rushed at him. He ditched his bag then ran at them, wanting to stop the men before they got too close to Harley. When almost upon them, he spun and kicked, hitting the man on the left. As he did so, he grabbed the other man, twisting his arm back, then flipping him on the ground. With all five lying on the road groaning, he went back for his bag, looking for his rope. He found it, then tied the men up.

"Harley."

Sitting, she observed the sight before her. "Are they dead?"

"No, not one."

He stalked over to the archer and grabbed the collar of the man's shirt, dragging him to the others. After tying him up, Ackley clutched a fistful of the archer's hair, forcing the man to look at him. "Why were you in the tree?"

The man spat at Ackley.

Using his arm, he wiped the spit from his chest, then pulled the short sword at his back, pressing the tip to the man's groin. Ackley narrowed his eyes and hardened his face.

The man flinched. "I was told to shoot anyone who approached." Sweat coated his forehead as he tried scooting backward.

Ackley pressed the sword harder, and the man froze. "Who gave you that order?"

"My superior."

Ackley wanted to smack the guy for his non-answer. "And who is your superior?"

"Lieutenant Cliffton."

"What about the five men who followed us?"

"They are supposed to follow anyone coming into the city."

Again, a reasonable response given the state of things. "Who gave them that order?"

"Lieutenant Cliffton. He's been in charge since Captain Lyle left."

"Why were you up in the tree on this property?"

"Someone of importance lives there. I was asked to protect the property. Look, I just follow my orders, I don't question them." His breathing came out short and fast.

"Do you know about the takeover?" Ackley inquired.

"Yes. But Russek never came here."

Again, a reasonable answer. "Do you know who the false king is?"

"False king?"

"Any idea who's sitting on the throne?" Ackley pressed the tip of his sword in harder, emphasizing his point.

"No," the man said, sweat coating his face.

"I'm escorting Lady Harley to her parents' estate. The very one you appear to be guarding."

The man's eyes bulged, and his face blanched.

"I would like to take her inside so she may see her parents." He scanned the area for additional threats, not seeing any. His gut told him to kill these men since they knew about his abilities. If they meant him or Harley harm, they could return with more soldiers and overpower him. He didn't want anyone else to know they were here.

"Lady Harley," he called out, gaining her attention. "Get my bag and head to your parents' estate. I'll be along shortly."

"What are you going to do?" she asked as she stood, brushing herself off.

"I have a few questions for these men."

She nodded and did as he requested.

As she walked away, he retrieved his weapons from the ground. Once they were all accounted for, he dragged the men off the road and into the nearby field, concealing their bodies in the tall grass.

Harley's back was to him as she headed toward her parents' home. Ackley crouched, withdrew his dagger, and severed an artery in each man's leg so they'd bleed out and die. Ackley wiped the blade in the grass and stood, sheathing it. As the life drained from each of them, he felt a tinge of remorse. However, as he'd been trained, it was kill or be killed. He turned and joined Harley.

"Did you learn anything important?" she asked.

"No." They walked down the path, nearing her parents' home. The large stone manor stood before them, smoke rising from one of the chimneys. The longer Ackley was there, the more uneasy he felt. "I'd like to see a map of Penlar. I assume there's one in the house?" More specifically, he wanted to see how Penlar fit into the kingdom and if it was feasible Russek would have spared it.

"Yes." The closer they got to the house, the more fidgety

Harley became, wringing her hands together, pushing the hair out of her face, and playing with the edges of her sleeves.

When they reached the front door, Ackley took a step back from Harley, gesturing for her to take the lead. She lifted her hand, dropped it back at her side, peered over at Ackley, and then raised her hand again. This time she knocked.

After several tense minutes, the door swung open, and an elderly woman dressed as a servant stood there. "Lady Harley?"

"Carietta!" Harley stepped inside, hugging the woman.

When Harley released her, the woman took a step back. "It's good to see you, Lady Harley. We all thought you were dead."

So they knew about the takeover then. Ackley tried to keep his face impassive.

"Are my parents here?" Harley's voice wobbled as she spoke.

Carietta looked Ackley over, scanning him from head to toe before answering, "Your parents are here. Come inside."

Ackley followed a few feet behind Harley as they were led down a long hallway. The walls contained portraits, several of which were faded, indicating how old they were. Five suits of armor, one between each portrait, were on the left side of the hallway. On the right side, several sconces had been lit, illuminating the way.

Carietta opened a door on the left, ushering them into a grand sitting room. Tall windows framed by heavy drapes covered the right wall. Several sofas facing one another were situated in the middle of the room before a large hearth, a fire roaring in it. Tapestries covered the left wall. A small round table stood in one of the corners, a game of chess on it.

"Please have a seat," Carietta said. "I'll bring some refreshments."

After she left, Ackley turned to face Harley.

Tears filled her eyes. "They're alive."

Ackley scanned the room again, taking note of all entrances and exits. He had a bad feeling about this.

CHAPTER TWELVE

HARLEY

"*M*ay I present Lady Mayle," Carietta announced from the doorway.

Harley turned to face her mother, who wore a beautiful emerald green dress, her hair braided atop her head. As always, Lady Mayle's appearance reflected her station and rank. Harley curtseyed. It took every ounce of strength she had not to run and hug her mother. However, her mother always insisted she behave as she should at all times, regardless of emotion.

"I'd like you to meet my escort, Prince Ackley of Marsden." Harley gracefully gestured toward Ackley, curious to see how'd he'd act. So far, she'd seen him as an assassin and a soldier, not a prince.

"Lady Mayle." He didn't bow or lower his head since he was a higher rank than her.

"Where's Father?" Harley asked, glancing behind her mother.

Lady Mayle looked from Harley to Ackley and then back

again. "He's not feeling well." Wringing her hands together, she glided farther into the room, her head held high but her arms trembling. "I didn't expect to see you here." She kissed Harley's cheek, then took a seat on the sofa. "You look and smell like you've slept with pigs. Why are you dressed like a commoner?"

Harley thought her mother would be happy to see her, not questioning her appearance. Perhaps her mother didn't know what happened throughout the kingdom. Or maybe Penlar had been spared completely. "Did you hear what transpired at the castle?"

Lady Mayle focused on her hands, not looking Harley's way. "I have," she whispered.

"Only a few cities survived," Harley said, hoping her mother would explain what had happened here.

"Thankfully, Captain Lyle didn't take many of his men with him to the castle. When word came that the Russek army was marching this way, we had ample soldiers to protect us. Russek just passed right on by. There wasn't even a scuffle."

Harley sat beside her mother, taking her hand and squeezing it. "I don't know how to tell you this, but Lyle is dead." Still no sadness gripped her at the mention of her husband's passing.

"He's dead?" Lady Mayle asked.

Harley nodded.

Her mother tilted her head to the side, as if trying to figure something out. She was probably trying to ascertain how upset Harley was over the matter. But she need not worry.

With that out of the way, Harley attempted to broach the subject of her brother. "And…" She couldn't even bring herself to say Hollis's name. The pain gripped her heart and made it hard to breathe.

"And Commander Beck?" Lady Mayle asked. "Any news of him?"

Walking over to the chess board, Ackley said, "He hasn't returned to Melenia if that's what you're asking." He reached down, taking one of the chess pieces and moving it.

Lady Mayle smiled, tears filling her eyes. Harley wanted to ask why she appeared so happy over the news about Commander Beck, but Carietta entered carrying a tray with a pot of tea, three cups, and some treats.

After setting the tray on the low table between the sofas, she asked, "Shall I pour the tea?"

"We'll see to that, Carietta," Lady Mayle responded.

The servant curtseyed, then left the room.

Ackley sauntered over to the fireplace, observing the picture of Lord Silas and Lady Mayle hung over the mantle. "You have a quaint country house."

Lady Mayle's brow furrowed, and she focused on Ackley. "Where did you say you were from?"

He turned to face her, a slow smile spreading across his lips. "Who are you, exactly? Lady Harley's grandmother?"

Lady Mayle's eyes widened in shock, and her right hand flew to her bosom.

Heat crept up Harley's face, making her want to crawl under the sofa and hide. This was not going well. To take their focus off one another, Harley reached for the tray, pouring the tea. "My mother and father are in charge of this province," Harley said, knowing Ackley was already aware of it and silently cursing him for choosing to be the arrogant prince today. Just once she would like to see him be charming. If that was even possible.

"Province? We have several of those in my kingdom. We also have people who oversee the provinces who then report to the king." He plopped on the sofa across from Harley, stretching his arms out across the back.

Harley handed him a cup of tea. He took it, not bringing it to his mouth. Seeing him purposefully not drink the tea made her afraid to take a sip—which was ridiculous. Carietta would never poison their tea. She handed her mother the last cup.

Lady Mayle clasped it, not bothering to take a sip either. "Prince Ackley, how did you come to be here in Melenia with my daughter?"

A cocky smile slid across his face as he leaned forward, setting his cup back on the table, then resting his elbows on his thighs. "I'm from Marsden. I'm here with King Owen as his personal guest." His smile turned lethal as his eyes locked onto Harley's mother. A challenge of sorts.

"King Owen?" Lady Mayle asked.

"That's what I've been trying to tell you," Harley said, exasperated that her mother wasn't showing more concern over her or even asking about Hollis. Since the moment her mother had entered the room, she'd seemed distracted. As if she had something weighing heavily on her mind or as if someone were even watching her.

"That's generally how it works," Ackley interrupted, cutting Harley off. "When the father dies, title and land pass to his son." He glanced at his fingernails, as if bored. "Unless your kingdom is so archaic that you have another way of doing things?" This time he glanced at Harley, expecting her to answer.

"No, you're correct," she said. "That is how succession works here. And yes, King Owen is the legitimate king." She focused on her mother. "When Russek invaded us, they killed the entire royal family except for Owen." She took a deep breath, preparing to explain how Hollis had been killed in Owen's place.

"I thought someone else was sitting on the throne," Lady Mayle mumbled.

"That's what we've heard," Ackley said. "Can you imagine King Owen's shock when he learned a lowly foot soldier had taken up the Melenia throne?"

The only sound in the room was the fire crackling as the wood burned.

Finally, Lady Mayle asked, "Why are you here?" Her focus remained on Ackley.

"We're just passing through," Ackley answered nonchalantly.

Harley knew him well enough to know this was all an act. Since Owen had told him that he suspected her parents of something, Ackley must have an idea of what it was. That, coupled with the fact that her mother was behaving strangely, made Harley squirm. She didn't want to face the possibility that something was amiss here. However, she'd be a fool not to.

"Why is a prince from Marsden here in Melenia? Why are you with my daughter?"

"I'm here because of a new treaty." He raised a single eyebrow, as if anticipating her response.

"A treaty between whom?" Lady Mayle whispered. "Did Commander Beck send you?" Her voice shook.

Instead of answering, Ackley stood. "We need to be on our way if we're going to reach our destination before nightfall."

The sky outside had turned dark.

"Where is your destination?" Lady Mayle asked, also standing.

"You don't need to concern yourself with your daughter. I'll take good care of her."

Lady Mayle considered him a long moment before responding, "You can remain here for the night if you so wish."

"No," Ackley replied. "That won't be necessary. I didn't even want to waste my time stopping here, but Lady Harley insisted." He glanced around, his face cringing. "Let's be on our way." He sauntered from the room. "My men will be wondering where we are."

Hurrying after him, Harley wasn't sure if her mother heard that last part, though she assumed Ackley had said it simply for her mother's benefit. Ackley was a man she couldn't even begin to comprehend. However, she knew without a doubt that everything he did, he did for a specific reason.

"Can I see Father before we leave?" While she knew his health had been declining, being confined to his room was something new. If she could just see his face, hold his hand, she'd feel better.

"He's sleeping, and I don't want to wake him." Lady Mayle followed them out of the sitting room and down the hallway toward the front door. "But you are welcome to visit with me longer. You don't need to leave so soon," she said a little louder than necessary.

Harley glanced over her shoulder at her mother, wondering again about her odd behavior. "Are you all right?"

Lady Mayle pushed a loose strand of hair off her forehead and glanced around, as if expecting to see someone lurking nearby. Lowering her voice, she said, "There are things you don't know. Factors at play you can't even begin to comprehend."

"Tell me," Harley insisted, taking her mother's hands in hers.

"You wouldn't understand."

"I will. Or I'll try."

Lady Mayle peered at Ackley. "I'm sorry, Harley. I'm forbidden from telling you."

Her mother always did take her oaths, secrets, and station seriously. "Can I at least see Father before I leave?"

"If you stay the night, you can see him in the morning."

Ackley's fingers slid around Harley's upper arm and he whispered in her ear, "We need to leave. Now."

"Please give Father my love." She squeezed her mother's hands, then released them.

"I will." She kissed Harley's cheek. "Always remember I love you."

Ackley practically dragged Harley out of the manor and along the road. He leaned in and mumbled, "As quickly as possible, we need to get to the house you lived in with Lyle."

Since it was dark out, heading straight through the city would probably be the fastest and easiest way to get there.

"And don't use any of the main roads."

That would be more difficult. Regardless, she nodded and led him off the road and onto the neighbor's property. "There are horses in the back pasture." They could ride around the city, reaching Lyle's house in an hour or so. "Why did we leave so quickly? What do you think was going on?"

"There was a sleeping tonic in the tea."

Which explained why he hadn't touched his drink. "How do you know?"

"I could smell it."

She supposed an assassin would have such skills. "I can't imagine why there'd be sleeping tonic in it." Neither her mother nor Carietta would intentionally harm her.

"Your mother seemed nervous. And she clearly knows

something you don't. Do you have any idea what she was referring to before we left?"

Harley hadn't come up with anything yet, so she shook her head.

Ackley opened the gate to the pasture, allowing Harley to enter first. "Why did your father have you marry Lyle?"

She bristled at the mention of Lyle. Being married to him had been lonely and degrading. Thankfully, she hadn't been married to him long. If she'd had to endure his negative and belittling comments for years, it would have destroyed her. Not wanting to discuss Lyle, she headed straight for three horses.

Ackley quickly deemed one suitable. When Harley went to get a smaller horse, he grabbed her arm, pulling her closer to him. "We'll ride together."

The intensity in his eyes and voice sent a jolt of pleasure through her. Not understanding her body's reaction to this arrogant, cocky, assassin-prince, she rounded her shoulders and responded, "I am perfectly capable of riding on my own." Just because he thought she was a weak, helpless female, didn't mean she couldn't take care of herself.

"It's too dangerous. I don't know what's going on here, but something is amiss. We stick together." His hands slid around her waist, and she yelped from the touch. His eyebrows rose. "Problem?"

"No." His hands remained firmly planted on her waist, making her body feel like it was on fire. He lifted her onto the horse, then climbed on behind her. As his body shifted closer to hers, an unbidden desire flared within her. "Is this really necessary?" she hissed. Every time he touched her, her body had these strange reactions. Maybe that was why he did it—to prove he had the upper hand.

Lowering his voice, he said, "Is what necessary?" He shifted closer as he urged the horse on.

She tried to twist around to slap him. However, with his arms wrapped around her upper body, she couldn't move. Feeling his strong arms below her bosom only fueled the fire building inside of her.

Licking her lips, she tried to rein in her rising desire. Maybe if she kissed him and got it out of her system, his voice wouldn't send ripples of pleasure through her and the mere touch of his hand wouldn't make her feel warmth blossoming within. Not once had any man made her feel a fraction of what Ackley did. "I'm perfectly capable of mounting a horse on my own."

"Even in a dress?" His voice held a hint of laughter.

"I just don't think it's appropriate for the two of us to be so physically close."

"I'm sorry. I didn't realize I was making you uncomfortable."

"You're not. I mean, I just don't think this is suitable behavior for a prince."

He chuckled and steered the horse up the hill so they could skirt around the city. "You're not saying anything I haven't heard before." He shifted his body, pressing against her as the horse traversed down a short slope.

Briefly, she wondered what being with Ackley would be like. With Lyle, he'd always been so quick and forceful with her, that she'd never enjoyed herself. She assumed she wasn't supposed to. She was there simply for his pleasure. After all, she was a woman. She couldn't own land or work and had no value in anything other than what she could give her husband.

This was the first time she considered that being with someone could be enjoyable based upon her body's reactions to this man sitting behind her. However, if she were to ever be with a man again, he would have to be kind and gentle. And this assassin-prince was neither of those things.

"Are you okay?" Ackley asked, his breath brushing past her ear.

"I'm perfectly fine, thank you."

"You never answered my question," he reminded her. "Why did your father have you marry Lyle?"

"My family is very wealthy. Commander Beck wanted his son to be a captain. My parents needed to appoint a new one. My father liked the idea of me living so close to home and being taken care of." Honestly, she knew what Commander Beck and Lyle had gotten out of the match; as to what benefit her parents received, other than having her married off, she had no idea. It wasn't like he was the only suitor—she'd had several. However, for whatever reason, her father deemed Lyle the most advantageous.

"We've reached the end of the city," Ackley murmured. "Where to?"

She blinked, trying to refocus. "Head east. Cut along the edge of the forest." Her house wasn't far from here. And she was going to take Ackley inside of it. What would he glean from this invasion into her life? Panic started to swell. "Is this necessary?" If he thought something amiss, shouldn't they just leave and return to Owen?

"Pardon?"

"Going to Lyle's house. Is it necessary?" Lyle was dead. There was nothing to be learned from intruding in on her privacy.

"Yes." He hesitated a moment before continuing. "Commander Beck wasn't a good man. Since Lyle was his son, I need to investigate."

That was what she feared. "Why?"

"I believe Beck was involved with the takeover. I'm going to see if there's anything that supports my theory."

She didn't know how Beck would have been involved since he was in another kingdom when the takeover happened.

"The commander and a large portion of the army were gone, which makes me wonder if this entire thing was orchestrated," Ackley said, answering her unasked question.

"Turn here," she instructed him. Although she understood the need to investigate Beck, she didn't know why Ackley wanted to go to Lyle's house. Beck hadn't lived there.

He steered the horse out of the forest.

"My house is right over there." Twenty feet from the tree line, a stone wall surrounded Lyle's property. The main house was the building on the right; to the left, the stables and Lyle's workshop. A small garden separated the house from the paddock. While it was a perfectly respectable house, it wasn't nearly as grand as her parents' manor.

Ackley pulled the horse to a halt and dismounted, observing the area.

Harley remained on the horse, silently waiting for Ackley to decide what he wanted to do.

"We're at the back end of the house?"

She nodded.

"So the road and the front of the house are directly on the other side from where we are?"

"Yes."

"Any other entrances?"

"There is a gate in the wall to your left." The dark night and thick fog made it difficult to see it, but she knew exactly where it was. She'd come out here at night often enough. "From there, you can access the back door of the house."

"Dismount. We'll head to the stables. If everything appears normal there, we'll enter the house."

"I'll remain here with the horse." There was no need for her to go inside with Ackley.

"I intend for us to spend the night here. I'll investigate while you sleep."

He'd need to sleep, too. She was fairly certain he'd stayed up all last night keeping watch while she slept. Glancing at the dark house in the distance, Harley took a deep, calming breath, then dismounted. Maybe going inside would be good for her. She could say goodbye to this part of her life so she could put it behind her. Thankfully, she hadn't been married long. If years or decades had passed, she wondered if Lyle would have broken her spirit. If she would have given up.

She walked on the horse's right side, Ackley on its left. He didn't make any sounds as they approached the wall. She unlatched the gate, pushing it open.

"I don't see anyone," he whispered. "Regardless, stay close to the horse just in case."

Neither spoke as they crossed the property. When they reached the stables, he stepped forward and slid the door open, inspecting inside before waving Harley in. She led the horse to an empty stall.

"How many horses do you have?"

"Four. But we took them to the royal castle."

"Good, since the stalls are empty."

She closed the stall gate and joined Ackley.

"How many servants do you employ?" They exited the stables.

"None. Lyle didn't want anyone around." She did all the work around the house.

"Why?"

"He was paranoid." He thought people were spying on him and reporting his movements to someone—who, she had no idea.

They reached the back door. Harley placed her fingers on the handle and froze. Taking this assassin-prince into her house felt too intimate. He saw details and understood things that most people didn't. Once he went inside, he would know Lyle mistreated her. Would he think less of her?

"Is everything all right?" Ackley asked as he scanned the surrounding land again.

"Yes." The answer came out weaker than she intended. Taking a deep breath, she slowly let it out and pushed open the door. The familiar smell of Lyle greeted her, making her want to gag. She stepped into the dark kitchen.

"You're shaking." Ackley closed the door. Instead of asking her why, he simply passed through the kitchen, pausing at the doorway. "Wait here. I'm going to make sure no one's in the house." He slunk away, melting into the shadows.

Harley remained standing there, wishing she was anywhere but back in the house she'd shared with Lyle.

A few minutes later, Ackley returned. "All clear." He waved her over.

She followed him into the narrow hallway, trying to see things through his eyes. No portraits adorned the walls, no flowers filled the vases, no knitted blankets were on the sofa, and there wasn't any cut wood for the fireplace.

In the sitting room, Ackley turned in a slow circle. "Where did Lyle spend most of his time?"

"His workshop." She pointed outside to the other building.

"What about here in the main house?"

"His office." She led him down a short hallway and to a closed door, gesturing toward it. She'd never been inside. Lyle hadn't allowed it. He said if she stepped foot in there, he would consider it a violation of his privacy. He said that this was his home, not hers, and as such, she wasn't afforded a private space of her own since he deemed it unnecessary.

Ackley reached for the door handle, but it wouldn't budge. He pulled a dagger from his sleeve, inserted it into the lock, and popped the pin, releasing the door. Slowly pushing it open, he peered inside. "Can you get me a candle?"

Harley went to the kitchen and procured two candles, lighting them. She went back to the entrance of Lyle's office, handing one to Ackley.

He took it and stepped inside. "You don't have to do this with me. You can go and prepare for bed. We'll leave first thing in the morning."

With her heart pounding wildly in her chest, she nodded. "You'll want to look through his workshop as well." She couldn't believe she was in Lyle's house with Ackley and that he was going through Lyle's possessions.

"I'll go there after I'm done here."

"Let me know if you need anything." She headed up the stairs, several of them creaking under her weight. At the top, she made her way to her bedchamber, hovering at the entrance, not really wanting to go in. But she needed fresh clothes and wanted to pack a few things to take with her.

She went over to the dresser, setting the candle in a holder. Glancing at her reflection, she gasped. Her knotted hair stuck up in all directions and dirt covered her right cheek. Her mother had been right—it looked as if she'd slept with pigs. Her first order of business would be to wash up.

Not wanting to bother heating the water, she grabbed two bucketfuls and dumped them in the wash basin. Then she scrubbed her body. Once she finished, she put on clean clothes and brushed her hair. Afterward, she packed a couple of dresses in her bag.

Since she hadn't eaten all day, her stomach growled with hunger. She went to the kitchen in search of food. Most of the items had rotted, so she trekked out to the garden. The dark night made it difficult to navigate through the various vegetables. However, she'd planted and maintained this garden, so she knew where each item was. She pulled up a few carrots, some potatoes, and a couple of onions. Back in the kitchen, she proceeded to make soup for her and Ackley.

Not hearing any noises coming from elsewhere in the house, she suspected Ackley had gone out to Lyle's workshop. The windows were covered and the door always locked, so she had no idea what was even in there since she'd never stepped foot inside. Hopefully, he'd find something useful.

Once the soup was done, she sat and ate in silence. Just like she always did. Lyle oftentimes worked late into the night. When he came home from work, Harley knew what he wanted. After he took his pleasures, he usually retreated to his workshop.

When she finished eating, she pushed the bowl away. The house was eerily silent. Perhaps knowing Lyle wouldn't come in gave it a new stillness.

Seconds, minutes, hours passed. Time lost all meaning.

Ackley entered through the back door. "What are you doing in the kitchen?"

"I made soup." She pointed to the pot behind her, hanging over the low fire.

He grabbed a bowl and scooped himself a large helping. Sitting on a stool across from her at the kitchen table, he started eating. After a few bites, he said, "I thought you'd be asleep by now. It's after midnight."

She didn't know what to say, so she didn't say anything. Exhaustion consumed her bones, but she couldn't make herself move.

"You look better," he said around a mouthful of food.

"I can't believe you let me walk into my mother's home looking like a servant."

"You know, this soup isn't half bad." He took another bite, then asked, "How long were you and Lyle married?"

"Not long, but long enough." She propped her chin on her hands. "Are you done looking through everything?"

"I am."

"And?"

He took a bite of soup before answering. "I found a few letters between Lyle and his father. I'm taking them with us. It is for Owen to decide what he wants to do with the information."

"In your opinion, did Beck have something to do with the takeover?"

His eyes darkened, and he focused on his soup. "I believe so. But I don't have anything concrete."

She wanted him to extrapolate, but he didn't.

"You're different here." He finished his soup, setting his spoon in the bowl.

"How so?"

"You're quiet. More reserved."

She hadn't realized that. Standing, she picked up the bowls, taking them over to the counter to clean.

"Is there a room I can sleep in?"

A laugh escaped her lips at the idea of another man spending the night in Lyle's house.

Ackley's eyes narrowed.

"What's that look for?" she asked, leading him out of the kitchen and to the staircase.

"I don't think I've seen you laugh." They went up to the second floor. "It's good to see you smile."

Her face warmed at the compliment. "You can sleep in here." She stopped before the door on the left. "I'll be in the room to your right."

"Is that the bedchamber you shared with Lyle?"

"No. It's a guest room."

"Can I see Lyle's bedchamber?"

"This way." She led him down the hallway and to the right. "In here." She opened the door.

He stepped inside and went over to the fireplace. Kneeling, he started to build a fire. Harley sat on the edge of the bed, watching him.

"Since you're so young," he said as he worked, "will you remarry?" He glanced over his shoulder at her. In the dim candlelight, she could just make out the smirk he gave her before he said, "After all, a woman needs a man to survive."

"Are you teasing me?" It was late, and she was too tired to deal with his jokes. The wood crackled as the fire took. "And why did you make a fire when no one is sleeping in here tonight?"

He stood, hands on his hips, observing her. "To answer your first question, yes, I'm teasing you." The room started to glow as the fire grew. Ackley began walking around the room, looking over the dresser, bed, and armoire, though he didn't touch a single thing. "To answer your second question, I want smoke to be seen from your chimney. I'm wondering if someone is looking for you."

Her eyes widened. "You set a trap?" And she was the bait?

"Yes. Since you won't be in this room, you'll be fine."

"Now I won't be able to sleep." She rubbed her face, remembering the men who'd followed them when they first entered the city. She'd been so overwhelmed seeing her mother alive that she'd completely forgotten about the encounter until now.

"I'm here. There's nothing to worry about."

Ackley sure thought highly of himself. She stood, ready to go to the guest bedchamber for the night. "Is there anything else you need before I retire?"

With his hands now clasped behind his back, he continued perusing the room. "I'm going to stay in here and look a little while longer. You don't need to stay with me."

A clear dismissal. "You won't find anything. I've already searched the room."

"The back of tapestries or on the rear side of portraits are generic places to hide items of value. Personally, I prefer to hide them behind drawers, especially in armoires. But my favorite is under a floorboard." He stopped and looked at her. "Did you check under the floorboard?" He pointed to one in particular. One that looked a little worn along the edge.

"No." She hadn't noticed that one before.

A sardonic smile slid across his face. "Like I said, I'm going to stay in here for a bit. Goodnight."

CHAPTER THIRTEEN

ACKLEY

*O*nce Harley left the room, Ackley knelt on the floor. He pulled out his dagger and wedged it between the boards, prying up the one in question. A part of him didn't want to find anything else. What he'd seen in the office and workshop had been more than enough for him to understand Lyle had been a ruthless soldier, dedicated to his profession, and unyielding. The scary part—Ackley saw a part of himself in Lyle. However, Ackley valued duty, honor, honesty, dedication, and family. He doubted Lyle felt any of that.

One thing Ackley knew, which Owen did not, was that Idina had written a letter to Russek letting them know Melenia soldiers were in Marsden, leaving Melenia short of men to defend the kingdom. She'd intended for the king to call his soldiers back to Melenia, thus saving her own kingdom in the process. However, Melenia had been invaded shortly thereafter and the entire royal family executed.

A takeover of this magnitude wasn't done simply because of

a letter his sister had written. There was no way Russek could have organized and executed such a thing so quickly and efficiently. Someone on the inside had been sending Russek information long before the takeover happened. Someone like Commander Beck. But to what end? Ackley couldn't implicate someone without having evidence. What he feared was that Idina would be the one to take the fall. Which meant he needed to find the letter and destroy it.

Laying the floorboard aside, he examined the contents beneath. There were two pieces of paper and a bag. He pulled out the papers and unfolded them. The first one was a detailed map of Melenia. Specific cities had been marked. The second piece of paper had a few words scrawled on it. *This should be enough to keep you quiet.* It was signed with a single letter: *C.* The king's name was Coden. That, coupled with the letters Ackley found in Lyle's office, convinced him that Beck had been blackmailing the king—and Ackley knew why. After setting the papers aside, he lifted the bag out, its contents jingling as he did so. Inside, he found a handful of money. Since he didn't recognize the currency, he didn't know the value of it.

Ackley knelt there, considering his next move. His man should have made contact with Kerdan by now and hopefully had established a time and place for them to meet. If ever there was a time to sneak into Russek and have a clandestine meeting with Kerdan, now was the perfect opportunity since the kingdom was in civil unrest. The problem with his plan— Harley. At first, he considered leaving her with her parents. However, the second he realized the tea was laced with sleeping tonic, he knew her mother couldn't be trusted. Which left him with the option of taking Harley with him. Traveling into Russek with her would be infinitely more difficult.

Although, she could provide a believable cover, an inconspicuous married couple not worth anyone's attention.

Going over to the dresser, he blew out the candle and found a comfortable place to sit. It was only a matter of time until someone snuck into the house searching for Harley. Not only had those men followed them, but Lady Mayle had tried giving Harley the sleeping tonic before attempting to get her to spend the night. It was why he wanted to leave the manor so quickly —to get away from whomever wanted Harley. He also needed to come here and investigate before anything could be destroyed. With that accomplished, all he had to do was sit back and wait for the person to come here looking for her.

His eyes grew heavy, a result of having stayed up all last night to guard Harley. As he watched the fire in the hearth, he wondered why Lady Mayle hadn't seemed surprised to see Harley. It was almost as if she knew she was coming. But Owen hadn't told anyone Ackley and Harley were going to Penlar.

He stretched out on the chair, not wanting to get too comfortable as he waited. Sitting there, he had nothing to do but contemplate how Harley connected everything together. The fire crackled. The hours wore on. His eyelids fluttered shut.

"Ackley," Harley whispered, her voice like a strand of smoke curling around his ear. She stood in the middle of the bedchamber in nothing but a thin nightdress, the soft glow of the fire highlighting the golden hair hanging around her shoulders.

Not knowing what to say, he watched as she hesitantly approached, desire flaring within him. When she moved, the nightdress hugged the curves of her body. He wanted to extend his arm so he could touch her, but he was afraid to move and scare her away. When she reached the chair, he spread his legs ever so slightly, just enough for her to stand between them. Her hands pressed against his shoulders, pushing him back in the chair. Then her right leg slid up alongside his left thigh. She did the same with her other leg until she straddled him. Unable to contain himself, his fingers found the hem of her nightdress, slowly lifting it.

Her soft lips hovered above his. "I've wanted to do this since the moment I met you."

Ackley startled awake, trembling.

Sweat covered his forehead and his heart beat frantically. Rubbing his hands over his face, he realized he must have fallen asleep. What a reckless and irresponsible thing for him to do. He stood and went over to the window, pushing the curtain aside and peering out into the dark night. Nothing moved below. Before he'd come inside, he'd set a few traps just in case he fell asleep. The last thing he needed was someone taking him by surprise. So far, none of his traps had gone off. Regardless, something had woken him.

With a dagger in hand, he put his bag over his shoulders and crept out of the bedchamber. In the hallway, he stood listening. Not a single sound or creak. Everything felt too still. He slowly made his way to the room Harley was staying in. Pushing open the door, he peered inside. Darkness greeted him. After a minute, his eyes adjusted and he stepped into the room.

Uneven breathing came from his right, about fifteen feet away. "Harley?" he whispered, knowing she wasn't asleep by the sounds she made.

"Yes?"

Hearing her voice eased a bit of his building tension. "Something isn't right." He felt stupid being so vague.

However, he'd learned through the years to always trust his instincts.

"I know." She sat up in bed.

"Get dressed. If you have pants, put them on. I'll be waiting right outside the door."

"I'd prefer if you stayed in here with me."

With the dream of Harley fresh in his mind, he had to take a slow breath, grounding himself in reality. Her request meant she was afraid to be alone—nothing more.

In the shadows, he could just make out her body sliding out of bed. Curling his fingers, making two fists, he turned his back. With his dream still fresh in his mind, the feel of her bare skin against his hands was almost tangible. He needed to clear his head. If he wanted to make it out of this alive, he had to be sharp.

While she changed, he considered where he'd set the traps: near the front and back entrances, near two of the larger windows, and a handful around the perimeter of the house. Since none had gone off, he didn't think anyone was inside yet. However, he couldn't be certain.

"Okay," Harley whispered, coming to stand alongside him. "What do you want to do?" She slid her bag over her shoulders.

The fact that she'd been packed and had clothes readily accessible spoke volumes.

"What? Why are you looking at me like that?" she whispered.

Instead of answering, he leaned in close to her right ear. "I don't know for certain if anything is amiss." Her hair smelled of lavender.

"I agree with you, something feels wrong."

He hesitated a moment before righting himself. Their eyes

locked. Originally, he'd intended to interrogate whoever was out there. However, with Harley standing before him, her eyes scared and trusting, he knew his focus had to change. Getting her safely off the property was now his primary objective. Then, once she was in a secure location, he could come back.

Since Harley had pants on, traveling would be much easier. He withdrew one of his daggers. Reaching out, he found her hand and placed the dagger on her palm, closing her trembling fingers around the hilt.

"We're going to try and sneak out of here without anyone seeing us."

Her hand gently rested on his chest, freezing him in place. "There's a servants' passageway that no one knows about. We could use that. It'll take us out to Lyle's workshop."

The hairs on the back of his neck stood on end. Ackley could almost feel a presence around him. "Does the passageway go between the walls?"

Harley nodded.

There were people in the servants' passageway right this very minute—he was certain of it. Without uttering a single word, he curled his fingers around Harley's wrist, leading her from the guest room. They had to get out of there. Quickly. Most likely they were outnumbered, and there were probably more men outside waiting for them. How could he have let this happen?

They needed a distraction. "You're not particularly attached to this house, are you?" he asked, releasing her wrist.

"I hate it."

That was all the answer he needed. He'd ponder her response later, when he had more time, because he was fairly certain Harley's relationship with Lyle had been one of abuse instead of love or respect.

Ackley ran back to the master bedchamber, Harley right behind him. When he got there, he grabbed a blanket, wrapping it around his hand and arm. Then he reached into the dying fire, gingerly picking up a log. He pulled it out and tossed it on the bed. The flames fluttered, almost dying out. He was about to get another log when a small flame licked out, sliding over the blankets. The fabric erupted in bright flames. Rushing over to the vanity, Ackley snatched the chair and smashed it against the armoire. Picking up a handful of the pieces, he went back to the bed, sticking the ends of the splintered wood into the flames. He waited for them to catch. Once they did, he hurried from the room, Harley following at a safe distance. Thick, black smoke filled the air. As he sprinted down the hallway, he tossed the lit pieces into the rooms, aiming for curtains and beds. When he reached the top of the staircase, he waved Harley past him, then flung the last piece down the hallway.

The sounds of men yelling and pounding came from within the walls. Without looking back, Ackley took the stairs two at a time.

Since the roads were probably being watched, their options were limited. "Do your neighbors have horses?"

"The neighbors to the east have several roaming in their pen."

"Get us to the eastern most window."

Instead of questioning him, she took off running. Ackley followed close behind. Footsteps pounded on the floor above them. They didn't have much time.

"In here." Harley shoved a door open, and they entered the dining room.

Ackley rushed over to the window, looking outside. Not seeing anyone on the property, he grabbed one of the dining table chairs and smashed it against the window, shattering the glass. Then he yanked the curtain down, putting it along the opening so Harley wouldn't cut herself.

Going feet first, Harley climbed out of the window. She remained next to the house while Ackley jumped out. He scanned the area again, still not seeing anyone.

"Let's go." They sprinted across the field, heading straight for the neighbor's property about a quarter of a mile away.

Shouts rang out behind them. Ackley glanced over his shoulder. Flames shot out of several windows, the glow illuminating a few people in the house and several running around the perimeter of it.

"Faster!" he said to Harley. They were about halfway to the wall separating Lyle's property from the neighbor's.

The distant whirl of an arrow flying through the air caught Ackley's attention. Without thinking, he flung himself at Harley, knocking her to the ground. She yelped in surprise. The arrow struck the ground next to them, less than a foot away.

"Stay low," he ordered. "Head in a zigzag pattern as you make your way to the wall."

Harley nodded as she crouched on the ground.

"Go." Ackley turned back to search the house, trying to find the archer. Based upon the trajectory of the arrow and how it landed, he suspected the shooter was level with him—whether that was from outside or inside the house, he didn't know. But at least the archer wasn't on the second floor looking down on them. If that were the case, it would make dodging arrows infinitely more difficult.

An arrow came at him, landing four feet away. He didn't think the archer could see him now that he wasn't moving. Hopefully the shooter wouldn't see Harley. Making a quick decision, Ackley jumped to his feet and ran toward the wall, making sure to sprint in an erratic pattern, trying to draw attention away from Harley and to himself. Another arrow soared through the air, landing behind him.

Harley reached the wall about thirty feet away, panting.

More shouts rang out. Ackley peered over his shoulder. Flames now engulfed the roof, the entire area around the house alight from the fire. Five men were headed straight for him. He'd hoped to escape without having to kill in front of Harley. For some reason, he didn't want to spill blood before her.

Unfortunately, that wasn't going to happen tonight.

Facing his oncoming attackers, Ackley palmed a knife in one hand, his short sword in the other. Tilting his head to the side, he stretched his neck, preparing for battle. As he always did before a fight, he slid on his mental armor, zeroing in on his attackers. Nothing existed but those who wished to harm him. There would be nothing but killing blows if he wanted the two of them to make it out alive. Strike hard and fast.

The closest man appeared to be five foot seven inches, a hundred and seventy-five pounds. Ackley aimed his knife, counted to three, and threw. The man collapsed to the ground, the knife protruding from his neck, blood spurting out.

One down, four to go.

Not wanting to lose any more weapons, he'd have to get a bit more creative. Zeroing in on the next two, Ackley saw the one on the right lift his longsword. That was a mistake. Ackley turned, ramming his short sword into the man's exposed stomach. As he did so, he used his momentum to kick the other one's head, knocking him down. Withdrawing his sword, he lifted it, plunging it into the one who'd fallen to the ground.

Three down, two to go.

The last two had almost reached him. Yanking his sword free, he twisted and sliced his attacker's neck.

Four down, one to go.

Where had the last man gone?

Ackley turned in a slow circle, searching for the last of his five attackers.

Dread filled him. He knew, before he spotted him, that the man probably had Harley. When he faced the wall, he saw a man standing there, his arms around her. In the shadows, Ackley could just make out the knife placed at her neck.

"Stay where you are," the man said. "Drop your sword and get on the ground. Put your arms above your head so I can see your hands."

Ackley chuckled, the sound menacing in the dark night.

"Do as I say or I'll kill her," the man snarled.

"What makes you think I care about the woman," he said nonchalantly, buying himself some time. The man was a head taller than Harley making him six feet exactly, about one hundred and ninety-two pounds. Since his neck was hidden by Harley's hair, Ackley would have to find another way to kill him.

The man took a step forward, keeping Harley in front of him as a shield.

Shouts rang out behind Ackley. More men were coming, which meant he was out of time. Sliding a dagger from his sleeve, he kept his eyes focused on the man. Once the dagger was in his palm, he flung it at him. The hilt hit his forehead, momentarily stunning him. Ackley withdrew the knife from his boot, throwing it. It struck the man's arm holding the knife against Harley's neck. When the man released her, she turned and rammed the dagger Ackley had given her into his stomach.

The man snarled and went to withdraw the dagger, now

covered with blood. Harley dropped to the ground, giving Ackley the opening he needed. He ran at the man, grabbing hold of the hilt and twisting it. Then he shoved the man away. The metallic smell of blood hung heavy in the air.

Seven men were running toward them, about thirty feet away and closing in fast. "Get over the wall. Now."

Harley clamored to her feet, then crawled over the wall.

Ackley grabbed his weapons, then climbed over after her. She was already sprinting alongside the wall, headed straight toward the forest, a good forty feet away. He took off after her, wondering why she hadn't gone for the horses. It would be easier to lose the men on horseback than running around dense foliage.

They reached the tree line. "There's a river not far from here," Harley said, breathing heavily. "I keep a boat there. We can use that to go downriver."

Another flipping boat? He cursed. At least it wasn't the open water of the ocean. A river he should be able to handle. "Don't you think the horses would have been faster and easier?"

"By the time we reached them, mounted, and got out of a *locked* pen, the men would have been upon us."

"I can pick a lock in two seconds."

"It doesn't matter!" she said a little louder than necessary. "It's too late for the horses, so stop arguing with me."

Footsteps pounded on the forest floor behind them.

"How much farther?" Ackley thought the men were falling a little behind now that they were running amongst the trees.

"Almost there." Harley ran with purpose, as if she'd done this a hundred times.

The trees abruptly ended and a river stretched out before them, the water rushing by. Harley slung a broken branch to the side, revealing a tiny boat barely big enough for the two of them. She dragged it to the water's edge, hopping in. Ackley gave it a shove to get it going, then he jumped in, the boat wobbling from his weight. Harley thrust two tiny oars at him. After sitting, he took them, steering the boat with the current and toward the other side, wanting to put as much space between them and their pursuers as possible.

Men came crashing through the forest, stopping on the river bank where the boat had been only moments before. Shouts rang out, then the men started running alongside the shore after them.

"Don't worry," Harley said. "I have an idea."

While they'd managed to grow their lead, Ackley could still see and hear the men chasing them.

"There's a bend up ahead. We'll jump out there, leaving the boat in the river. About a half mile after that, there's a waterfall. Hopefully, they'll think we went over it. It should buy us enough time."

Considering the plan, Ackley looked for holes. Given their circumstances, it seemed a solid idea. "Okay."

"Keep us on course. When I say, steer us to the left."

He nodded and rowed as fast as he could. His shoulders burned, but he welcomed the pain.

"Now."

He steered to the left just as the river curved the other direction. As soon as the men were out of sight, Harley launched out of the boat, the water up to her knees as she clambered onto the shore. She ran into the cover of the trees. Leaving the oars in the boat, Ackley got out then grabbed the tip of the boat, shoving it back into the middle of the river. Satisfied, he sprinted after Harley. They headed deeper into the forest, neither one speaking. After about ten minutes, he grabbed her arm, pulling her to a stop. They stood there, listening.

An owl hooted. Leaves rustled in the wind. No sounds of footsteps or voices could be heard.

"What's our next move?" Harley asked, her voice barely audible.

While Ackley didn't like the idea of traveling in the dark, they didn't have an option tonight. It would only be a matter of time before the men discovered he and Harley hadn't perished in the waterfall. They had an hour at most before people came looking for them.

"I'll explain everything later, but right now, I want to get us to Landania." He believed they needed to head southeast. He gave her a second to consider his words.

She tilted her head up, her brows pulling together as she looked him in the eyes. "You don't intend to meet up with Owen?"

Eyeing her sidelong, he asked, "How would you feel about going on an adventure...with me?"

CHAPTER FOURTEEN

HARLEY

*a*n adventure…with an assassin-prince. Harley didn't know what to think about that. When they were at her parents' home, he'd exhibited the side of him that screamed he was an arrogant prince. Then at Lyle's house, Ackley had revealed the ruthless assassin side of him. The part of him that could kill without hesitation. When he'd fought those men, he'd reminded her of a panther. Lean, sleek, and lethal.

"I don't know." Because she didn't. Even though he scared her at times, she felt safe around him. Somehow, she knew he had her best interests at heart. But going on a mission with him took things to another level. One she was not sure she was prepared to go to. "What do you have in mind?"

When he didn't immediately respond, she thought perhaps he hadn't heard her. She was about to ask again when he said, "I'm going to Russek."

Not *I'd like to go to Russek* but *I'm going.* Somehow she knew this wasn't a spur of the moment thing. And she was inclined to think Owen had no idea about it.

"I need someone who understands the culture and people so I can blend in," he explained. "I need your knowledge and expertise."

"What makes you think I know anything about Russek?" She'd never been there before. The only people she'd met from the kingdom were the barbaric soldiers who'd invaded Melenia.

"As neighboring kingdoms, you must know something about them. Plus, you were at the castle during the takeover. You've seen them, the way they speak, the way they dress. All of that is valuable knowledge. Knowledge I need to survive a mission like this."

Mission.

With shaking hands, she started walking again, having a vague notion of which way to go. If she was headed the wrong direction, Ackley would let her know. Not hearing any sounds behind her, she glanced over her shoulder to be sure he was following. He was. Silent as a panther.

"Why do you want to go to Russek?" Perhaps he intended on assassinating someone. She wouldn't mind getting her hands on the man who'd murdered her brother.

"The less you know, the better. That way you can't accidentally give information away if you're questioned."

"How long will we be there?"

"I don't know; however, I don't want to be there any longer than necessary." His voice sounded even closer to her, giving her chills at the nearness of him.

Excitement and terror coursed through her. So far, everything that happened had happened to her. She was constantly acclimating to the changing world around her and had no control over her life. Now, Ackley was giving her the chance to be a part of something—whatever that may be. To be an active participant. To change things. After what she'd been through, she believed herself capable of helping him. "What makes you think I can survive a mission like the one you're planning? I have no fighting skills." The last thing she wanted was to be a liability.

"Just because you don't know how to fight doesn't mean you are useless."

She came to the edge of the forest and stopped, afraid to traverse over open land. Behind her, she could almost feel Ackley's body heat radiating from him.

"You are not useless to me," his soft, caressing voice murmured mere inches from her ear. He took a step forward so he stood beside her. "I won't lie. It might be easier without you. I could move quicker and wouldn't have to worry about defending you. But I've learned over the course of our short time together that you're smart, and I value intelligence. I've also learned through the years that you don't have to fight to be strong. You can be strong in other ways." He nodded ahead and took the lead, maintaining a southeasterly course.

Harley felt oddly exposed now that they were out in the open. Thankfully, Ackley maintained a quick pace. Exhaustion began to take root from everything they'd been through the last two days. Her feet became slow, her eyelids heavy. The sky lightened as dawn approached.

"Let's stop here," Ackley said, his breath coming out in a white puff from the chilly morning air. "We need to rest for a few hours."

"A few hours?" Her body could easily sleep for an entire day.

"We can't afford to waste the daylight. We'll each sleep for two hours and then continue on. When night comes, we'll sleep longer." He dropped his bag on the ground.

As much as she wanted to complain about only getting two hours of sleep, she understood his concern and agreed with him. When that man had held her at knifepoint, he'd whispered in her ear that someone was waiting for her. She shivered. She was definitely safer with Ackley. "I'll go with you."

"Excuse me?" He stretched out on the ground.

"To Russek." She yawned.

He turned to look at her. "Are you sure?"

No. She nodded.

A wicked smile slid across his face, making her toes curl. "Excellent."

"There is something I'd like to know beforehand, though."

"Ask away." He propped his head on his bag.

"How do you do it?"

"Do what?"

"Kill people." Her hands still shook whenever she thought about all the death and destruction she'd seen at the castle. Unable to imagine taking another person's life, she wondered how soldiers did it repeatedly. Thinking back to her altercation with the man who'd held her at knifepoint, she'd had no qualms about stabbing him. In fact, she'd wanted him dead—not simply injured so she could escape. That thought terrified her. How Ackley did it time and time again and lived with himself was beyond her understanding. That he still managed to see the good in those around him said something about him being able to cope remarkably well.

"I don't do it for pleasure." His words were sharp and clipped. "If I didn't kill my enemies, the people I love would be dead. You'd be dead."

"I'm sorry. I didn't mean to imply that you enjoy killing." Placing her bag on the ground, she rested her head on it.

He rolled away, his back to her. "Perhaps one day I will tell you how I came to be an assassin. But where I'm from, I'm known as a knight. We're the protectors of our kingdom. A secret organization that maintains peace. However, if you only want to look at it as a killer squad, go ahead. Just don't forget you benefitted from my skillset."

Stunned, she realized she'd upset Ackley. Someone as tough and strong as him had been hurt by her words. She'd basically implied he was a cold-blooded killer. "I'm sorry. I didn't mean to offend you."

He didn't respond.

Each step felt like knives stabbing into the bottoms of Harley's feet and ankles. When she'd hurried and dressed two nights ago, she hadn't had socks. She'd slid her feet into her boots, assuming she'd packed socks and could put them on later. Well, she forgot socks. So after two days of walking without them, her feet were covered in blisters, most of which had popped. Ackley probably had a spare set in his bag; however, she didn't want to ask him for anything. He'd been cold and distant the past two days, barely talking to her.

As the sun set, tears threatened. She thought they would have reached Landania by now. Maybe Ackley, who never hesitated in which direction he went, had made a mistake—if that were even possible.

The wind blew gently. "It reeks of death." The heady scent made her want to gag.

"Russeks truly are barbarians," Ackley muttered. He'd stopped a few feet in front of her, at the top of a small rise.

"Is it another town?" She couldn't bring herself to see another burned village with the remains of the inhabitants charred. There was only so much heartache she could handle.

He hesitated a moment before facing her. Adjusting the bag on his back, he said, "Not quite." There were shadows in his eyes as if haunted by what he saw.

Scared, Harley moved slowly to the top of the hill, stopping beside him. About half a mile ahead, a row of spikes stuck out of the ground for as far as she could see in both directions. On top of each spike was a severed head. Some of them small enough to indicate it belonged to a child. She fell to her knees, clutching the grass, trying to keep the screams inside.

Ackley crouched next to her. "I didn't think anyone capable of so much evil. And I've seen evil firsthand." Carefully reaching out, he took hold of her fingers, squeezing them. "We must reach Landania before it's fully dark. I'm guessing this is the border between Melenia and Landania."

She nodded, unable to speak.

He stood, pulling her up alongside him before releasing her hand. "Stay right behind me. Focus on my back and nothing else."

They were going to have to pass the line of severed heads, walking directly between them. The smell would only intensify the closer they got.

Ackley began the trek down the hill, keeping a swift pace.

Harley did as he said and kept her focus on his back, never wavering from it. She would not look at the decaying heads on the spikes. "We need to take them down." They couldn't leave her fellow citizens in such a state.

"I agree, but now is not the time."

"They deserve to be buried."

"If we had the necessary help and supplies, we could. However, that is not our mission right now. We must remain focused. If you want Russek to pay, we need to stay our course."

What he said made sense. Yet, it didn't stop the fact that she wanted to do something to help these people.

Ackley's hand slid around hers, gripping it tightly. "I'm here to help you. But right now, I need you to help me. Keep walking." He pulled her alongside him, quickening their pace.

Once they'd passed the line of spikes, Harley focused on what she saw in the distance. Smoke rose from over a dozen spots in a clustered area. "Do you think that's a town in Landania?"

"That's my guess. Probably one with a heavy military presence."

Even though they'd passed the heads, he didn't release his hold on her. "You can let go," she said. "I'm not so fragile I'll fall over or cry." Though she wanted to.

"Have you considered the possibility that I'm holding your hand not for your benefit, but for mine? That I'm the one who needs comfort? That I want to be grounded in another human so I don't do something stupid?"

The confession startled her. She had no idea how to respond, so she simply squeezed his hand, trying to provide as much comfort as she was receiving.

The two of them continued walking as darkness overtook them. The closer they got to the town, the better Harley could make out the buildings. There were far more than she'd originally thought. When they reached the outskirts, Ackley slowed, walking casually as if he didn't have a care in the world. Harley tried to mimic him. He steered them toward the middle of the town, where the buildings were denser. People were out walking, no one paying them any heed. Much to her relief, no Landania soldiers were visible. Hopefully no one would question where they were from or what they were doing there.

Up ahead, a group of people stood laughing. To the left, a sign hung with the word *Tavern* painted on it.

"They speak the same language as us," Ackley whispered. "Though their accent is more along the lines of yours."

She didn't have an accent, Ackley did.

"When we go inside, you'll need to do most of the talking," he said.

"We're going into the tavern?" She had no desire for a drink at this hour. A bed was what she wanted.

"Yes. We need to hear the local gossip. I want to make sure it's safe to remain here for the night. If it is, we'll find an inn."

Harley hadn't thought to bring any money with her. All she'd packed were dresses. Hopefully Ackley had some on him; otherwise, they'd be stuck sleeping in a barn or out under the stars again.

"Besides," he said. "I'm starved. I could use a real meal."

As if on cue, her stomach growled.

Chuckling, Ackley led her around the group of men. He pushed open the door, and they entered the tavern. Two dozen people filled the room, taking up most of the bar and about half of the tables. Ackley chose a table close to two occupied ones.

As Harley took her seat, she noticed another woman wearing pants. Relieved she wouldn't stand out, she leaned back in the chair and moaned, thankful to be off her blistered feet. She was certain her boots were soaked with blood.

A server approached, and Ackley peered at Harley.

"Uh, two bowls of stew," she muttered. Ackley kicked her under the table. "Oh, and two drinks. Thank you."

The woman nodded and left.

"Why'd you make me order ale? I don't want any." The last thing she needed was alcohol.

He shrugged. "Neither do I. But you can't come into a tavern and not have a drink. It would look suspicious."

"I suppose." The low ceiling made Harley feel caged in.

"How are you holding up?" Ackley asked, leaning in closer to her.

She opened her eyes, not having realized she'd even closed them. "I'm fine."

He raised a single eyebrow. "My sister told me whenever a woman says she's fine, she is anything but."

The server set two bowls and two mugs on the table, then hurried away.

Harley pulled one of the bowls closer to her, taking a tentative bite of the stew. "If you want to know the truth, ever since my cousin's birthday celebration, my life has been a living nightmare. I keep expecting to wake up and find my brother alive." Tears filled her eyes.

"You saw it happen?"

Even though his question was rather vague, she knew what he meant. "Yes." She'd witnessed her brother's brutal beheading. It was something she would never forget. Could never unsee.

"I can't imagine witnessing that." He took a bite of his food. "Considering what you've been through...both before and after...you're a remarkably strong woman." He took another bite, not looking her way.

She didn't know what to make of that statement. When he'd said *before*, he had to be referring to her marriage to Lyle.

He'd probably seen something in Lyle's house that revealed how her husband had treated her. Her face warmed with embarrassment. She couldn't even look at Ackley, only exemplifying that she was anything but strong. Just because she'd managed to survive, that didn't make her strong.

"Eat," Ackley said. "I haven't heard anything of concern from any of the other patrons. Since things seem calm here, we'll find an inn for the night, then I'll sneak out and investigate while you sleep."

"What do you hope to discover?" And didn't he ever sleep?

Setting his spoon down, he peered at her. "Just some basic information about Russek. I don't want to cross their border without knowing as much as possible about what I'm getting us into."

When the server returned for payment, Ackley pulled out a few coins, handing them over before inquiring about an inn. The server recommended the establishment directly above the tavern.

"How did you know how much to pay her?" Harley asked as she stood.

"I didn't. I just guessed. That's why I asked her a question —to distract her." He led the way to a narrow staircase at the back of the tavern.

Climbing the stairs, Harley winced. Her feet hurt even worse than before.

On the second floor, they found the innkeeper sitting at a desk. Ackley paid him for one room. After obtaining the key, Ackley led Harley down the hallway to the last room. He pushed open the door, allowing her to enter first.

The single bed took up most of the space. At this point, she didn't care whether she slept on the bed or the floor—she was happy to have a roof over her head. Before she had a chance to ask Ackley if he wanted the bed, the vision of them sharing it shoved its way in. She imagined removing his tunic, tracing the lines of his stomach, then lying next to him, pressed together. She shook her head, unable to believe she'd stood there daydreaming for a minute. She must be delirious from lack of sleep.

"Here." Ackley helped her remove her bag. Then he placed both of their bags on the empty chair in the corner of the room. "Go to sleep," he commanded, his deep voice husky in the dimly lit room. "I'm going to head out. Make sure to lock the door after I leave."

She sat on the edge of the bed, untying her boots. "Will you be gone most of the night?"

"Probably."

"Please be careful." She removed her right boot, wincing as she did so.

"Your foot is bloody."

"It's just a few blisters. I'm fine." She removed her left boot, dropping it to the floor along with her other one. Both of her feet throbbed with stinging pain.

Shaking his head, Ackley left the room.

After locking the door, Harley stretched out on the bed, not even bothering to change into her nightdress or climb under the covers. The bed practically hugged her body. Since she didn't want to get blood on the blankets, she kept her feet dangling over the end of it.

The doorknob rattled, and her eyes flew open. Ackley opened the door, pocketing the key. He held a bucket in his other arm. "Sit up."

"Aren't you supposed to be out investigating?"

After closing the door, he set the bucket on the floor. "I said sit up."

"I'm half asleep." And she had no intention of sitting or doing anything else for that matter.

"Fine." Gingerly, he slid his hands around her waist, flipping her body over onto her back. Then he slid his hands down her legs to her knees. He gently pulled her toward the end of the bed until her calves hung over the edge.

"What are you doing?" she asked, horrified. She hadn't bathed in days, and she smelled.

He lifted her right leg, shoving her pants up. Then he placed her foot in the bucket filled with blissfully warm water.

A moan escaped her lips. "What's in that?"

"Healing oils," he answered, his voice amused.

Some part of her wanted to protest at him touching her so intimately, but she couldn't bring herself to say anything. The warm water felt too luxurious to complain about his hand holding her calf.

After a couple of minutes, he removed her right foot from the bucket, inserting her left foot into the water. While it soaked, he dried her right foot and applied something cold and gooey on it. Then he repeated the same ministrations to her left foot. She vaguely felt him lift her legs back onto the bed, tucking her under the blankets.

Harley awoke. Blissful sunlight poured into the room, warming her. She sat up, stretching.

"Are you finally awake?" Ackley asked from somewhere on the floor next to the bed.

She peered over the side and found him lying on his back, crammed between the wall and the bed.

"Please tell me you didn't sleep on the hard floor." Not that there was much room on the bed for him or that sharing would have been appropriate.

"I spent most of the night going to different taverns and talking with the locals."

He had to be exhausted. "Would you like to sleep on the bed for a few hours?"

"I'm good." He yawned. "I was able to confirm most of what we already knew about Russek." He went over to the window, glancing outside.

"King Drenton is truly dead?" The man responsible for sending his troops into her kingdom was dead?

"He is."

"Did you discover who killed him?"

He shook his head. "Jana is sitting on the throne while Kerdan is in exile. The kingdom is torn on who to support."

"What do you think?"

"That things are going to get even worse for Russek. I also confirmed Princess Allyssa of Emperion has been killed. Emperion has amassed their army along the Russek border. They intend to attack." Leaning against the window sill, he folded his arms.

"Any word about who's sitting on Melenia's throne?"

"Everyone knows Melenia is ravaged, the royal family slaughtered, and a Melenia soldier has declared himself the new ruler, but no one knows his name. No one seems to care right now with a massive war brewing."

Harley twisted the blanket between her hands hoping her family would still get justice for their senseless murders. With Drenton dead and Russek about to be invaded, she feared retribution would not come. Maybe the destruction of Russek would be enough. She peered at Ackley, this assassin-prince who could deliver the revenge she wanted. He could make sure those responsible died—whether Owen gave the order or not. "So what's our plan?"

"We're going to Russek, we'll meet with Kerdan, and then return to Melenia." He made it sound so simple.

"How do you intend to meet with a man who is in exile?"

Instead of answering, he pointed at her feet hidden beneath the blankets. "Are you going to be able to walk?"

She pushed the blankets off. Her feet looked significantly better and felt wonderful. "Whatever you did to them worked." Her eyes widened in horror as she recalled him tending to her last night. She'd been too tired and in too much pain to protest.

"I bought you some socks and fur-lined boots for the journey." He nodded at the end of the bed. "Put them on, and we'll get going." He pushed off the window ledge.

Unable to move, she sat there staring at the boots and socks he'd bought for her.

"Is something the matter?" he asked tentatively.

She shook her head, horrified. Not even Lyle would have taken care of her like that. This man who was practically a stranger—and a prince no less—had cleaned and tended to her feet. Her face went flaming red with embarrassment.

He took a deep breath, letting it out slowly. "What is it?"

"I'm sorry you had to do that last night." Her feet had been covered with blood, blistered, and they had to have smelled.

He shrugged. "I'm sure you would have done the same for me. Let's go."

While Ackley didn't seem to consider it a big deal, Harley did. Only her mother had ever tended to her like that before.

The thick socks were soft to the touch. She slid them on before putting on the fur-lined boots. When she stood, her feet felt as if they were wrapped in clouds. "Thank you." She finally looked him in the eyes. "You didn't have to get these for me. I appreciate it." His eyes were two pools of warmth, making her want to step closer to him, even hug him. She imagined his hands taking hold of her face and kissing her. As desire built inside of her, she had to look away.

"My pleasure." Even his voice had a charming allure to it.

They exited the room and headed down to the tavern where a handful of people were sitting at the tables having breakfast.

"Let's eat before we head out," Ackley suggested.

Harley thought that a wise idea. This time, Ackley chose a secluded table in the corner of the room. When the server approached, Harley ordered oatmeal for the both of them. While they waited for their food to be brought, Ackley pulled out a piece of paper, unfolding it. He flattened it on the table between them.

"You have a map," she said, looking over the detailed rendering of the mainland. Villages, rivers, and borders were all marked. "Have you had this the entire time?" She'd assumed he had an uncanny sense of direction.

His lips twitched. "I have." He was on the verge of laughing at her.

"Why are you choosing to share this with me now?" She should have known he had a map. There was no way he could have led the way out of Melenia to Landania, arriving at this town without some sort of guidance.

"We're going to head north to this village." He pointed at the map. "There, I'm meeting with one of my men."

As in, this had already been arranged. How long had Ackley planned on going to Russek? "Does my cousin know we're doing this?"

"My man has already requested an official meeting between

214

Prince Kerdan and myself. As a prince, I can do this on my own."

Without Owen being involved or knowing about it.

He folded the map, tucking it away. "From here on out, we're going to pretend to be a married couple." His eyes shone with mischief, as if he knew playing such a part would make her uncomfortable. He raised his right eyebrow, waiting for her to protest.

"Why not brother and sister?"

He leaned in closer, taking a lock of her blonde hair between his fingers and twirling it. "Not as fun."

"But more appropriate." She pulled her hair free even though she rather enjoyed the idea of a man flirting with her. Not to mention what that simple touch had done to her insides.

"You of all people know how brutal Russek is. When we step foot in that kingdom, you are my wife. I can't risk anyone trying to take you, hurt you, or use you. Having you be unmarried is too risky."

The server set two bowls of oatmeal on the table and left.

Taking a bite, Harley almost believed that Ackley cared for her. However, she was certain Owen had made him promise to bring her back safely. Any commitment to protecting her stemmed from that promise and nothing more. When she swallowed her oatmeal, she had no idea why it felt like thick mud going down her throat, making her stomach sour.

CHAPTER FIFTEEN

ACKLEY

*A*ckley stood there, once again not quite believing what he saw ahead. Crossing from Landania to Russek should have been simple. Easy. He rubbed his face, then looked at Harley. "I'm sorry."

"Do you think those are more Melenia citizens? Or are they Russek?"

He had no idea what kingdom the severed heads on spikes belonged to.

"If they're from Melenia, what are they doing all the way out here between Landania and Russek?" Harley asked. "And if they're Russek, how could their own countrymen do this to them?"

"Let's not stand here out in the open," he said. He began walking toward the line. The spikes were about ten feet apart. He aimed so he'd cross in the middle between two, trying to put as much distance as possible between them and death.

Harley reached out, clutching onto his arm. "I don't know if I can do this."

Surprise washed through him at the fact that she was touching him. He didn't think she'd voluntarily do so.

She glanced at her hand on his arm and jerked, suddenly releasing him. "I'm sorry."

"For what?" He needed to get her focus off the severed heads and on him. If he did so, he could get her into Russek without her panicking about her fallen countrymen.

"It was inappropriate for me to touch you so informally." A slight blush graced her cheeks.

He chuckled. "I washed your feet last night." He leaned down closer to her ear. "I've touched far more intimate parts of your body than your arm." He hoped his teasing distracted her. The blush on her cheeks deepened, indicating he'd done his job.

She squared her shoulders, composing herself. "Regardless," she said, her chin slightly raised. "You're a prince. Someone of my standing should not touch you without invitation."

He almost burst out laughing. Lowering his voice, he murmured, "So if I asked you to touch me, you would?"

Her eyes widened, and she leaned away from him. "I wasn't saying that at all!" She quickened her pace so she was walking slightly in front of him. "I'm sorry for implying anything like that."

She marched straight past the spikes, her hands balled into fists.

Once they'd passed the line, he could feel a change in the air. They were in Russek, land of savage men. Harley slowed, as if sensing the change as well. If Ackley had done his calculations correctly, they had about another mile to walk

217

until they reached the small village where his man was waiting for him.

"Stay beside me." He didn't want Harley walking behind him. Not only could he not see if she limped or started to fall behind, but he had this odd compulsion to talk to her. To get to know her better. Which was strange because he didn't like talking all that much.

"I've never done anything dangerous or risky like this before," she said as she joined him, rubbing her hands together then blowing into them.

The air seemed to turn colder with each step they took. Ackley would have to find them warm cloaks to wear so they wouldn't freeze. "I think managing to sneak out of the great hall during the invasion constitutes risky behavior. Not to mention being brave enough to light the signal fire and speak to Kerdan." He tilted his neck to the side, cracking it. While her being the only noble to get out of the castle alive did seem questionable—he didn't think she had anything to do with, or had any knowledge of, the takeover. Unless she was fooling him.

She laughed, staring up at the sky. "I hardly call that brave. It was simply survival. First, being driven by saving my brother, and then myself. Doing something like this," she waved her hand between them, "would never have happened before."

"Before?"

"With Lyle. He didn't like me leaving the house. He thought my place was inside—cooking, cleaning, and tending to his needs."

Ackley had to force himself to remain calm so she'd continue to confide in him. "Even though you're a lady, he had you doing the work of servants?" And he'd seen the closet. It had been cleared out, there was a chain around the door handle, and the inside had scuff marks from someone kicking and banging. He couldn't figure out why Lyle would have locked Harley in there.

"Lyle didn't allow servants in the house. Someone had to do the work."

Lyle had married a person of wealth and social standing for a reason. He should have taken advantage of it. There was no reason to force Harley to do the work of servants and treat her so abominably. "I would have thought he'd want to show you off." Usually when a man married a woman as beautiful as Harley, he enjoyed taking her to balls and gatherings. It seemed strange to want to hide her away. But then he thought about the woman his brother had wanted him to marry. She was a pretty little thing who he didn't care for. If they'd married, he probably wouldn't have wanted to take her anywhere and would have preferred ignoring her. Thankfully, that engagement had been severed. He shivered, grateful to have gotten out of that one.

"Maybe he would have with time." She folded her arms, gazing out at the scenery.

A few wooden huts came into view, which meant the village had to be close by. Ackley glanced at Harley. Her beautiful, long blonde hair stood out like a beacon. "I think you should braid your hair. Try to look a little less conspicuous."

"Good idea." She quickly braided her hair then slid it under her tunic.

He tried not to think about what it would feel like to run his hands down her bare back. Such thoughts would do him no good. She was not his type.

"When we reach the village, what are we going to do?"

"Find the tavern."

"Of course. It seems all business dealings are conducted at

219

such establishments." Her voice dripped with sarcasm.

"Maybe try not to speak so refined when we're near other people. Try and mimic those around you." More buildings came into view. "Use some slang. Curse."

"I most certainly will not curse. I can, however, use some slang as you call it."

He chuckled. "This should be good fun."

A cart neared. The driver didn't even bother to glance their way as he steered the horses past them.

"No wonder Russeks wear those fur things."

"Excuse me?"

"It's so cold here. I'm sure the fur wraps keep them warm. At first I thought it was to intimidate others, but now I see it's for survival."

They would stand out even more without cloaks of some sort. Especially if Harley kept shaking like that.

The cart stopped in the middle of the road ahead of them. Ackley stepped in front of Harley, a dagger already in his right hand.

The man driving the cart chuckled, then climbed down. "You from Melenia?" he asked in a thick accent. He was six feet four inches tall and about two hundred fifty pounds. His long dark hair was pulled back at the base of his neck.

While Ackley didn't visibly see any weapons, the man probably had one in his boot and maybe one hidden on his back. The way the man held his body, along with his muscled arms, indicated he was well versed in the art of fighting. He probably didn't need a weapon—his hands were deadly enough.

Yet, he hadn't made any move against Ackley or Harley. Weighing his options, Ackley decided to shrug.

"I've been waiting with your *friend*. When he saw you pass

by, he sent me after you." He folded his arms, tilting his head to the side, studying Ackley. "He didn't expect you to bring a woman along."

Ackley shrugged again. "What difference does it make?" He hoped having Harley there didn't prevent him from meeting with Kerdan.

"Just wasn't part of the plan," he replied. "Your friend who arranged everything never did tell me your name."

"I'm Prince Ackley of Marsden."

The man threw his head back, laughing. "You've got balls, I'll give you that."

Harley moved closer to Ackley. He wished she hadn't moved because by doing so, she drew attention to herself.

"Who's the woman?"

"Lady Harley of Melenia."

The man squinted. "She looks familiar."

"I recognize you," Harley said, stepping beside Ackley. "You were in the kitchen that day during the takeover."

His eyes darkened. "That I was." He waved them forward. "Get in the cart before someone else sees you. I'm taking you to Kerdan."

Interesting that the man didn't use a title with Kerdan's name. "How far away is he?" Ackley asked.

"I should have you there tomorrow sometime. I can't give you any information beyond that."

Ackley took hold of Harley's hand, leading her to the cart.

"The name's Gelik Wolf." He smiled wryly as he climbed onto the driver's bench.

Ackley thought he was missing something with the name. Regardless, Gelik felt trustworthy, so he helped Harley up into the back of the cart, climbing in behind her. The cart lurched forward, heading away from the village.

"At least we don't have to walk," Harley whispered, settling in beside Ackley, closer than necessary. The back of the cart was empty save for a few pieces of straw.

"I was looking forward to getting a room for the night and having nothing to do but tend to my wife." It was a bold thing to say, but he felt like pushing the boundaries. Her eyes widened, and her lips parted slightly. He longed to lower his head, kissing her. However, that was one line he couldn't cross.

"I've never met anyone like you," she whispered.

He hadn't expected her to say that. "No, I suppose I'm one of a kind." He stretched his legs out before him, crossing his ankles.

Her hand reached out, resting on his forearm. He held still, surprised she was touching him again. "I think that's a good thing. I'm not sure the world could handle two of you."

A laugh escaped him. "Who knew you were so funny."

"Likewise."

<hr />

Arriving sometime *tomorrow* ended up being a rather liberal use of the word. They'd been riding in this cart for well over twenty-four hours. Darkness had descended for the second time. Ackley was pretty sure *tomorrow* was at an end. At least Gelik fed them. Granted, it was bread. But food was food.

Harley hadn't spoken much. She'd remained at his side, resting against him, not attempting to make small talk. Which was good. They didn't need Gelik overhearing their conversations.

"I didn't think it possible, but it's getting even colder," Harley mumbled, snuggling closer to Ackley as the cart trudged along. "I can't feel my fingers, but I can feel my toes." She wiggled her feet. "Thank you for the socks and boots." She'd thanked him over a dozen times already.

He wrapped his arm around her shoulders, tucking her in close. Since it was so frigid out, she didn't even argue and instead, seemed to melt against him. Their nearness was out of necessity, nothing more.

The cart finally came to a stop. Ackley glanced around, not seeing any signs of a town or village nearby.

"We're here," Gelik announced.

"It doesn't look like we're anywhere," Harley commented as she climbed out.

There were at least two men in the nearby trees. Ackley couldn't see them, but he could feel them. "Are they your men?"

Gelik smiled. "You could say that." He whistled.

A man swung down from the tree to Ackley's right, landing deftly on his feet.

"These two are here to see Kerdan," Gelik told the man.

He nodded. "I'll take care of them."

Gelik thumped the guy on his shoulder, then swung back onto the driver's bench. He gave the command, and the horses took off.

Harley remained four feet to Ackley's right, not moving.

"That won't be necessary," the man said, eyeing the dagger hidden in Ackley's palm. "You can put your weapon away."

"Forgive me for being prudent," Ackley said. "It's not often I'm dropped off in the middle of nowhere."

"You're not in the middle of nowhere. Kerdan is close by. We couldn't risk bringing the cart any closer to the manor."

Because Kerdan was in exile. Ackley put his dagger away and reached for Harley's hand. She took it, holding on tightly.

The man neared.

"You're also one of Kerdan's men," Harley said, her voice soft in the quiet night.

"I am. And you saved his life." He lowered his head. "Thank you. Now, if you'll come with me." He turned and headed off the dirt road and into the cover of the trees.

They followed him, trying to stay close since it was so dark out. They traveled in silence for about a mile. Standing at the tree line, a large manor stood in an open field before them.

"Kerdan is staying there. You will meet with him tomorrow."

Harley moaned. "Please tell me we're not sleeping out here tonight because if we are, I won't have any fingers come morning."

"Of course you're not staying outside. Who do you think we are? Barbarians? Wild wolves?" He shook his head. "Follow me." He led them over to a large rock. Kneeling on the ground, he removed a square wooden door. "Climb in."

Ackley went first. He climbed down the ladder to a tunnel about seven feet tall by four feet wide. Harley joined him a moment later.

"Take the tunnel to the other side. Knock twice, then once, then five times. Tell them Gelik sent you." He closed the door, plunging them into darkness.

Harley clutched onto him. "I can't see."

"Shocking."

She smacked him.

"Just hang on. I'll lead the way."

"Excellent. That way if you fall into a crevice, I won't."

"Not if I drag you down with me." He started walking, his right arm out in front of him, feeling the way. Plodding through the tunnel, he contemplated this new side of Harley. She was funny and clever. He sort of enjoyed being around her.

Which was dangerous—especially considering one of the plans he was leaning toward in regards to her.

When he came to a dead end, he felt around until he found a ladder. He climbed it. At the top, he knocked as he'd been instructed. When the door opened, a large Russek greeted him. Ackley quickly introduced Harley and himself, telling the man Gelik had sent them and they were there for a meeting with Kerdan.

The man nodded once, then waved them up. Ackley climbed out of the tunnel, finding himself in a square room lined with weapons. It appeared to be some sort of indoor training facility. Once Harley joined him, the man led them from the room and into the main portion of the manor. He took them up a flight of stairs to the second floor.

Halfway down the hallway, the Russek stopped. "You can stay in here." He opened one of the doors. "There will be a guard posted out here all night. If you need anything, let him know. Do not leave this room. Food will be brought to you. Once it's time for your meeting, I'll come and get you."

Ackley and Harley stepped into the room. The door shut, the lock sliding into place.

"This is a beautiful house," Harley said. "I wonder who lives here."

Ackley had been contemplating the same thing. "I'm just glad we have a roof over our heads and we're not in that cart any longer." He surveyed the room. One bed, two armoires, and a wash table. No settee, which meant he'd be sleeping on the floor. Again.

Harley removed her bag. "I'm going to change into something more comfortable."

He continued examining the room, searching for a hidden door, weapons, anything of importance. The room appeared to be a regular guest suite. Sitting on the edge of the bed, he took off his boots. When he glanced up, he saw Harley had her back to him as she removed her tunic, revealing her bare back.

Ackley froze. She was changing...in front of him.

She pulled on her nightdress over her head, letting the fabric slide down her body. Then she reached under the material, pushing her pants off.

He wiped the sweat from his brow.

With her back still to him, she unbraided her hair, running her fingers through it. When she turned around, her eyebrows rose in surprise. He hadn't meant to sit there, frozen in place, watching her like a miscreant. To make matters worse, Harley's nightdress was so thin, he could see hints of what lie hidden beneath. The temperature of the room increased, and he could barely breathe.

Harley rushed over to the chair, snatching the blanket draped over the back of it, wrapping it around her body. "I can sleep on the floor this time."

The desire to pull the blanket away from her inundated him. Only, he didn't want to stop there. He'd remove her nightdress, caressing her luscious body beneath. He needed to get a hold of himself. He couldn't let her know the power she held over him. "I can't allow you to sleep on the floor." His voice sounded normal, surprising him. "Please take the bed. I won't have it any other way."

She chewed on her bottom lip, hesitating.

He took the top blanket from the bed, laying it on the floor, not giving her a chance to argue. When he laid down, he was happy to not be able to see her. It helped clear his head. Harley was Owen's cousin. His future brother-in-law's only kin. And she'd recently lost her husband.

"Why don't you sleep in the bed," Harley suggested, her voice barely above a whisper. "With me."

He must have heard her wrong. His heart pounded so hard he feared she could hear it.

"It's large enough for the both of us. We can even put pillows in the middle, separating our bodies. We're both adults. It shouldn't be a problem."

He swallowed, unsure he could share a bed with her—even if it was platonic.

"Otherwise, I'm sleeping on the floor, whether you take the bed or not."

Sucking in a deep breath, he stood. She was on the other side of the bed, standing there, not meeting his eyes. "Fine." The bed was large. "I'll take this side." He stretched out on top of the blankets, using the one he'd had on the floor to cover himself.

Harley slid under the blankets, turning away from him.

If he'd gotten under them with her, he didn't think he could make it through the night knowing she was only a few feet away. The covers kept a barrier between them—one that couldn't be penetrated.

"Without a fire, it's rather cold in here," she whispered. "I've had the warmth from your body all day." She shivered, the bed shaking slightly.

Those words almost undid him. He had to turn away, his back to her. "Goodnight, Harley."

"Goodnight."

As he laid there, he considered his precarious plan once again. Before, it had just been an idea. Now, he was seeing firsthand how love could be a dangerous weapon. Dare he harness that power? Because if he chose to, it could be the key to everything.

CHAPTER SIXTEEN

*H*arley woke up but kept her eyes shut as she tried to remember where she was. Warmth surrounded her along with strong arms. The events of last night gradually came back to her. She and Ackley were in Russek, waiting to speak to Kerdan. And she was in bed. With Ackley.

Slowly, she opened her eyes and found Ackley's alert face in front of hers.

"Good morning," he said. "I've been afraid to move and wake you."

"Why are we hugging?" Because as much as his arms were around her, hers were equally clinging to him.

"Um, I'm guessing we were cold?" He raised a single eyebrow.

"That makes sense." The lower half of their bodies were separated by a few covers. It had been smart of him not to climb under them alongside her. Who knows what state they would have woken up in.

He wiggled his arms free and sat up, running his hands over his face and through his hair.

Harley stretched, trying not to think about how she'd just been tangled together with Ackley.

"You should dress. That way when someone comes for us, we'll be ready." He went over to the window, his back to her.

Harley climbed out of bed, then padded over to the chair where she'd left her bag. Folded on top of it were thick wool pants and a fur-lined cape. "Ackley, did you procure these items for me?" Her hands shook at the possibility of someone coming into their room last night while they were sleeping.

"I asked the guard on duty if there was anything lying around that you could wear. He found the items, not me."

Again, his thoughtfulness surprised her. She dressed quickly, thankful for the warmer clothing, all the while trying not to think about this softer side of Ackley.

"I'm sorry if I made you uncomfortable last night," he said, his voice gruff. "It was not my intention."

When she turned to face him, she found him staring out the window. "I know. And the same goes for me. I didn't mean to cling to you like a harlot."

Laughing, he turned to face her. "You always surprise me."

"What do you mean?"

"You never say or act the way I expect you to."

She felt the same way about him. She was about to tell him so when someone knocked on the door.

Ackley hurried over and opened it.

"Kerdan will see you now," someone said from out in the hallway.

They gathered their belongings and followed the man to the first level. He stopped outside the training room. "Kerdan is waiting for you." He made no move to follow them.

They entered and found Kerdan standing alone in the middle of the room. As before, he wore a fur draped over his shoulders and had war symbols painted on his face. Even though he reeked of intimidation, Harley rushed forward to greet him.

"Prince Kerdan, thank you for seeing us today." She curtseyed.

His focus remained on Ackley.

"This is Prince Ackley of Marsden, a kingdom across the ocean."

The two men stood there staring at one another for what felt like forever.

"Since you are from Marsden, I assume you'd like this." Kerdan withdrew a piece of paper from his pocket and handed it to Ackley.

Ackley took it. "I'm not often surprised." He tore the paper in two before shoving it in his pocket.

"If you're wondering," Kerdan said, "that letter did not reach us in time. It had no bearing on events."

Harley really wanted to know what the paper contained, but she kept her mouth shut.

Kerdan folded his arms, then looked at Harley. "I want to thank you for saving my life." Again, his kind voice was strangely at odds with his rugged appearance. "I am deeply sorry for the loss of the royal family. That was not supposed to happen."

A mixture of anger and understanding warred within. "Perhaps if you hadn't invaded my kingdom, my family would be alive." Actions had consequences. Even though he didn't intend for her family to perish, they had.

He nodded. "I believe that is a much more in-depth discussion that neither one of us is prepared for today." Kerdan glanced at Ackley. "Your man said you needed to speak with me."

"Yes. I have questions I hope you can answer."

"Before we begin, he told me Marsden is working with Melenia."

"We are," Ackley answered.

"He said you will guarantee an alliance."

Harley curled her fingers into fists. An alliance? Ackley couldn't make such bargains without Owen. And what about revenge?

"Yes. In exchange for your cooperation and bringing those responsible for killing Harley's family to justice, Marsden will sign a treaty with you, Prince Kerdan. Not anyone else in Russek."

"Agreed."

Ackley was making a deal with Kerdan on her behalf? Her breathing sped up. This was what she'd hoped for all along. And Ackley was going to make it happen. Anticipation swelled within.

"I'd like to know who you've been working with in Melenia."

"I haven't been working with anyone."

Ackley's eyes narrowed.

"Queen Jana is responsible for this. If you want revenge, she's the one you want to kill."

Although Kerdan said it simply, Harley heard the hatred seeping through his words. "Why her?" she asked.

"She wants to destroy Emperion. Since Russek's army isn't large enough to go to war against them, she coaxed my father into taking soldiers from Melenia."

"But you planned the invasion?" Ackley asked.

"I did. My father intended to march across Melenia, taking the men for soldiers and slaughtering the women and children. I decided to step in. I thought I could get soldiers from Melenia without killing innocent people. It looks like I was wrong. And for that, I am sorry."

"If you weren't working with anyone in Melenia, who was?"

"After Jana killed my father, I went through his office. I found correspondence between him and Commander Beck. Detailed information about Beck's departure from Melenia along with a large portion of the army."

"I overheard Soma speaking to the traitor," Harley said. "Can we interrogate Soma and find out who it is?"

Both men looked at her with odd expressions on their faces, as if she'd said something funny.

"Prince Soma is dead," Kerdan replied, striking that idea down. "I searched his room, but nothing revealed who the Melenia traitor is."

"What about Queen Jana?" Harley asked.

"I am in exile, so I haven't had the opportunity to go through her quarters."

"Who's controlling your army?" Ackley asked.

"A little more than half are loyal to me; the rest are blindly following Jana." He focused on Harley as he said, "Please know that as soon as my father died, I gave the order to withdraw all Russek troops from Melenia."

Probably because he needed them here in order to overthrow Jana and reclaim his throne.

"They never should have been there in the first place. I'm sorry I didn't get them out sooner."

Ackley folded his arms. "What about the Melenia soldiers Russek took?"

"They're free. They were told to go home. If they haven't returned, they're probably in Kricok, Fia, or Landania. No one knows what's going on in Melenia or who's in control of the kingdom right now. Since I'm in exile, I haven't been able to do much more than pull my soldiers out and free Melenia's citizens."

"What's your next move?" Ackley inquired.

"I'm going to kill Jana and retake my kingdom. What's yours?"

Ackley smiled. "The same. We're going to oust the traitor king and put Owen on the throne."

Kerdan nodded. "Once we've each accomplished our goals, let's meet again."

"Agreed."

"I have two horses saddled and ready to go. Hopefully the next time we meet will be under better circumstances. If you'll excuse me, I have some guests arriving shortly, and I must prepare."

"Second spear on the south wall?" Ackley asked.

Kerdan smiled. "Yes. And it's nice to meet a fellow warrior-prince." He left the room.

Harley had a million questions for Ackley, but now was not the time.

Ackley rushed over to the spear, pressing on it. A door in the floor opened, revealing the tunnel they'd entered through yesterday.

They made their way back through the tunnel. When they

climbed out, they found two horses saddled and loaded with the necessary provisions for a week of traveling.

Harley wrapped the cloak around her body, then climbed on the horse. They traveled about a mile before she spoke. "What did you think of Prince Kerdan?"

"He will be King Kerdan soon, of that I have no doubt."

He did seem the sort of man who succeeded in all he did. "I've never met anyone like him before."

"Neither have I." He adjusted the reins in his hands. "He is far more complex than what I thought upon first meeting him. He seems to be an intelligent man. And skilled in fighting. I wouldn't want to go up against him."

"Why?" she asked, the desire to taunt him rising. "Would you lose?"

Ackley eyed her sidelong. "No."

"I can understand your hesitation. He was a foot taller than you and twice as wide."

He chuckled. "I wouldn't want to go up against him because then I'd have to kill him. And I rather like the guy."

"You have that much faith in your skills?"

"He's a trained soldier. I'm a trained assassin."

The words hung heavy between them. She finally found the courage to ask what had been bothering her all along. "Why train a prince to kill?" They had soldiers for that sort of thing.

The wind whipped down the mountainside, blowing against them so forcefully Harley felt the horse shift. She pulled her cloak tightly around her.

"It's a long story. The gist of it is I was used and manipulated. I was made a weapon to take down my father and his legacy."

"I thought you said the knights were the protectors of the kingdom?" Didn't that include the king?

"They are. But what I became, who I became, was something else."

"But why you?"

"Let me ask you a question," he said, his voice suddenly softer. She gestured for him to continue. "Who's more dangerous? An assassin who sneaks into a castle late at night to kill the king? Or the woman lying in bed with the king while he's sleeping soundly?"

With that analogy, she understood why a prince would make the perfect assassin. "You have access to people and places normal people do not."

"Exactly." He adjusted the reins in his hands. "I knew my way around the castle, I knew the castle's secrets, where my father liked to go to be alone."

The sky darkened. The wind whirled by so violently that the sound made the hairs on her arms rise. "Am I to understand that you enjoy being a knight but not an assassin?" Or was she reading too much into what he'd said?

"I enjoy helping my kingdom and my family. I love the freedom being a knight gives me."

It seemed like there was more he wanted to say. There was definitely more she wanted to know, especially since he hadn't addressed the second part of what she'd said about being an assassin.

However, he kept glancing at the sky. "I think it's going to start raining. We should find shelter." A large mountain loomed to the north, a forest to the south. Ackley led the way between the towering trees. After fifty feet or so, he stopped. "I don't want to go in any farther and risk getting lost."

Harley dismounted. "Lost? You? I didn't think it possible."

"There's even a tent in these supplies," he mused.

"You take care of that, and I'll tend to the horses." Harley led the animals over to a low-lying branch, which she tied them to. Then she patted them down and gave them some water. After she finished, she joined Ackley inside the tent. They shared a loaf of bread.

"I hope the storm passes through while we sleep. Then we can be on our way tomorrow first thing." Ackley handed her a blanket. "There's only two. One for each of us."

The temperature continued to drop now that the sun had set. Harley feared it would snow instead of rain. "Maybe we should share." She didn't look at Ackley's face because she didn't want to know what he thought of her suggestion. While they might have shared the bed last night, she didn't want him to think she was coming on to him. "I also have my cloak. It seems better to share than for each of us to be cold and not sleep." Although, he probably intended to keep watch and wouldn't bother sleeping.

"Harley." His gruff voice made her toes curl. She loved when he said her name like that. "Are you sure?"

She looked at him then. "I'm certain. It's not like it means anything. We're just trying to stay warm."

"Okay." He spread out one of the blankets on the ground and then laid down.

She stretched out next to him, being careful not to touch him. Then he covered them with the other blanket, placing her cloak on top of that.

"It's going to get a lot colder," he said. "If you need to nestle next to me, I'll understand."

"I think the blanket will suffice."

He chuckled. "Why are you afraid to touch me?"

"I'm not afraid to touch you."

"Prove it."

She jabbed him in the ribs. "See?"

236

"No one will know if we're snuggled up together or not."

"Did you just use the word snuggled? You? Ackley? An assassin-prince?"

"I thought the word might be more enticing. All I'm thinking about are my toes. If you're next to me, my toes will be warmer. And really, that's all that matters."

She wanted to roll over and curl her body next to his. But she couldn't. He was a prince, and she only a lady. They weren't even from the same kingdom. And her husband had recently died. She should be in mourning, not lying beside another man.

"You're not eager to cuddle since you have those warm socks on," he teased. "The ones I purchased for you back in Landania."

"You're right. I am rather warm from the socks and pants. Too bad you don't have warm socks and pants like me. What'll I do if I wake in the morning and find you dead? What if you actually freeze to death?"

"It'll be your fault for not snuggling with me."

"Isn't snuggling just another word for stealing my body warmth?"

"If you don't want to share your body with me, Harley, just say so."

She sucked in a breath, not knowing how to respond. She'd thought they were simply teasing one another, but now, she wasn't so sure. Was there a kernel of truth to what he said? Did he truly want to cuddle with her? Not for warmth but for need? Every moment she'd spent with Ackley, she'd learned more about him. While he was still the arrogant prick she'd first met, she'd also discovered that he was sincere, kind, compassionate, and considerate. Her entire body warmed thinking about being intimate with someone like him.

And that was why she couldn't get too close. He was slowly chipping away at the steel cage she'd erected around her heart. The cage that protected her from men like Lyle. Men who only used. If she let Ackley in, it might be wonderful for a while. But it wouldn't last. He'd return home and find a princess to marry. Someone equal to him in every way. And she'd be left here to pick up the pieces. She wouldn't do it. She would never give herself to a man. Now that she was finally free from Lyle and her marriage, she would be her own person, not owned by another man ever again.

In the darkness, she could barely see the outline of Ackley's body, only a foot away.

"Stop worrying that pretty little head of yours," he whispered. "I'm just teasing you. In case you haven't noticed, I like to tease. Now go to sleep. We have a long day ahead of us tomorrow."

Traveling via horseback was much faster than being stuck in the back of a cart traveling over a rickety dirt road. The horses were strong and quick, taking them to the Russek and Melenia border late the following day.

"Let's cross before we stop for the night," Ackley suggested.

"Good idea." While Kerdan had been kind, she didn't trust other Russeks to behave the same way. The sooner they were in Melenia, the better.

"The horses may be a little skittish when we cross," he said, implying that the animals wouldn't handle the rotting heads on spikes well.

She couldn't blame them—she could barely handle it

herself. The only way to survive was to ignore what she saw. Because if she allowed herself to dwell on the death and devastation around her, it would be too much to recover from. Keeping a tight hold on her horse's reins, Harley steered her way between the line of death. Once her horse stepped foot in Melenia, a sense of relief filled her. "Is this the sort of thing you do back home?"

"What do you mean?"

"This. Going on missions. Meeting with important people in secret."

"Yes."

"Do you usually go on them alone?" Even though she'd gotten to know Ackley better over the past few days, she didn't know much about his personal life. Like if he had a woman back home. The thought didn't sit well with her.

"It depends. Sometimes my brother accompanies me. I have a group of men that I travel and work with. Why do you ask?"

"I've enjoyed our time together," she admitted. "I've gotten to see more of the world this trip than I have previously seen."

"You sound like my sister." He adjusted in the saddle. "It is one of the reasons she came here. She wanted to see more of the world."

Harley understood. "How long do you plan on remaining in Melenia?" Perhaps she could go on another mission with him.

"Until my sister is married, crowned, and I feel Melenia is safe for her. Then I will return to Marsden."

So he wouldn't be here for more than a season or two. She needed to stop becoming attached to this man. This assassin-prince.

They crested a low hill. At the bottom, a long, narrow road stretched out before them. About a mile ahead, two people on horses blocked the way.

"Who do you think that is?" she asked. It couldn't be Russek soldiers. Not only did they have a different build, but she didn't think they'd be in Melenia. That only left two possibilities. Either they were soldiers under Owen's command, or soldiers under the traitorous king.

"There's only one way to find out."

CHAPTER SEVENTEEN

ACKLEY

*A*ckley knew exactly who the one rider was, and she'd only be here if there was a problem. A complication. And he'd much prefer if there were none of those right now. However, one thing was always certain—things never went according to plan.

"Is that Ledger?" Harley asked as they rode down the hill.

He squinted, trying to get a better look at the second rider, who appeared to be Ledger. An interesting pairing. Yet, somehow it made sense.

As they approached, Gytha's eyes narrowed, watching the two of them. She probably didn't recognize Harley in pants.

"Is my sister okay?" Ackley asked when they were close enough for Gytha to hear.

"Your sister is well."

"Then what is it?" he asked, pulling his horse to a halt.

"Not here," Gytha said.

He turned his horse in a slow circle, verifying that they were indeed alone, not a person around for miles.

"Is my cousin okay?" Harley inquired.

"Yes," Ledger replied. "No harm has come to him."

"Then let's have it," Ackley said, wondering why all the hesitancy.

"It's getting dark," Ledger stated. "I'd like to get farther away from the Russek border before we're forced to stop for the night. Once we're in a secure location, Gytha is permitted to repeat King Owen's message."

"Then lead the way," Ackley said, now more nervous than before, not buying the bit about them being too close to Russek. He suspected they didn't want him doing something stupid. By waiting until dark to tell him, it limited his options.

They kept to the road, heading west, deeper into Melenia. Gytha and Ledger rode in front, Ackley and Harley behind them.

"What do you think it is?" Harley asked, chewing on her lip. She did that when she was nervous or thinking about something.

Ackley pulled his horse to a stop so he could look her in the eyes. Her blue eyes were clear, open, wanting an honest answer. "I don't know. Owen chose to send someone I trust and someone you trust. Whatever it is, it must be important." Especially since Gytha had left Idina's side.

"What are the two of you doing?" Gytha demanded. "We need to keep moving. Let's go."

"Does she always speak to you that way?" Harley inquired.

"She does." He smiled. "It's one of the reasons I like her."

"Oh." Her head jerked back slightly.

"Now!" Gytha snapped.

Chuckling, Ackley nudged his horse.

"I didn't realize you and Gytha had an arrangement."

"An arrangement?" He had no idea what she meant by that.

"Or whatever you call it where you're from."

"An arrangement," he repeated, trying to understand her.

"I didn't realize the two of you were involved romantically." She raised her chin, her focus on the road ahead of them.

He burst out laughing. "What gave you that crazy idea?"

"You just said you liked her." Her brows furrowed in confusion.

"I do. I like her as a friend and a soldier." He mulled over how much to tell her. "We've been through a lot together." She didn't need to know the details. He didn't want to relive them anyway.

"Oh." She chewed on her lip again. "You're not married, are you?"

"Me? Most certainly not."

"Engaged?"

"No way."

"You say that like it's a bad thing."

He threw it right back at her. "Did you enjoy your marriage?"

She pursed her lips. "No."

"Because of your position, you had to make an advantageous match. You weren't consulted about who you married, were you?"

She shook her head.

"So you can see how someone in my position would be forced to make a political match, as well."

She nodded.

"That's my problem. I refuse to marry for someone else's agenda." He couldn't believe he was talking about this with Harley.

"It would be nice to marry for love," she said so softly he almost missed it.

"Love?"

She nodded again.

Curiosity got the better of him. "Have you ever been in love?"

"Once when I was much younger. He was my brother's friend." She smiled. "When my parents found out I fancied him, he wasn't allowed to come to our house anymore. I never saw him again. My brother said he wasn't good enough for me."

Strange that they considered Lyle good enough for her. "I imagine a great many men aren't good enough for you."

"There's an abandoned barn up ahead," Ledger announced. "We'll sleep there for the night."

"We passed it on the way to meet you," Gytha added. "We checked it out. It's safe."

As the sky darkened, the four of them reached a small, secluded barn on the outskirts of a village. There were no horses in sight, leaving Ackley to believe that Russek must have taken them. He dismounted, observing the area. The walls had holes, and the roof was in dire need of repair. If a storm came through, he wasn't certain the barn would hold up. Perhaps there weren't any horses because no one lived here and the place was abandoned. However, it would be better than sleeping in a tent for the night.

While removing his horse's saddle, Gytha approached.

"We need to talk," she whispered.

Harley dismounted, and Ledger rushed over to help her. He removed her saddle, irritating Ackley because she was perfectly capable of doing it on her own.

"What's your take on Lady Harley?" Gytha whispered.

"Why? What's going on?"

"Owen wants to know if you have any hesitations about

trusting her implicitly? Something about depending on how it went with her parents?" Her face remained expressionless, although Ackley could tell she wanted to know the details.

"I trust her. Owen doesn't need to worry."

She nodded.

"Why?" he asked.

"Your answer determined our next course of action."

"Which is?"

"There's a well not far from here," Ledger said, interrupting them. "I'll get the horses water."

"And I'll handle supper," Gytha said.

"Harley and I will see to the horses."

"We'll finish this conversation later," Gytha whispered before going over to her horse and grabbing a bow and arrows. She slunk into the nearby forest.

"Is Ledger from these parts?" Ackley asked Harley when they were alone.

"I have no idea."

It surprised him that she didn't know much about the man, considering she'd spent several weeks with him.

Once all the saddles had been removed, Ackley slid the barn doors open. Harley led two of the horses inside while he brought the remaining two in. After situating each in its own stall, they found some hay and fed the animals. Ledger returned with buckets of water, putting one in each stall.

Toward the front of the barn, Ackley pushed a few farming tools out of the way, making a space large enough for them to sit comfortably.

"If we keep the doors open, we can have a fire here," Ledger said.

Ackley eyed the hay and half rotten wood all around them.

"Never mind," Ledger mumbled. "I'll make a fire outside and cook the food there."

"Good idea," Ackley replied, patting the man on his back. "I suggest you get to it."

Once Ledger exited, Ackley closed the doors, trying to keep the cold air out even though it was futile.

"There's a loft in the back." Harley pointed up behind them.

"The ladder looks somewhat questionable." Several of the rungs were missing.

Harley shrugged. "Want to go up?"

"Sure." They had nothing else to do until it was time to eat. As Ackley climbed the ladder, the entire thing shook. Most of the rungs bowed under his weight. At the top, he observed the area. There were a few bales of hay and a couple blankets. There was enough room for him to move around, though he couldn't stand up straight without hitting his head. The flooring looked solid—no holes that he could see.

Harley yelped.

Ackley peered down in time to see a rat running by her feet. He descended the ladder.

"I'm sleeping on my horse tonight," she hissed. "There's no way I'm going to be where a rat can crawl on me."

He chuckled. "Or, you can sleep up there." He pointed at the loft. "There are even blankets. It looks safe enough." Not that a rat couldn't crawl up there, but she didn't need to know that.

"Then that's where I'll be."

The barn doors slid open, revealing Gytha. "Time to eat."

Outside, Ledger and Gytha sat by the fire. Harley and Ackley joined them. Ledger cut the cooked rabbit meat, handing each of them a plateful. The sky had turned dark, hundreds of stars dotting the night.

Ackley had been waiting for Gytha to tell him what was going on. As they ate in silence, anxiety started to take root. Unable to handle it, he set his plate aside. "Tell me why the two of you are here."

Ledger glanced at Gytha.

"Something happened," Gytha announced.

Ackley rolled his eyes. "Get to the point."

"Shortly after the two of you left, a messenger from the royal castle arrived."

"A messenger just rode right up to Owen?" he asked in disbelief.

Gytha sighed. "Well, no. He rode into our camp. Apparently, the traitorous king got wind that the army had returned, so he sent a messenger."

Ackley rubbed his forehead, knowing he wasn't going to like whatever Gytha said. "Continue."

"He had a letter for Commander Beck. When we informed him the commander was no longer with us, he asked to speak to whomever was in charge."

"He didn't want to speak to Owen?" Ackley asked.

"Correct. When Owen stepped forward, the messenger seemed confused." Gytha glanced at Ledger. However, he shook his head, so she continued. "He handed over the letter. It said that the king has a list of every soldier from Melenia who made the journey to Marsden. It also said that each soldier's wife and children are being held in an undisclosed location. Once the soldiers return to the castle and swear fealty to the new king, he will reunite them with their loved ones."

A smart move to ensure loyalty. "Who is claiming to be king?"

"The messenger didn't give a name," Ledger said around a mouthful of food.

"And did the message explicitly state what happens should the soldiers not return to the castle and swear fealty?" Ackley inquired.

"He said the soldiers would find their loved ones' heads on spikes," Gytha answered.

Ackley had several possible plans running through his head. "And the two of you," he looked from Gytha to Ledger, "came here to find Harley and me simply to tell us this information?" While the news was important, it didn't warrant them coming all this way.

Gytha fumbled with the hilt of her dagger. "There's more." She wouldn't meet Ackley's eyes.

He had to force his temper to remain in check. "Just tell me and get it over with."

Gytha's shoulders rose and fell. "Fine." She took another deep breath. "Please don't kill me. I'm only the messenger."

Harley reached over and clutched Ackley's hand. The simple gesture helped him remain sitting there by the fire, across from Gytha, and not jumping up and strangling Ledger. Not that any of this was Ledger's fault. He just didn't care for him.

Gytha's attention went to Ackley and Harley's clasped hands. Her brows drew together slightly, then she shook her head. "As I was saying. I'm only doing my job. Owen ordered all Melenia soldiers to proceed to the castle without him. They are to swear loyalty to the new king and get their loved ones back."

Ackley refrained from saying anything. He waved his hand, gesturing for her to continue. Because there had to be more to it than that.

"He ordered all Marsden soldiers to head south. You are to join with your men as soon as possible. Once you reach Kricok, you're to ask for an audience with Empress Rema. Owen wants you to let her know you seek temporary asylum. Then, once Owen is ready, he'll contact you."

Once Owen was organized and the soldiers had their loved ones somewhere safe, Ackley assumed he would rejoin Owen to help him retake the throne. "I'll leave first thing tomorrow morning to meet up with my sister and the Marsden soldiers. I assume you'll be going with me, Gytha?"

"Yes. But..."

"But what?" he said.

Harley squeezed his hand harder.

"Your sister didn't go south with the Marsden soldiers."

"I'm not sure remaining with Owen is a wise move," he replied. "Why didn't you stay with her? I gave you explicit instructions."

"That's the other part I need to tell you." Gytha continued fidgeting with the hilt of her dagger. "I am not protecting Princess Idina any longer."

Everything suddenly went silent around Ackley as he processed the information. "Why?" The word sounded loud, demanding.

"Owen and Idina married," Ledger said.

Ackley blinked. Once. Twice.

"Idina thought it best for them to marry," Gytha explained. "That way she could stay with Owen and help him."

That was something his sister would do. But he'd missed her wedding. And she'd married a man with a target on his head, thus putting her in even more danger. If word got out, she would be the perfect person to kidnap to get to Owen. He rubbed his forehead with his free hand. "Where are they going to go? And who is with them?"

"They are going to Kreng. He took six of his most proficient men."

Only six men to protect Owen and Idina. Ackley's headache worsened.

"There are soldiers in Kreng," Harley said. "He is probably going there to try and rally them."

Ackley tried to look at the situation objectively. He tilted his head to the right, cracking his neck. He wanted to immediately rush out of there and seek Idina. He knew he could ensure her safety. The problem was, as a Marsden prince, he was responsible for the Marsden soldiers. But his sister was his family. He couldn't choose between duty and family.

"What about me?" Harley asked. "Am I going to meet up with Owen?"

His first reaction was to say no, that Harley would remain with him. However, it wasn't his place.

"Yes," Ledger answered. "I'll escort you to Penlar," Ledger said. "Owen and Idina will meet you there. Then you'll travel to Kreng together."

"Owen doesn't even know if Penlar is still standing," Ackley pointed out.

"He said it didn't matter. He just needed a spot for us to meet."

Ackley wasn't keen on the idea, especially since his run-in with those soldiers there.

"I'll ensure she makes it safely to her cousin," Ledger insisted.

The idea of Harley traveling alone with Ledger grated on Ackley's nerves. But he knew he shouldn't object.

Harley released his hand. "I'm tired," she announced, eyeing the barn wearily.

"We should sleep so we can leave at first light," Gytha said. "Ledger, if you can take the first watch, I'll take the second, Ackley the third." Both men agreed.

Ackley stood, pulling Harley up alongside him. "I'll walk you to the loft." Turning to Gytha he said, "I made room for us right inside the door."

"I'm going to do a perimeter run for Ledger and then I'll be in."

Ackley led Harley to the barn. Earlier, he'd spotted a lantern just inside the door. He found and lit it.

"In Kreng, I was working at the inn so I wouldn't have to sleep in the barn with the animals."

Ackley chuckled. "At least there're only horses in here."

"It's still a barn and horses are animals."

At the bottom of the ladder, he held the light out so Harley could see as she climbed up. Once she reached the top, he couldn't see her in the darkness. "Do you want me to bring the lantern up to you?"

"Yes, please."

He looped the handle over his arm then climbed to the top, praying the ladder didn't slip and he didn't light the entire barn on fire. When he reached the top, he pushed the lantern toward Harley.

She grabbed it, dragging it closer to her. "Thank you." She glanced at him, her brow furrowing.

Something in his chest tightened. "Do you want to talk?" Gytha and Ledger had revealed quite a bit of information, and Harley had barely said two words. "I can be a friend if you need one."

She bit her bottom lip, then scooted back. "If I wanted a friend, I'd seek Ledger or Gytha out."

The comment stung.

"I don't think you fit the definition of a friend," she revealed.

Ackley took a deep breath, figuring she only thought of him as an assassin or prince, not as a person. Not as a friend. "Of course. Well, if you need anything, I'll be right down there near the door." He started to descend the ladder.

"Wait." She reached out, as if to grab him. "Let me explain what I mean. Please, join me for a minute."

His body moved of its own accord. The next thing he knew, he was sitting beside her, his leg brushing hers.

Her lips curved into a small grin. It was enough to bring a smile to his face.

"I'm sorry, I didn't mean to imply that you are less than a friend."

He had no idea what to say to that.

"I don't have a lot of friends, so maybe I'm bad at this." She sighed. "It's just that I consider you...as something more."

More? Had he heard her correctly?

"We've traveled across the kingdom," she explained. "We've pretended to be married and, well, I don't know. You just seem to be more than a friend to me."

He turned so his body faced hers, allowing him to look into her beautiful eyes. "I wasn't sure you even liked me."

Her focus went to her hands, playing with the hem of her cloak. "I wasn't sure I liked you, either. Until I got to know you better. I'm sad we'll be parting ways tomorrow."

So was he, but he didn't know how to say that. This beautiful woman sitting before him was stronger than any woman he'd ever met, but he couldn't tell her that. He didn't know how to bring up what he'd discovered at her house. The type of man Lyle had been. A ruthless soldier who took what he wanted. Including Harley. What she'd been through and experienced with Lyle had to be atrocious. Ackley didn't know how she was sitting there before him with a smile. It had to take a tremendous amount of strength to get through a marriage like that—which made her perfect for one of his plans. But he'd think on that later. Right now, the desire to reach out and touch her face overwhelmed him. He wanted to show her what real love was. He wanted to show her that he could be gentle and caring. She deserved a man who treated her well. He could be that man.

His eyes widened and his head jerked back, unable to believe that he'd just had those thoughts.

"Is something the matter?" she asked. "You look like you've seen a ghost."

He shook his head, dumbfounded that he was falling for this beautiful woman before him. She wasn't his type. In fact, she was the opposite of his type. She couldn't even lift a sword.

But strength came in different forms.

And Harley was strong. She was a fighter. Just not the kind he was used to. But somehow, someway, just the sort he needed.

CHAPTER EIGHTEEN

HARLEY

*H*arley couldn't figure out why Ackley had that strange look on his face. "Are you okay?" she asked.

"I'm fine," he replied, his voice hoarse.

She bit her bottom lip, noticing his potent eyes. An intense yearning filled her. She wanted to know what it felt like to touch his face, to taste his lips against hers, to have his strong hands on her back. No other man had ever sparked such desire in her.

"I should go." His leg brushed hers.

"Stay." Horror filled her that she'd just blurted that out loud. While she wanted him to stay, she didn't want him to think her desperate.

"As a friend?" he asked, his piercing eyes making her feel naked before him. He reached over, taking hold of her hand, lightly touching each of her fingers.

She had no idea how to answer that since she was still

sorting through her own feelings on the matter. "Can I ask you a question?" she whispered, focusing on their joined hands.

"Yes."

"Will you answer honestly?" She peered at his face. The intensity in his eyes made her shiver from head to toe.

"I will on one condition. I get to ask you a question, and you must answer honestly as well."

"Deal." Perhaps his question would reveal his feelings for her—if he had any.

"You go first," he whispered, his soft voice like the lick of a flame at night.

Here, in the loft, the only light came from the lantern next to them, casting the rest of the barn in darkness. "I want to know what you're thinking right now." She glanced at their joined hands again, afraid to hear his answer. Afraid to meet his piercing gaze that saw too much. That understood too much.

"I have to be honest?" He squeezed her hand.

"Yes." The word come out all breathy. Waiting for his answer, her entire body tingled with anticipation.

"I very much want to kiss you."

She froze, unable to believe he'd said that. She licked her lips and looked into his eyes, a sea of emotions swirling inside them. He was staring at her as if she were the most precious thing in the world. Almost as if he wanted her the same way she wanted him.

"Now I'll ask my question." He scooted a touch closer, their thighs touching. "Can I kiss you?"

Harley looked at his lips, wondering if she could handle one kiss or if it would leave her greedy for more. She licked her lips again. It would be worth it. A single kiss. She nodded, unable to form a word with him staring at her with hooded eyes.

His face softened, making him appear younger, more innocent somehow. Letting go of her hand, he reached forward, sliding his fingers against her cheek. Her entire body tingled at his touch. His thumb brushed over her lips and she sucked in a breath, not expecting a smoldering fire to flare to life inside of her. He tilted his head, leaning in closer, hovering mere inches from her. Unable to take the anticipation, she shifted forward and kissed him. She closed her eyes, savoring the feel of this man before her.

Then he moved his lips over hers, gently caressing her. She parted her lips, inviting him in. His tongue cautiously slid into her mouth. Her hands clutched his hair, holding his head in place as she moved her lips along with his. She shuddered as his mouth slid down the column of her throat, touching her like she'd never been touched before. The heat and power of Ackley overwhelmed her.

His hands slid to her back, pulling her body closer to his. She straddled him, cursing that she had pants on instead of a dress. She pressed her body against his, feeling the hardness in his pants. She wanted him. All of him.

Taking hold of Ackley's face, she kissed him again, this time trying to express what she felt. What she desired. Not missing a beat, he scooped her up, laying her on her back, his body on top of hers. She reveled in the feel of him on her.

He pulled back, gazing down at her. "What are we doing?"

An excellent question. "Enjoying each other's company," she replied, her voice airy.

"It's good to see you smile."

"If you want me to keep smiling," she teased, "then kiss me again."

He hesitated. "I don't want you to do anything you'll regret."

"The only thing I'll regret is if this doesn't happen." She reached up, pulling his head down toward hers.

"You're certain?"

She was. "Do you not want this?"

His body shook as he chuckled. "I've never wanted anything more."

"I feel the same way." She didn't have to say it a second time. His lips devoured hers. Savoring every moment, she was in no hurry to rush this along. Her legs tangled with his. His hands slid up her sides, pulling her shirt off. His fingers trailed over her bare skin, making her shiver. Wanting to feel him, she lifted his tunic up over his head. In the faint light, she saw several scars from swords, a testament to his profession.

His lips slid down her neck, her shoulder, and to other parts of her.

Once would never be enough with this man. Somehow, she'd fallen for this assassin-prince.

Harley peeled her eyelids open. A beam of sunlight cut through two of the boards on the side of the barn. Smiling, she stretched and rolled over. Ackley lie stretched out beside her, asleep. A blanket covered him from his naval to his knees. Resting her head on her arm, she admired the lean cut of his muscles. His face was smooth, youthful, innocent, and...happy. She couldn't help but smile. Last night had been perfect. Everything she hoped it could be with the right person.

Reaching forward, she gently trailed her finger down the side of his face. Where would they go from here? She had to travel with Ledger to Penlar where she'd meet up with Owen. Ackley had to go south to lead his army. She'd gotten so used to having him around that she couldn't envision not having him by her side. And after last night, she didn't want to be separated from him. However, they were from different kingdoms and each had their own set of duties to attend to.

Ackley's hand wrapped around her wrist, yanking her to his chest. She squealed as she fell against him.

"Morning," he said, his voice gruff and husky. He smiled, the simple act lighting up his face. "I think I could get used to this."

So could she. Unable to help herself, she kissed him, savoring the feel of his lips on hers. Her stomach growled. Apparently, she'd worked up quite the appetite last night. "We should get dressed." She kissed the tip of his nose. Turning, she located her clothes strewn all over the loft. She quickly gathered them, pulling them on.

"I didn't realize it was so late." Ackley cursed.

"What's the matter?"

"I was supposed to be on watch after Gytha." He pulled on his pants.

"Sorry," she said sheepishly, not really sorry for having monopolized his time last night. The most perfect night of her life.

"What happens now?" he asked.

"You go meet up with your army, and I'll meet up with my cousin."

"I mean between us." He slid his shirt over his head.

"I don't know." He'd eventually return to Marsden where he belonged. It wasn't like he'd stay in Melenia for her. He was a prince. And she couldn't go to Marsden with him since her life was here.

He nodded. "When you figure out what you want, let me know." He grabbed his boots and headed down the ladder.

No one had ever asked Harley what she wanted before. She'd never been given that luxury. Her life had been dictated and controlled by her parents and then Lyle. The idea of doing something simply because she wanted to was so foreign to her, she didn't know how to respond.

She followed him down the ladder. At the bottom, Ackley stood holding the ladder for her. When she reached him, she grabbed his shirt, forcing him to meet her eyes. "What do you want?"

He tried to look away, but she firmly held him in place. "I want whatever you want," he answered.

"Why give me the power? I don't understand."

He leaned his forehead against hers. "Because you deserve to be happy."

"What about you being happy and getting what you want?"

He closed his eyes. "Harley." He said her name like a soft caress. "I was at your house."

She jerked away from him. "What are you saying?"

"I know your marriage to Lyle wasn't what you wanted. I think after dealing with him, you deserve better. I refuse to push something on you for my own personal reasons. Otherwise, I'm no better than Lyle."

Her hands shook as horror filled her. Ackley knew how Lyle had treated her. But then there was that second part about him wanting something—her—but was afraid to push himself on her. If he was asking her to choose him, then she would.

"I want you," the words slipped out of her mouth.

His forehead creased as he considered her words. Then his face softened. "I was hoping you'd say that." He kissed her.

"How's this going to work with us going separate ways?" she asked.

"We'll figure it out. Once we get rid of the false king, we can sit down and come up with a plan. I promise."

For the first time in what felt like forever, happiness swelled inside of Harley.

"You have the most beautiful, infectious smile," Ackley said, running his thumb over her lips. He took hold of her hand, kissing it. "We need to get going before Gytha and Ledger come looking for us." Not releasing her hand, he led her from the barn.

Outside, Gytha and Ledger had the four horses saddled and ready to go. Which meant they'd been inside the barn when Ackley and Harley were sleeping up in the loft. She hoped they hadn't seen anything.

"Now that everyone's here, we'll set out," Ledger said. "There's food in the saddlebags."

Harley mounted her horse. The sun was already rising, putting the time at mid-morning. Ledger had said he wanted to leave at first light. "How far until we part ways?" she asked.

"About two hours."

She only had two hours until she said goodbye to Ackley.

The four of them set out, heading into the forest.

No one spoke as they rode.

Harley kept reliving moments from last night. She was sure she had a dopey smile on her face; however, she couldn't help it. She had never felt this wonderful before.

When they came to an intersection, Ledger stopped. "Let's take a short break together before parting ways." He dismounted and led his horse under the shade of the nearby trees.

Harley dismounted and stretched. She let her horse graze nearby while she nibbled on a loaf of bread from her saddlebag.

Gytha drained her water.

"Would you like some of mine?" Harley asked, holding out her waterskin.

Gytha glared at her. "I don't want anything from you."

Harley wondered what she did to upset her.

"I'm sorry I didn't take a turn on watch last night," Ackley said. "I'll make up for it tonight. I'll take watch so you can sleep."

"Are you sure you have the energy after last night?" Gytha asked, glaring at Ackley.

Harley wanted to disappear into the tree behind her. Gytha knew that Harley had been intimate with Ackley, and she clearly didn't approve. Unable to tolerate the woman's piercing glare, Harley turned and walked deeper into the forest, needing some space. There was no reason for the warrior woman to be so upset. Gytha was a soldier, and Ackley was her superior. She had no right to speak to him that way.

Having gone far enough from the road, Harley hugged herself, trying not to let Gytha's sour mood ruin her happiness.

Leaves crunched not far away, but she didn't see anyone approaching.

"Ackley, wait," Gytha hissed. "I just want to talk to you. How could you be so stupid?"

"You're out of line," he snapped. "Now leave me be. I need to go and find her."

"Out of line?" Gytha said, her voice rising.

"It just happened."

"Things with you don't just happen. Everything you do, you do for a reason. You have plans and backup plans."

"I don't know why you're so upset," Ackley said. "This isn't any of your business. Stay out of it."

Gytha chuckled. "Why do you think I came on this trip?"

"To keep an eye on Idina."

"You still can't say her name, can you?"

"I can say her name just fine. And she has nothing to do with this."

"So sleeping with Harley had nothing to do with Reid?"

"That's Queen Reid to you," Ackley said, his voice low and furious. "And no, it had nothing—*nothing*—to do with Reid."

Harley wondered who this woman was. He'd referred to her as the queen, so she must be the queen of Marsden. Was Ackley in love with her? A sharp pain pierced Harley's heart. Had Ackley used her to forget about Reid?

"So you suddenly have feelings for Harley?" Gytha demanded.

Harley heard the sound of more leaves crunching.

"How could you?" Gytha asked, her voice cracking. "Harley...she can't even wield a sword. She's weak. I didn't think you liked weak women."

Harley found herself kneeling on the ground. *Weak.* Because she couldn't defend herself. She was a useless woman.

"Ackley?"

"Go back to the horses," Ackley said. "This conversation is over."

What had Harley done? She hadn't thought of how Gytha would react to her and Ackley spending the night together. She hadn't even considered her finding out.

A hand rested on her back. "Are you okay?" Ackley asked, crouching beside her.

She covered her face with her hands. "Who's Reid?"

He sat next to her, never moving his hand from her back. "Reid is the queen of Marsden. She married my cousin, Dexter."

"Did you care for her?"

"Yes. But we were only friends—nothing more."

So he'd cared for someone before her. And Harley had been married. They both had a past. But did they have a future? "Do you think we made a mistake last night?"

"Does it feel like a mistake to you?"

Lowering her hands she said, "No. But I didn't think about our actions affecting others." She'd been so wrapped up in what she felt for Ackley that she hadn't stopped to consider the consequences. She felt terrible for hurting Gytha. She hadn't realized the warrior woman cared for Ackley until she'd heard the pain in the woman's voice. "What about you? Do you think we made a mistake?" She peered at him, trying to read his face. As always, his emotions were concealed, his features blank.

"I don't regret last night." His face softened.

That was all she needed to hear. She didn't think she could live with herself if he did.

He leaned toward her, whispering in her ear, "I wouldn't mind doing it again."

She shivered. "Neither would I."

Standing, he reached down, pulling her up alongside him. "It will give me something to look forward to."

"I can't believe we're about to part ways."

He ran his hand through his hair. "Promise me you'll be careful. You're smart. Trust your instincts."

"I will."

Reaching in his bag, he withdrew a small sword no bigger than her forearm. "I want you to have this." He handed it to her.

"It's beautiful." On the hilt, the grip had been wrapped with red leather. The guard had a beautiful swirly design. Along the edge, markings had been etched.

"It belongs to a set. That one I call Sword of Rage."

"Do you have the other?" she asked.

He handed her the scabbard for it. "I do. It's called Sword of Desire. When you fit the pommels together, they lock and form a double-edged sword."

Sliding the sword into the scabbard, she considered the two names. Rage and Desire. She supposed one needed to have both emotions to use a sword to kill. The two sentiments were also something she felt quite often since the takeover and meeting Ackley.

"For now, you can slide that in your cape. I believe there's a hidden pocket made for a weapon such as that."

She removed her cape, examining the interior portion of it. Sure enough, there were several pockets sewn on the inside. It took her a couple of tries, but eventually she found one that fit the short sword.

Ackley helped her put the cape back on, buttoning it at the neck for her. "If you ever need to kill someone quickly," he said, staring into her eyes, "put the tip of your sword here." He touched the base of her throat. "Then thrust it in and pull it sideways."

"Why are you telling me this?"

"You can also cut someone here." He pressed her shoulder. "Or here." He pressed her upper thigh. "Both places have arteries. Slice either of those spots, and the person will bleed out."

"Why are you telling me this?" she asked again.

"I gave you a sword. You should know how to kill with it. Just in case."

She nodded. Maybe she would practice using the weapon when she had a chance. Pressing it into a potato or something to get the feel of stabbing someone. Not that she planned to go around killing people, but if Ackley thought she should know this information, then she would be prepared.

"I also want you to give these to Owen." He pulled out a handful of neatly folded letters. "This is correspondence I found at your house."

She stood there staring at them for a moment. "Can I read through them?" she asked, finally reaching out and taking the letters.

"That's something I can't answer for you."

"Did you read them?"

"Yes."

"I'll make sure my cousin receives these." She found a smaller pocket on the inside of the cape for the letters.

"We need to get back to the others."

"I'm sorry I've complicated things between you and Gytha."

"There is no me and Gytha. She is a soldier in the Marsden army. She came here to protect my sister. We're friends. That's all."

She nodded, pretending she believed that. But she knew better. Gytha was in love with Ackley.

When they reached the others, Harley mounted her horse, ready to get this goodbye over with. Ledger mounted and came alongside her. They were heading west and would take the road in front of them. Ackley and Gytha would take the road to the left.

Ackley mounted, then pointed at Ledger. "Take care of her. If anything happens to Lady Harley, I'll kill you myself."

"Funny, Owen said the same thing."

Ackley looked at Harley. He winked, then turned his horse, riding away from her. Gytha followed, not once looking back.

"Shall we?" Ledger asked.

As Ackley rode away, it felt as if a piece of Harley's heart were leaving with him. She missed him already. "The sooner we reach Owen, the better."

"I know you like the guy," Ledger said, "but I don't trust Ackley."

She didn't feel like having this conversation right now, so she didn't respond. There was no point in arguing with Ledger if his mind was already made up.

"I mean, do you really think a prince would come all the way here and then go on a mission alone?" He shook his head as if the idea were absurd.

Harley wanted to point out that Owen had done the exact same thing, but she decided to keep her mouth shut. She felt a headache coming on and didn't need to antagonize it any more.

"Word among the soldiers is that Ackley killed Commander Beck back in Marsden." He steered his horse alongside Harley's. Lowering his voice, he said, "Did he tell you about that?"

She looked Ledger straight in the eyes. "No, he never spoke of murdering my father-in-law." Shock rolled through her. While Owen had told her Beck betrayed them and tried killing him, he'd never revealed Ackley was the one to kill Beck. Ackley singlehandedly saved the Melenia royal line by protecting Owen and ending the commander.

"Harley." Ledger reached over, grabbing her horse's reins and pulling her to a stop. "I'm sorry I brought up Commander Beck's death. You must still be feeling the deaths of your family members acutely." He released her reins, running his free hand over his thigh. "I just...I'm afraid Ackley is using you. Please be careful."

"Using me?" How in the world would Ackley be using her? She nudged her horse, and it resumed walking.

"He killed Commander Beck, came here to Melenia, and now he's leading a portion of the Marsden army across our kingdom. He has Owen's trust. All I'm saying is we need to be careful. You shouldn't be so quick to trust him."

She glanced back at Ledger who followed close behind her. "I'm always careful. You have nothing to worry about." Looking forward, she decided to ignore him. Logically, she knew he was only being overprotective. He cared about her, and they'd been through a lot together.

"What were the two of you doing in Russek?" he demanded. "Did you meet with someone?"

Her skin prickled. "How'd you know we were in Russek?" It hadn't dawned on her before now to question how he and Gytha had known where to find them.

"Ackley told Gytha where he was going before the two of you left." He steered his horse in front of hers, blocking the road. "Now answer my question. What were you doing in Russek?"

"When I get to Owen, I will answer any questions he has for me. Until then, I will keep my time with Ackley a secret."

"A secret? Is that what Ackley told you? To keep it quiet and not tell anyone?" He huffed. "Typical. You have to see he can't be trusted."

"Actually, it was Owen who insisted I keep everything a secret. Now, if you don't mind, let's focus on traveling instead of talking."

He mumbled something unintelligible before steering his horse to the side of the road alongside hers.

Harley didn't care what Ledger said. She trusted Ackley.

CHAPTER NINETEEN

*A*s Ackley rode behind Gytha, he couldn't help but notice her rigid posture and the lack of conversation. Not that Gytha had ever been particularly chatty, but she hadn't said a single word since they'd left Ledger and Harley.

"If you're not talking as a form of punishment," he said, "you should've thought of something else. I don't mind it being so quiet."

"A form of punishment? The thought never crossed my mind."

"Then why aren't you talking?" he asked.

"I have nothing to say to you."

Like hell she didn't. He almost wished she'd just unleash on him and get it out. He'd have to ask her to spar with him once they stopped for the night. That would probably get things back to normal between them. It always had in the past.

"You know what," the warrior woman said. "I do have something to say. I'm disappointed in you."

He hadn't expected that. He steered his horse alongside hers so he could hear her better. "Disappointed? That I've moved on?" He didn't understand why she even cared.

She shook her head. "There's a lot going on right now. The last thing I expected was for you to sleep with Owen's cousin. What if Owen doesn't approve? What's that going to do for relations between our kingdoms?"

He rubbed his head. "You're right."

"Excuse me?" She pulled her horse to a stop.

"I said you're right. I hadn't thought about that." His focus had been on Harley, not on Owen or his approval.

"You threw me," she said. "I didn't think you'd go for someone like her."

Given Gytha's comments earlier in the day, he knew what she was referring to. "Strength comes in many forms."

"I never thought you'd go for the most beautiful woman in the room. I always thought you were attracted to a stealthy warrior woman."

"Because of Reid?"

She nodded.

"You know, I didn't even realize I'd fallen for Reid until it was too late. I'd spent so much time trying not to be tied down to any woman that she took me by surprise."

"And with Harley?"

With Harley he saw how smart she was. The woman hidden inside that needed to be unleashed. The person she could become. He saw a lot of himself in her. He just didn't know how to articulate it to Gytha. At least not yet. With time, she would see and understand.

"I don't think you should be getting involved in any sort of relationship right now," she said while patting the side of her horse's neck. "You have a job to do."

"I always do my job."

"Good. Then focus on that so we can go home."

Right now, he wasn't sure he even wanted to go home. He wouldn't mind exploring more of the mainland. However, what mattered most was ensuring the hundreds of Marsden soldiers here did make it home. Many had families to return to. "Let's get moving." The sooner he reached his men, the better.

"I'm curious to meet this Empress Rema I've been hearing so much about," Gytha said. She nudged her horse, and it started walking again.

Ackley guessed Gytha was no longer upset with him. He gave the command and his horse set out. "I'm interested to meet her, as well." Since the empress was married, he found it interesting that most people referred to her as being in charge instead of her husband. It was the sort of thing Reid would find fascinating. "Do you still care for Dexter even though he's married?"

Gytha's shrugged. "For years I assumed I'd marry him. When he chose another woman, I was disappointed. Don't get me wrong, I like Reid and think she makes a suitable match for him."

An answer that really wasn't an answer. Since spending so much time with Harley, Ackley hadn't thought about Reid.

"Why are you smiling?" Gytha asked.

He hadn't even realized he was smiling. He hurried and tried to make his face blank.

"You need to focus on the task at hand," she chided him.

Rolling his shoulders back, he forced himself to scan the land around them, needing to pay attention. He also wanted to use this time to come up with a couple more plans. He had to reach his men, then get them safely into Kricok. After that, he'd establish some form of communication with Empress

Rema. He'd probably send a letter and ask for a meeting in person. Ideally, he'd like to deliver the letter himself. However, he'd need to remain with his men. Maybe he'd send Gytha. She'd probably like that.

The road led them to a ravine. Since the sun was starting to descend, Ackley said, "Let's make it through here and then stop for the night." The banks on either side of the road were only fifteen feet high, topped with thick, lush trees.

"Okay."

The spot sort of reminded Ackley of something. "Wait." Pulling his horse to a halt, he scanned the surrounding area, not seeing any movement. He'd set up an ambush once in a place similarly situated.

Gytha dismounted, checking her horse's hoof. "You thinking what I'm thinking?" she asked, not really inspecting the hoof.

Assuming they were being watched, he needed to act casually so they wouldn't alert anyone that they were on to them. Withdrawing his knife, he made a show of handing it to Gytha to use on the horse's hoof, as if something were stuck in it. He dismounted, inspecting the animal alongside Gytha.

"We need to get out of here," he mumbled.

"If we back up, they'll suspect we know," she mumbled.

"They might not have seen us yet." He took his horse, leading it from the road. Still not seeing any movement, he urged Gytha to do the same.

"Now what?" she asked.

"We have to figure out who's there." Because it wasn't Russek.

"So it's not enough to merely escape death," Gytha said sarcastically.

"You not up to the challenge?"

"For once I'd like something to go according to plan."

"No such thing." They backed up a tad more, trying to melt into the trees. Since they couldn't ride their horses here amongst the vegetation, they had two options. One, tie the horses up and hope no one stole them. Two, keep the horses with them. The problem was that the horses were loud and noisy. However, they would serve as nice shields should someone try shooting at them.

"Let's leave the horses here," he said. "Then scale a tree and see if we can spot anything of concern." While he didn't know for sure someone was out there, he felt it in his bones. If he had to guess, he'd say about a dozen soldiers. He didn't think they were Owen's men, and he knew they weren't Russek's. If they were Melenia soldiers, well, that was something he didn't want to consider at the moment.

"Is it really necessary to identify them?" Gytha asked while tying her horse to a tree.

"Yes." If they were from Melenia, it changed everything.

After securing his horse, Ackley felt for his weapons, ensuring they were there. One was missing—the short sword he'd given to Harley.

"These trees are too flimsy," Gytha whispered. "If I climb one, the limbs will shake the leaves."

Plan B then. He tilted his head to the right. Gytha gave him a thumbs up. Taking a deep breath, he steeled his heart and prepared to hunt. His feet became lighter, his movements fluid as he made his way through the forest. The rise remained to his right. Most of the trees were only eight feet tall with long branches, half the leaves on the ground.

Gytha swung out wide, about thirty feet away. She had a sword in one hand, a dagger in the other. Ackley had a short sword and a knife. Moving between the trees, he became one with his surroundings. Crows cawed, then took flight straight ahead, about forty feet away. That had to be where the soldiers were hiding. Not bothering to see if Gytha followed, he slunk between the trees, heading to the area in question, all the while keeping his ears open to the sounds around him. The last thing he needed was to be taken by surprise by a man he didn't see lying in wait.

If these men were Melenia soldiers, that meant someone had sent them to kill Ackley and Gytha. The most logical person was the false king. What scared Ackley about that was twofold. First, it meant the false king knew Gytha and Ackley were traveling south. If he knew that, then he probably knew Harley was meeting up with Owen and they were going to hide in Kreng. Second, it meant someone was feeding the false king accurate information. After dealing with this ambush, Ackley needed to make sure Idina, Harley, and Owen were safe. Then, he needed to find and kill the informant.

Nearing the spot in question, he scanned the rise to his right, not seeing anyone. However, thick leaves, which could easily conceal people, covered the ground. Crouching low, he slid from trunk to trunk, constantly scanning the ground. Thankfully, the trees weren't sturdy here, so he didn't have to worry about someone hiding in them and attacking from above.

Ackley needed to leave one man alive so he could interrogate him; the rest he would dispose of. Since he didn't know how many there were, he couldn't waste his weapons.

Then he heard it—the silence that in a forest means only one thing: an intruder. Or, in this case, an unknown number of intruders. Ackley froze, taking it all in and feeling his surroundings. The enemy was close by. A calmness settled over him. He breathed in and out.

"Where'd they go?" someone whispered, fifteen feet to the left.

"I can't see them," another said, five feet dead ahead.

Ackley would have to take out the man in front of him first. Then the man to his left. As soon as he struck, Gytha would step in and help, but he couldn't rely on her. Palming his knife, he prepared to make the first kill. He lifted his arm, about to throw, when three men stood fifteen feet in front of Ackley, their backs to him. Each man had a bow in hand with full quivers strapped over their shoulders. Change of plan—he'd have to kill them first.

He reached down and withdrew two additional daggers. Taking a step closer to the man lying on the ground, he kept his eyes on the archers. Each archer's focus remained on the road not far below.

As he always did, he chose where to strike each man to ensure a swift death. He threw his first dagger, then the second, and then his knife. All three archers went down. Jumping forward, he slammed his right foot against the head of the man on the ground. Withdrawing his knife from the archer closest to him, he slashed the guy to his left, killing him.

Chaos ensued.

Men shouted all around him—he quickly counted five. Since he'd taken out five men, he assumed this was a unit of ten. Crouching low, he stole one of the archer's bows. He grabbed two arrows and shot them simultaneously, killing two soldiers with bows slung over their backs running toward him. He needed to keep moving.

Seven down, three to go. He was vaguely aware of Gytha a little farther down the hill fighting with two men. Knowing she could handle herself, Ackley turned to face the last man. With his short sword in hand, he twisted, allowing him to come in closer. He sliced the man across his abdomen while continuing to turn. Then Ackley kicked him, knocking him to the ground. He repositioned his weapon, slamming it straight down into the man's chest, killing him. Not wanting to waste time, Ackley withdrew his weapon, wiping the blood off on the man's shirt.

The only one still alive was the one he'd knocked unconscious. Turning, he looked for Gytha. The two men she'd fought were lying on the ground. He approached her. "Dead?" he whispered in case they had another unit of men coming to attack them.

She nodded. Blood coated her hands, and she had a nasty bruise already forming on her right cheek.

"Are you injured?"

"No," she responded. "My ribs are sore from a punch, but I'm fine."

"I left one alive." He nodded up the hill to where the man was lying. "Go and grab a bow and arrows. Hide near the top and cover me. I'm heading to the other side of the ravine to see if there are men over there as well."

She nodded and hurried toward one of the fallen archers.

Ackley retrieved his weapons from the dead soldiers, then ran back toward the horses. If there were additional men out there, they'd probably heard the commotion and would be coming to help. Which meant they'd have to cross the road and enter the forest near the horses.

Assuming there were ten additional men, the easiest thing to do would be to draw them out, exposing them on the road so Gytha could shoot them. He stretched his arms, preparing for hand-to-hand combat.

If the men were organized similarly, there would be five archers and five scouts. He doubted all ten would come at the same time. They'd probably send two first—one archer and one scout.

Ackley spotted the horses, munching on some tall grass about ten feet away from his current location. He rounded the end of the low rise. On the other side of the ravine, two men crouched between the trees, nearing the road. Ackley took a large, jerky step, making sure the men saw him, then he slunk behind a trunk so the archer couldn't shoot him.

He heard the familiar sound of a hiss as an arrow sailed through the air, followed by what sounded like a man hitting the ground. Ackley peered around the trunk. The archer was sprawled in the middle of the road. Not wanting to run forward and fight the other soldier out in the open, he waited as the other man neared. Once the man was close enough, Ackley reached out, yanking the soldier into the cover of the forest.

Shouts rang out. He knew Gytha would strike any man running across the road. Not having time to spare, he released the man, then plunged his knife into him once. Twice. The man fell to the ground, dead.

Ackley turned to face any men Gytha missed. One soldier was about half-way across the road when an arrow soared through the air, striking the man's throat. It was a well-placed shot which Ackley admired. That was the third man down. Five men hovered on the other side, afraid to cross and be struck. That meant there were still two men, an archer and a scout, up on top of the ravine, looking down. Ackley would have to lure those men out as well. Although, that could take too long since time was of the essence right now.

There was a quicker—albeit more dangerous—way. He bolted across the road, zig-zagging, then he dove for the closest soldier, tumbling to the ground. Arrows rained down, but all missed him since he hadn't gone straight across. He rammed his dagger into the soldier's side while twisting so the man's body was on top of his, providing protection. He withdrew his dagger then flung it toward the man on his right, striking him. Reaching out with his other hand, he grabbed a man's ankle, knocking him down.

He flipped the body off him, then kicked, swiping one of the soldier's legs, knocking him down. The last man standing pointed an arrow right at Ackley. The guy dropped to the ground, an arrow protruding from his back. Even though all five men were on the ground, only three were dead. Ackley grabbed a dagger, embedding it into the soldier on his left. The last one scrambled to his feet.

Ackley almost made a severe tactical error and looked into the man's eyes. Once again, steeling his resolve, he neared the man. Five foot seven inches, one hundred sixty pounds. He pretended to throw a punch but instead, kicked the guy's side, knocking him down. He quickly plucked a dagger from one of the fallen bodies and flung it at the man's neck, striking true.

That left the two on top of the ravine.

Ackley slunk deeper into the forest, hoping the last two soldiers weren't already tracking him.

A twig snapped. Twisting, he dropped to the ground and threw his knife. An arrow sailed inches above Ackley's head. Ackley's knife struck the archer's side, not doing enough damage. The scout ran at him. Out of weapons, he sprang to his feet, wrapping his arms around the man's torso. He turned, and an arrow embedded into the soldier's back. Ackley lifted the man and ran at the archer. The archer shot another arrow, striking the soldier a second time. Ackley threw the body at the archer, knocking him down. Without stopping to think, Ackley knelt next to the archer, grabbed his head, and twisted as hard as he could.

He scanned the area, looking for additional threats. Not seeing any, he stood and counted the bodies on the road and lying around him. All ten were accounted for.

He whistled, and Gytha answered with an identical whistle. All clear.

His steady hands started shaking. He balled them into fists, forcing his body to remain calm and in control. Just because this immediate threat was over, didn't mean he could relax. He had a man to interrogate.

After wiping his hands off on his pants, he began retrieving his weapons. While doing so, he compiled a list of questions to ask the soldier.

Gytha stood on the other side of the ravine. "The man woke up, so I tied him to a tree." She scanned the road in both directions, her bow nocked and at the ready as if she expected to be ambushed at any moment.

"Twenty men is a lot," Ackley commented. "If the false king sent them, then he had to know both you and I are trained soldiers."

"You believe these men are from Melenia's army?"

"I do." The side of Gytha's face was already black and blue. "I want you to stay here. Monitor the road for threats. I'll be back in five minutes."

"Only five?"

He gave a grim nod. It was all the time he needed.

Approaching the man, Ackley looked him over. Early twenties, six feet, one hundred fifty pounds. His arms had been tied together behind the trunk, his head resting against it.

"You're from Melenia's army," he said by way of greeting.

The man looked up at Ackley but didn't respond.

Ackley crouched near the man's feet, trying to decide if he should slice the soldier's leg open and be direct, or start out kinder and work his way up. "Did the false king threaten your family members, too?"

The man's brows drew together. "How'd you know about that?"

A wicked gleam flashed in Ackley's eyes as he smiled. "The false king isn't the only one with someone on the inside." Taking one of his daggers, he dangled it between his fingers, drawing the man's attention to the weapon. "Were additional soldiers sent out on missions?"

Sweat covered the man's face, and his breathing came out hard and fast. "Yes."

Panic took root, but he shoved it away. Panic would not help him right now. "How many groups?" He pressed the tip into the man's thigh.

"One other unit went out."

Ackley slid the dagger into the man's leg. "Who did they go after?" Owen and Idina? Or Ledger and Harley? Not that either was acceptable to him.

"Are you going to kill me?"

He pressed the dagger in harder. "I will if you don't answer me."

The man pinched his eyes together, his breathing labored.

"They went after another group. A woman and several men, I think."

"And their mission is to kill them?"

He nodded.

Ackley removed the dagger, letting it dangle between his fingers again. "Who's sitting on the throne?"

"A Melenia soldier, but I don't know his name."

"Who gave you the order for this mission?"

"Lieutenant Flan. He said this was a mission for the king."

This man was just a foot soldier, lacking valuable

information. Ackley didn't want to kill him since he wasn't the enemy and he'd done nothing wrong. However, since the man had been sent to kill him, he couldn't let him live. At least Ackley could make it a quick death.

"Do you know where the king is holding your family members?"

"No."

Ackley leaned closer to him, then quick as lightning, rammed his dagger into the man's neck. Unable to watch the life drain from him, Ackley sheathed his weapon and walked away. He tried not to gag at the heady smell of blood.

CHAPTER TWENTY

HARLEY

*S*itting on her bedroll, Harley picked at her bread, not really hungry. She'd spent the entire afternoon riding her horse, all the while thinking about Ackley. Not once did she question his trustworthiness. He'd proven himself time and time again. Last night still consumed her thoughts. The way his lips felt on hers, how his hands explored her body, and the way he made her feel. She sighed, wishing he were here with her right now.

"Do you mind if I sleep for a couple hours?" Ledger asked.

"No," she answered. "Go right ahead." After all, he'd been on watch half of last night while she'd been asleep.

"Wake me when you're tired."

She nodded.

He stretched out on his bedroll, facing away from her. He'd been curt and distant all afternoon, but she didn't mind. It afforded her some much needed alone time.

As she stared into the fire, she remembered the letters Ackley had given her. Once Ledger's breathing evened out, she withdrew them, curious. She traced the words on the top piece of paper. The handwriting wasn't familiar. Ackley had entrusted her to deliver these to Owen. He hadn't said she couldn't read them.

She untied the string holding them together. Unfolding the first letter, she discovered it was from Commander Beck. It talked about the need for change. He said that too many of the cities were starting to see uprisings. He informed Lyle that the villages were revolting, and the military was being sent in to regain control. Commander Beck wished the king would allow more representation among the people.

Harley sat there stunned. While she'd known about the occasional uprising, she hadn't realized there were so many or that the military had to get involved. There were a few scuffles in Penlar, but they had been easily dealt with. Her father never spoke about unrest throughout the kingdom.

Setting that letter aside, she opened the next one and read it. Again, it was from Beck to his son. This one discussed the lack of leadership from the king. Beck claimed the king was more concerned with gaining wealth and throwing elaborate parties than he was in making sure the commoners had food on their plates and roofs over their heads. He said the rampant poverty seen in Melenia was not the case in other kingdoms.

Harley's hands shook, furious that Beck had the nerve to accuse her uncle of being negligent. Her uncle cared about his subjects; of that she was certain. As far as the poverty suffered throughout the kingdom, she was aware of that issue. She saw it firsthand in Penlar. However, if there was a way to feed and shelter everyone, surely her uncle would have done something about it.

Looking at the rest of the letters, she debated whether she should continue reading them. Obviously, Ackley wanted Owen to see them for a reason. Maybe to establish why Commander Beck committed treason when he tried to kill Owen in Marsden. However, there could be more to it than that. A sick feeling took root in her stomach.

With a shaking hand, she picked up the next letter and read it.

Lyle,

You won't believe what I discovered. The king has a dirty little secret. We can use this information to our advantage. Break off your engagement with Naia, I have someone else for you. Someone that will give us everything we want.

I'll tell you about it the next time I see you. Stay safe. I know training under Captain Murgis is hard. Hang in there, for I'm certain your status is about to change.

Sincerely,

Your father

Setting it aside, Harley pulled her legs to her chest, wrapping her arms around them, contemplating what the king's dirty little secret could be. No gossip hinting at something scandalous had ever reached her ears. And as for Lyle, he must have broken off his engagement with Naia to marry Harley instead. A queasy feeling overcame her. Beck could have used whatever information he discovered to blackmail Harley's parents into accepting Lyle's proposal to elevate Lyle's position. Which led her to believe that her parents had to somehow be involved with the king's secret. Her mother had said there were things Harley didn't know. And she'd never understood why her parents had signed the marriage contract with Lyle in the first place. Since she was headed to Penlar, she could confront her mother, demanding to know the truth.

Little thoughts started to surface, scaring Harley. Things like why she spent every summer at the royal castle without her parents. Her mother had told her the king wished it to be that way. She'd never thought to ask why. How stupid and naive she'd been to not question things.

Glancing at the letters, she decided to scan through them to see if any mentioned her uncle's secret.

Lyle,

Do not argue with me. See that it's done. If we plan this right, she'll be the only one left. Then we can reveal the secret. I got him to write a letter admitting to it all. I have it safely hidden. When I return, I will see you elevated to the position you deserve. Together, we can right the wrongs and make Melenia a better place.

Sincerely,

Your father

Nausea rolled through Harley. She was going to be ill if this letter meant what she thought it did. There was no way possible for her to be the king's daughter, in line to the throne. Her mother loved her father and was the queen's sister. It couldn't be true.

However, deep down, she knew it was. It all made sense. The summers she'd spent at the royal castle, her mother's refusal to visit the place, the way the king treated her with an almost fatherly love similar to Princess Oriana. Regardless, she wanted to be sure she wasn't reading too much into it. Perhaps there was a reasonable explanation.

The following day, Harley and Ledger set out early. Since she'd barely slept, exhaustion racked her body. She couldn't stop thinking about the letters and what it all meant.

"Do you have the letters Ackley gave you in a safe place?" Ledger asked when they stopped around midday to rest the horses and take a quick break.

"How do you know about those?"

"Ackley told me."

"They're safe." She lifted her arm to pat the inside of her cloak where she had the letters tucked into a pocket. However, she refrained from doing so, not wanting to give away their location. Maybe she'd spent too much time around Ackley and was being paranoid. However, she figured better safe than sorry. An idea came to her. She patted her horse's saddlebag.

As she feared, Ledger's focus went right to her bag. She pretended not to notice as she led her horse to a stream so it could drink.

"I don't know why Ackley bothered going to Penlar in the first place," Ledger said, leaning against a tree.

She didn't want to discuss her mission with Ackley. Owen had asked him to go. He'd wanted to know if her parents were alive—which they were. They'd also discovered Penlar was untouched. "I keep wondering if our soldiers hadn't been in Marsden, if they'd been here for the invasion, if we would have been able to fight off Russek."

"I don't know. With a vast majority of the soldiers stationed at the castle gone, security was sparse the night of the takeover."

"You were at the castle," she said, thinking out loud. "But not on duty."

"Correct. I was sleeping. My watch didn't start until much later that night."

Lyle had been needed because they were short on men. And he'd already been on duty all day. Why hadn't they used Ledger and his unit? Funny she'd never thought to question it before now.

Once the horses were rested, they continued on. Ledger insisted he lead the way in case they encountered any danger. Harley obliged.

The day wore on and the temperature dropped, the clouds moving in. She hoped it didn't rain. As Harley rode, she thought about some of the things Ackley had taught her. Like to always trust her instincts. And right now, she didn't trust Ledger. Once she reached Owen, she would express her concerns to him.

When they came to one of the main roads that led to the castle, Ledger took it. "Which way are we going to Penlar?" she asked.

"The fastest way," he replied, glancing over his shoulder at her. "You don't have to worry about getting lost, I'll lead the way. I know where I am."

He must truly think her daft to assume she wouldn't know where she was. She'd traveled from Penlar to the castle dozens of times. Granted, it had been in a carriage and not on horseback, but regardless, she knew where they were and where they were going. Unable to fathom why he was deviating from the plan, she followed him trying to figure out why he was lying to her.

Ackley told her to never make a rash decision because that was how mistakes were made. So while she wanted to turn her horse around and run far away from Ledger, she couldn't. He'd simply chase after her. If she wanted to get away, she needed to be sneaky about it. She considered what Ackley would do in her place. Well, he'd probably just kill Ledger and be done with it. While she'd originally asked the question to try and figure out how to get away from Ledger, this new idea about killing him wasn't necessarily a bad one. Last night, she took the first watch for a few hours while he slept. If they did that again, all she'd have to do was use the short sword Ackley had given her.

But first, she needed to decide if she could stomach killing Ledger. When that man had held her at knifepoint, she had no trouble ramming the dagger into his stomach, though she didn't think she killed him. That was why Ackley had pushed the weapon farther in. She glanced at her shaking hands.

To be honest with herself, she didn't know for certain that Ledger deserved to die. Since taking a life couldn't be undone, she couldn't kill him. Which left her with trying to get away. Leaving now would only mean a chase. She was certain Ledger was the better horseman, and he'd overtake her in no time. It would have to be tonight then. When she went on watch and Ledger slept, she'd sneak away. She could lead the horse about a half mile away and then mount, riding all night to put as much distance between herself and Ledger as possible. She had enough provisions to reach Penlar.

That night, Harley offered to take the first watch. Ledger readily agreed and stretched out on his bedroll. Once his breathing became heavier, she got to work. She slowly stood, trying not to make a sound. The fire they'd used to cook their supper had almost died. Under the cover of the trees, it was easy to hide in the shadows.

She slunk to the next tree, then waited to see if Ledger moved. If he woke and questioned her, she would say she was either going to relieve herself or just standing while keeping watch. When he didn't stir, she moved to the next one. As she neared the horses, she hoped they didn't make a noise and wake him. Horses could be so finicky.

At her horse, she untied the reins from the branch. As she did so, sharp shooting pains exploded across her hands. A cry escaped her, and she fell to her knees, the pain intensifying as it slowly crawled its way up her arms. She didn't think anything had stung her. Having no idea what was going on, fear took over.

"Harley?" Ledger said as he ran toward her. "What's the matter?"

"My hands…"

He stood, hovering over her. "Did you touch the horse's reins?"

"Yes," she ground out, the pain now up to her shoulders. It was unlike anything she'd experienced before.

"I always put a little something on the horses' reins at night so they're not stolen." He squatted next to her. "What were you planning to do?"

She didn't bother answering. There was nothing she could say to explain why she'd been trying to untie the horse. The pain strengthened, tears streaming down her cheeks. "What is it?" She prayed it would go away and she wouldn't lose the ability to use her hands.

"It's not harmful," he said as he scooped her up. "But it lasts a few hours."

Thankfully, the pain hadn't gone past her arms. Still, it was enough to prevent her from being able to walk. She curled into herself, trying to take slow, steadying breaths.

"Go to sleep, Harley. In the morning, you'll feel better."

She wanted to tell him sleep was impossible in this much pain and near someone she didn't trust. However, she didn't want to accuse him of anything. The more compliant and naive she appeared, the better. Once the pain subsided, she would run away.

"This will help." Ledger reached forward. She was about to question him when he pinched her nose. Furious her arms wouldn't do as she wished and smack his hands away, she finally sucked in a breath. When she did, he put something in her mouth that tasted tangy. She tried spitting it out, but he clamped her jaw closed. He released her nose so she could breathe. Whatever he put in her mouth started to melt.

A deep heaviness overcame her. She couldn't keep her eyelids open.

CHAPTER TWENTY-ONE

"Are you okay?" Gytha asked, eyeing Ackley's bloody hands.

"I'm fine." He wanted to find a stream so he could wash up, but there was no time.

"What did you learn?"

Ackley cracked his neck, then looked up at the sky, trying to think through everything. First, he had a duty to his kingdom. "I need you to go south." He folded his arms, mentally going over the various plans he'd been considering and which one was most likely to succeed. "Meet up with the Marsden soldiers. You will command the army until I get there."

Gytha pursed her lips. "Okay."

He could tell she wanted to say something but refrained from doing so. "I'm going west. Another unit of Melenia soldiers went after Owen and Idina. I need to find my sister before she stumbles into a trap like this." He waved toward the ravine.

"She's with Owen and six soldiers. She'll be fine."

While Ackley knew Owen was a capable fighter who could protect Idina, he couldn't leave the fate of his sister in the hands of others. Not when there was something he could do to help. "Once my sister is safe, I'll come and find you."

"I'll be in Kricok waiting."

"The king knew we were heading south to meet up with our army. We have to assume he also knows we're going to Kricok."

"Where shall I lead the army then? Back to the shore where we first disembarked?"

"No, you need to get out of Melenia as quickly as possible." He'd been in Landania and hadn't seen anything of concern. "Take the army to Landania. Then get a letter to Empress Rema of Emperion." He withdrew his map of the kingdom, handing it to her. "Show me where you parted ways with Owen and Idina. I also want to know how many days ago that was."

Gytha studied the map. "Here." She pointed to a location west and slightly south of the castle. "Five days ago."

"Keep the map. You'll need it."

Gytha nodded. "Very well. Anything else?"

"Be careful." He didn't like the idea of her traveling alone; however, it couldn't be helped. "I'm placing my army in your hands. I trust you."

Clasping her right hand on his shoulder she said, "Please be careful as well."

"I will."

She bowed and then went over to her horse, mounting it. "Don't take too long."

"I won't. As soon as I know my sister is safe, I'll join you." Not wanting to waste any more time, he mounted his horse. Looking at Gytha, he nodded and then was off.

He urged his horse to run as fast as it could. Thankfully,

he'd studied the map of Melenia and knew the way he needed to go. Owen and Idina would be backtracking to Penlar. Guessing the route they'd most likely take, he just had to figure out where an ambush would take place and then intercept Owen and Idina before they reached that spot.

If he didn't make it in time, his sister would be slaughtered.

The mere thought made him furious. He would not let anyone kill Idina. Sweat coated his forehead. His stomach rolled with nausea. Faster—he had to go faster.

He wouldn't stop until he reached his sister, even if it meant he had to travel all day and night.

He'd gone over it in his head a hundred times. The soldiers should have arrived at Penlar first. Owen and Idina would be walking, taking them longer to reach the city. If Ackley headed a little farther north, he should be able to cut them off before they reached Penlar.

Riding low on his horse, he kept his focus reined in and sharp. A little voice in the back of his head kept reminding him about Harley. He'd read the letters between Beck and Lyle. It seemed Harley was the old king's illegitimate child—putting her in line for the throne. If that was the case...he shook his head. He needed to save his sister first. Once Idina was safe, he'd deal with Harley. If everything was as he thought, no harm would come to her.

His horse started to tire. He should be reaching the road Owen and Idina were traveling on. He wouldn't put it past Owen to have the group hiking just off the road for safety reasons.

When he came to the road, he steered his horse north,

knowing his sister would be close. The map he'd taken from Lyle's house had been exceedingly accurate. Without it, he wouldn't know where he was going now, and he wouldn't have been able to determine which way Owen was traveling either.

Ackley had estimated he'd overtake his sister right around here. So where was she? He cursed. His nerves were on edge, causing his heart to beat frantically. He needed to calm down and think rationally. He'd saved his sister once before, he'd save her again. Or so help whoever touched her—he would slaughter them all.

The horse trudged on. Each minute brought more anxiety and unease. What if the soldiers decided to spring a trap somewhere else? What if his sister was being attacked right now?

Something caught his attention. Slowing the horse, he glanced back, not seeing anything. He dismounted, leaving the horse in the middle of the road as he slunk into the forest, listening. Even though he didn't see anyone, he knew someone was there. Not only could he feel it in his bones, but he didn't hear any of the normal wildlife that was expected in the forest.

On a whim, he whistled the first part of Idina's favorite childhood song. A couple of seconds later, someone whistled the next melody. Relief filled him, and he stepped away from the tree, heading back to the road where he could be easily seen. The horse nickered, probably thankful for the rest. It was the first time the animal had stopped since Ackley set out yesterday.

Something red caught his attention. He turned and saw Idina running toward him, her red hair a beacon against the green forest. She needed to wear a hat to cover it. But knowing her, she'd refuse to wear something unless it was fashionable.

"What are you doing here?" Idina demanded as she wrapped Ackley in a hug.

Owen approached behind Idina. "What's wrong?" he asked, his voice low and soft.

"Gytha and I were attacked by Melenia soldiers."

Owen's face paled. "Where's Harley?"

Ackley released Idina. "I questioned one of the soldiers. He said another group was sent out after you and Idina." The six soldiers accompanying Owen approached but remained off the road, near the cover of the trees. "He didn't say anything about soldiers going after Harley."

"Where's the attack to take place?" Owen asked.

"Penlar. Whether that's in the city or just outside of it, I can't be sure." Ackley scanned the area, his nerves still on edge. "Regardless, you need to steer clear of the area."

"If Harley and Ledger are headed to Penlar, we need to stop them before they reach it," Idina said.

"I think we should go straight to Kreng," Owen said. "We can't afford to wait for Harley to catch up. It would only give the soldiers time to locate us."

"I agree," Ackley said. "However, I'm not sure it's wise to go to Kreng."

"Why not?" Idina asked. "We need to convince the commander there to support us. They have a standing army that could help ensure Owen's victory. We should be safe there."

"The false king knows that's where you're going," Ackley answered.

"I don't know how he found out," Idina said, her brow furrowing.

"Your sister thought there could be a spy in our midst after the messenger from the castle showed up," Owen explained, "so we didn't tell anyone our plans." Using his arm, he wiped the sweat from his forehead. "After I sent the Marsden soldiers —minus Gytha—south, I kept six Melenia soldiers and Ledger with me, sending the rest to the castle. Once everyone was gone, I told Ledger and Gytha to go and intercept you and Harley. I told Ledger to bring her to Penlar where we'd meet up."

His words hung heavy in the air as everyone processed them.

"So the traitor is either one of the six soldiers accompanying us, or Ledger," Idina said, her voice barely above a whisper.

"These six men are loyal," Owen said, vouching for them. "I can't be so sure with Ledger."

"Why not?" Idina demanded.

"I've worked with these six men; that's why I chose them to accompany us. I only met Ledger once or twice before he showed up with Harley. The only reason I kept him around was because she trusted him."

"I never liked the guy," Ackley said, rage seething within him. Ledger was with Harley. If Ledger touched her, Ackley would make him suffer the most unimaginable pain.

"I'm sorry to point this out," Idina said, "but Ledger probably killed Harley by now. There's no point in going after her." She rubbed Owen's arm, offering him comfort.

"I don't think he killed her." Ackley looked at Owen, unsure how to voice his suspicions. He'd hoped Owen came to his own conclusions once he read Commander Beck's correspondence. "I think Ledger is following orders and taking her somewhere."

"Where would he take her?" Owen asked, his eyes hardening. "And whose order is he following?"

Idina sucked in a breath, making an odd noise, her eyes widening. "She's only valuable if she's in line for the throne." She grabbed Owen's arm. "With her husband dead, whoever is sitting on the throne can force her to marry him. Then there would be legitimacy to the title."

Idina always figured things out before everyone else. "I concur." Ackley rubbed his chin. "But I think you're wrong on one point."

"Wait," Owen said, shaking his head. "Harley's my cousin, not my sister."

"I believe she's your half-sister," Ackley admitted.

"What part am I wrong about?" Idina inquired.

"You, of all people, haven't figured out who's sitting on the throne yet?"

Idina's eyes widened. "It can't be."

CHAPTER TWENTY-TWO

*P*eeling her eyelids open, Harley found herself lying in bed. She sat up, rubbing her eyes, recognizing the room as one of the guest suites in the royal castle.

She stood, trying to remember what had happened. Her hands tingled slightly, and she recalled touching the horse's reins covered with some kind of poison. Her head pounded, probably from whatever Ledger had shoved in her mouth to knock her out.

She had to assume Ledger brought her here. Going over to the window, she peered outside, finding it light out. She couldn't tell what time of day it was since dark gray clouds filled the sky, concealing the sun. Tents covered the entire east side of the castle. Soldiers moved about the muddy ground.

Letting the curtain slide shut, she tried to determine why Ledger would have brought her here. She rubbed her throbbing head, still reeling from whatever she'd been drugged with.

Unclasping the cape at the base of her neck, she removed it, setting it on the chair. Since no one else was in the room, she felt through the heavy fabric until she located the sword Ackley had given her, safely tucked inside. She withdrew it and the letters, examining the room. Ackley preferred hiding things in armoires. She went over to the armoire and opened the door, finding several shelves and one drawer. Pulling the drawer open, she reached in behind it. There wasn't much room, but it would make the perfect hiding spot. She slid the sword and letters in there, then closed the drawer and door.

Now it was time to see if Ledger lurked out in the hallway. Going over to the door, she reached for the handle, finding it unlocked. Peering into the hallway, she didn't see anyone. She stepped out of the room. This was the second floor and most of the guest bedchambers were located in this wing. She quietly made her way along the hallway and down the staircase, heading toward the great hall.

Harley paused at the threshold, taking it all in. This was where it had started—at her cousin's birthday celebration. Instead of a night of dancing, it had been a night of terror. Inside, the room had been cleared out. The only furniture remaining were the two chairs on the dais—her uncle and aunt's throne chairs. Her breath caught. Not her uncle. Her father.

She crossed the room to the throne chair, tracing the lines carved into the arm. She wished someone would have told her who her real father was. She wondered if her mother been secretly in love with the king. Maybe she'd thrown herself at him. Or he could have pushed himself at her. A tear slid down her cheek. She had no idea of the circumstances behind her conception—and she wasn't sure she wanted to.

"There you are," a familiar voice said, making the hairs on her arms stand on end.

Harley turned from the chair and looked at the man walking toward her. "Lyle?" Her entire body started to shake. It felt as if her heart were frozen, her stomach a raging sea, and her head a pounding storm. "I thought you died during the takeover."

"That explains your look of surprise at seeing me." His hands took hold of her elbows, and he kissed her cheek. "I'm not sure why Ledger didn't tell you I was alive and well." He held her at arm's length, looking at her.

"Ledger knew?" Her brain had trouble processing everything that was happening. Some part of her was in shock.

"Of course, darling. He's been working for me for years."

She looked up into his eyes.

"He says you have some letters for me?"

"Letters?"

His eyes hardened. "Don't play dumb."

"I don't have any letters." She kept her eyes wide and frightened.

"Where are they?" he snarled.

"I have no idea what you're talking about." She needed to avert his anger so she could figure out what was going on.

"Ledger," Lyle snapped. "Come here."

"Yes, Your Majesty?" Ledger said, coming into the great hall.

"Your Majesty?" Harley repeated. She turned in a slow circle.

"Have you honestly not figured it out?" Lyle asked.

Her hand went to her throat as she tried to process what was happening. "You're the false king?"

His lips curved into a sly smile. "Not a false king. A true king. Just like you, my wife, are a true queen."

"But..." She wanted to say that Owen was the true king; however, she didn't want to bring attention to her cousin. "If Ledger is working for you, then why did he lie to me?"

"A good question." Lyle faced Ledger. "Why didn't you tell my wife I am alive and well?"

"I didn't tell her because I was too busy spying for you and uncovering information."

"Uncovering information? You sent me generic reports on troop movement. There wasn't much intel."

"I saved the best to deliver in person." Ledger glanced at Harley. "I discovered who killed your father."

Harley knew Ledger was going to blame Ackley for killing Beck. Once Lyle knew Ackley had killed his father, he would stop at nothing to eliminate him. There had to be something she could do to prevent Lyle from learning this knowledge. Ackley had taught her a lot of things, and deflection was one of them.

"Ledger," she cried out. "How could you?" She pretended to be horrified.

"What?" he stammered.

"You lied to me! You told me my husband was dead. You came into my bed and insisted I give my body to you. You told me it was okay." She let the tears flow, which wasn't hard. "If I had known Lyle was alive, I never would have allowed you to touch me. I can't believe you did that to me." She dropped to her knees, sobs raking through her body.

"No," Ledger said, backing up. "It wasn't me. It was—"

Lyle withdrew his sword, the sound of steel slicing through the air. "Kneel," he commanded.

Without hesitation, Ledger did as he said. "I serve you, Your Majesty. I swear I never touched Harley."

"Harley? That's Lady Harley, soon to be Queen Harley, to you."

"I took care of her this entire time. I delivered her here

300

safely to you. Please," he begged, terror welling in his eyes. "I'm loyal. I swear."

A tinge of guilt pushed its way in, and Harley had to shove it aside.

"Yet, you never told her I was alive?" He took a menacing step closer to him. "It took you weeks before you even established communication with me. Was that because you were enjoying my wife?" His voice sounded lethal as a snake, and Harley had to force herself not to tremble.

"She was grieving over her brother. I didn't think it wise to tell her you killed him."

Lyle snarled, then thrust his sword into Ledger's chest. A sickening sound reverberated through the room. Harley squeezed her eyes shut and covered her ears with her hands. She was going to vomit.

Harley regretted using Ledger as a scapegoat. Ackley's words came back to her. He'd told her that he never enjoyed killing. However, sometimes it was a matter of kill or be killed. And in this case, Ledger's death saved Ackley.

"Your Majesty!" a man said, running into the room.

"Not now," Lyle snapped. "Harley, honey." Lyle knelt before her, his hands pulling hers away from her ears. "Look at me."

The last thing she wanted to do was to look into the eyes of a monster. However, she needed him to believe her compliant so he wouldn't murder her.

"The royal family is dead. We are the sole surviving heirs," he said. "Regardless of what happened or how, we have to be strong and rule this kingdom together." He pulled her to her feet.

Lyle had discovered her true parentage, married her, then planned this elaborate takeover so the royal family would be killed. Now, he intended on using her to rule the kingdom. It almost made her want to laugh. Almost.

Instead, rage boiled inside of her. Hollis and the royal family were dead because of this man before her. She looked into his eyes, evaluating his strengths and weaknesses.

"Your Majesty!" the messenger said again. "Word just came. The soldiers you sent out are dead."

"What?" Lyle asked, staring at her, his hands still holding her tightly.

"The two units you sent out. They failed. They were killed. All of them."

Lyle's head tipped back, his focus on the ceiling as his skin turned red. "You mean to tell me, the *twenty* men I sent south to kill *two* soldiers are dead?"

"Um, yes, that's the report."

"And the *thirty* I sent after Owen and his bodyguards are dead as well?"

"Yes, Your Majesty."

Harley had to conceal the smile from her face. Owen and Ackley were alive.

"How is that possible?" Lyle snarled.

"I don't know, Your Majesty. They're all dead, so we couldn't question them."

Lyle swung around to face the messenger. "Get out!"

"If Owen is alive," Harley said, trying to keep a straight face, "then I'm not the queen, which means you're not the king —Owen is."

"I'm the king."

She tried to keep her focus on Lyle, afraid to look down and see Ledger's body lying in a pool of blood. "Of course you're the king. You're the one in the castle commanding the soldiers."

His eyes narrowed.

"I'm sure all the neighboring kingdoms will support you. What can Owen do?"

"I want him dead."

"He's my cousin."

"I'm your king and husband."

She hated him. "Of course. I will support you in any way I can."

This entire time, Owen had been trying to get information about the false king. He'd wanted to know who he was, where he was, and what he intended to do. Now, Harley was inside the castle, privy to that information. She could report what she learned back to Owen. Not only that, but if she could discover the location of the soldiers' loved ones, she could free them. Once they were freed, the Melenia soldiers could support Owen again. With the might of the army behind him, he could retake his throne.

Ledger, the man who'd infiltrated Owen's army, learned their secrets, and reported back to Lyle, had unknowingly brought a spy and assassin into the castle. For that was what Harley decided to become.

Ackley's words came back to her. He'd asked her which assassin was more dangerous. The one who snuck into the castle to assassinate the king, or the woman sleeping beside the king at night. He'd given her his sword and showed her where to make the killing blow.

Right then and there, Harley swore to avenge her brother's death.

Then she would avenge the royal family.

She would save the soldiers' loved ones.

She would put Owen on the throne.

And Harley would do whatever she had to do to keep Ackley safe.

Lyle needed to suffer for what he'd done. A quick death would be a disservice. She would find a way to seek her revenge, and when the time was right, she would plunge the sword into him.

She would take her sword of rage and use it to right all the wrongs.

ABOUT THE AUTHOR

Jennifer Anne Davis graduated from the University of San Diego with a degree in English and a teaching credential. She is currently a full-time writer and mother of three kids. She is happily married to her high school sweetheart and lives in the San Diego area.

Jennifer is the recipient of the San Diego Book Awards Best Published Young Adult Novel (2013), winner of the Kindle Book Awards (2018), a finalist in the USA Best Book Awards (2014), and a finalist in the Next Generation Indie Book Awards (2014).

Visit Jennifer at:
www.JenniferAnneDavis.com

facebook.com/AuthorJenniferAnneDavis
twitter.com/authorjennifer
instagram.com/authorjennifer
bookbub.com/authors/jennifer-anne-davis
goodreads.com/jenniferannedavis
pinterest.com/authorjennifer